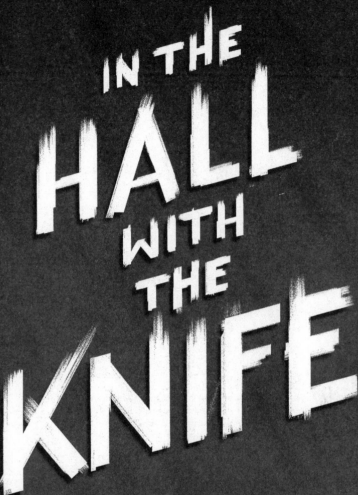

IN THE HALL WITH THE KNIFE

A **CLUE** Mystery

BY

DIANA PETERFREUND

AMULET BOOKS
NEW YORK

The Library of Congress has cataloged the hardcover edition as follows:
Names: Peterfreund, Diana, author.Title: In the hall with the knife / by Diana Peterfreund.Description: New York : Amulet Books, 2019. | Series: Clue mystery ; #1Identifiers: LCCN 2019011724 | ISBN 9781419738340 (hardback)Classification: LCC PZ7.P441545 Ih 2019 | DDC [Fic]--dc23

Paperback ISBN 978-1-4197-4696-3

Book design by John Passineau

Published in paperback in 2020 by Amulet Books, an imprint of ABRAMS. Originally published in hardcover by Amulet Books in 2019.

Printed and bound in U.S.A.
10 9 8 7 6 5 4 3 2

Amulet Books are available at special discounts when purchased in quantity for premiums and promotions as well as fundraising or educational use. Special editions can also be created to specification. For details, contact specialsales@abramsbooks.com or the address below.

Amulet Books® is a registered trademark of Harry N. Abrams, Inc.

ABRAMS The Art of Books
195 Broadway, New York, NY 10007
abramsbooks.com

1

Orchid

The office of the headmaster of Blackbrook Academy looked like a high-budget, if not particularly imaginative, movie set. Glossy wood paneling shimmered with the polish of a century, and leather-bound volumes of old yearbooks stood in rows as a testament to all the scholarly glory that had come before. As Orchid McKee entered, her gaze landed on the gilded wooden engraving of the school's crest mounted right above Headmaster Boddy's door.

TO MAKE MEN OF KNOWLEDGE AND INTEGRITY

Naturally, they never changed it after the school went co-ed. She wondered what they planned to do with the women.

The hard-backed wooden chairs lined up along the wall outside his door seemed crafted to be the most uncomfortable seats imaginable, the better to impress upon the occupants that they were in trouble and they'd better get used to squirming. There was already a student sitting in one.

Orchid perched on the very edge of another.

She wasn't in trouble, and she hadn't squirmed in years.

Of that she was sure. Orchid had crafted her entire existence at Blackbrook to make sure she would never be noticed for anything. The oversized, hooded sweaters, the mousy-brown hair, the glasses and the headphones and the ever-present, fat book—all were a perfectly crafted costume saying a single thing: *boring*. Her homework was always meticulously done and turned in early, if she could at all manage it. She didn't party or sneak off campus to drink in the woods near the ravine. She'd never even gotten dragged into the usual dorm-room drama, though it probably helped that she'd also paid the private room premium on her boarding bill ever since freshman year.

Orchid liked her privacy.

Which was why, when the person seated next to her nudged her elbow and asked, "Whatcha in for, McKee?" she just shrugged and returned to her book, letting her too-long bangs fall over her face. You could deflect quite a lot of conversation with a simple shrug. Orchid had been perfecting hers for a decade.

But Phineas Plum, seated in the hardback chair beside her, wasn't much for going unnoticed. If you *were* making that luxe boarding school movie, you couldn't have cast the part of hipster nerd any better. Cute, and boy did he know it. Smart, and he made sure everyone knew that part, too. At a school like Blackbrook, the resident genius enjoyed all the popularity of other schools' star quarter-backs or head cheerleaders.

"I don't know, either," he barreled on, as if Orchid had invited conversation. "Though, I guess, since it's the middle of junior year, it might have something to do with academic honor societies."

Possibly. Orchid's grades were excellent, and everyone at school knew that Finn was the best student in the class.

"Though I don't see Scarlett." he added.

Make that the best *male* student. Scarlett Mistry lived down the hall from Orchid, and, curiously, always seemed to have insider knowledge on every student's academic ranking, which she'd regularly announce to any person within spitting distance. She was also class president, the head of the Campus Beautification Committee, and—in Orchid's opinion—a complete pain in the butt. Orchid hadn't moved to Maine to get mired in the same compet-itive, mean-girl drama that had devoured so many of the young women she'd known back in California. It's not like Orchid kept up with the news from back home—but some stories you couldn't avoid. The tabloids made sure of that.

No, she'd come to Maine to stay out of trouble. And the fact that Scarlett wasn't also sitting in the headmaster's office right now did not bode well for Finn's honor society theory.

"Or maybe we screwed up," she suggested to him.

He laughed weakly. No, she bet Finn could never *imagine* doing anything wrong at all. Not Blackbrook's golden boy, the scientific genius who would uphold the campus legacy of innovation.

Half a century ago, Richard Fain, still a student at the school, had somehow stumbled upon a formula for some sort of mega-powerful industrial glue, which had made him—and Blackbrook Academy, which shared the rights to the patent—millions.

Not the most glamorous of inventions, glue. Not like a microchip. Orchid doubted anyone would actually make a big-budget biopic of a glue inventor. But it was still enough to put the tiny boarding school on the map.

For decades, it had been the premiere destination for the dedicated science student. At least those who didn't mind the remote setting, out on the tip of a rocky peninsula, so far into the wilderness of Maine it was practically Greenland.

They said if you came to Blackbrook, you were either a complete genius or hiding from something.

Orchid preferred to let people think she was a genius.

From behind the closed door to the headmaster's private chamber, there came a loud thump, followed by the murmur of raised voices.

"You can't do this to me!" That was a girl's voice. Orchid and Finn exchanged glances.

"...calm down..." Headmaster Boddy was heard saying.

More words, shouted over one another. Orchid couldn't make out much, until:

"No, *you* will live to regret this. I'll make sure of that."

The door flew open, and standing on the threshold, feet planted apart like she was some avenging Amazon, stood none other than the six-foot-tall terror of the tennis court—Beth "Peacock" Picach.

Well, that's what her fans called her. Orchid was never much for sports, and she thought the nickname was stupid, but Beth Picach had embraced it, as well as the cawing that ensued in the stands whenever her matches began. She'd even dyed the tips of her signature blond ponytail a vibrant blue, a color which was currently contrasting furiously with her crimson cheeks.

"Beth," Headmaster Boddy warned.

Peacock looked at the two students sitting in the chairs and scowled. This was the stare that struck fear in the hearts of her opponents.

Finn flinched. Orchid gaped.

Peacock fled.

Headmaster Boddy called to his secretary, then paused. "Oh, that's right. Ms. O'Connor is proctoring the freshman bio exam, isn't she?"

"I wouldn't know, sir," Finn replied. Suck-up.

In truth, most of the staff had packed up the second their last exams were finished and headed for the mainland to spend the break with friends and family. It was always dead at Blackbrook over the holidays.

Orchid knew that all too well.

"All right," Headmaster Boddy said. "I'll take care of it later. Miss McKee, I believe you're next?"

She felt a sudden dread, deep in the pit of her stomach. She didn't care what Finn's theory was. No way were they being called in here to be informed, one by one, of some dubious academic honor. She'd screwed up. Somehow, despite all her careful planning . . . she'd screwed up.

"Good luck," Finn said to her, as if they were friends. They were *not* friends.

She shrugged again.

Headmaster Boddy's private chamber was cozy, softer than the imperious presence of the office waiting room. Here there were the stern, frowning pictures of the head-masters—always male—who had come before him. But there was also a merry fire burning in the grate, and mis-matched plaid cushions on the armchairs across from the great wooden desk.

He swiped a heavy-looking brass candlestick from the rug, replaced it on the mantel, and chuckled ruefully. "Let's try to keep this civil, okay?"

That must have been the object they'd heard thunk-ing around. Had Peacock actually thrown it? At Boddy? Knowing Peacock's serving arm, Orchid was shocked the man had survived.

Everyone loved the headmaster. He'd been at Blackbrook for more than a decade, after a long career as a professor of chemical engineering at a college on the mainland. He liked cats and pipes and cheering for the school sports teams from the front row. A jolly old grandpa; at least as long as you stayed in line.

For a moment, Orchid stopped wondering what she'd done wrong and started wondering what Peacock was in for.

"Yes, sir." She closed the door and took a seat in one of the wingback chairs.

"Now, you." He shuffled through some papers. "Ah, yes. Miss McKee. We wanted to wait until you were finished with your exams so as not to disrupt the semester's academic record, but given that a situation has arisen . . . Well, when *was* the last time you spoke to your parents?"

"Oh, I speak to them a few times a week, over phone or email," she replied evenly. Cecily had called over Thanksgiving, ranting about her check, but Orchid had resolved that. The sperm donor, of course, she'd never met.

"It's just . . . There seems to be a problem with your last tuition payment. And when we tried to contact your parents in the Caymans, the number we have on file was disconnected."

"I don't know how this could have happened." Other than that the number was a total fake.

"If you could call your parents now . . . Maybe their cell phones . . . I'm sure we can resolve this. We wouldn't want a problem going into next semester."

"Of course not," Orchid said, thinking fast. "The only thing is, I think they are on safari in Kenya at the moment, so I don't know if I can get them."

"Safari." Headmaster Boddy looked unimpressed, as if

it were not the craziest thing he'd heard about his over-privileged students; probably not even the craziest this week.

"Yeah." She pretended to consider options. "Oh, I know. I can call our accountant. I'm sure she can tell me if there's a mix-up with the accounts."

"You know the number of your parents' accountant?"

"Sure." She gave a rich-girl shrug. *That* probably wasn't the craziest thing the headmaster had heard this week, either.

Then she called *her* accountant. The same one she'd had for over a decade. The only member of her original team left. Her accountant's secretary, unfortunately, was new, and momentarily confused by the name *Orchid McKee*, which Orchid had to repeat entirely too many times for comfort in front of the headmaster.

"I'm sorry," the secretary said. "She's out of the office today, but I can check on that transaction for you. Please enter your security PIN on the keypad."

This was why Orchid kept them around. Their commitment to keeping their clients' privacy was exquisite. She entered her PIN.

"All automatic transactions for this client were canceled last month."

Well, that explained why Cecily had been upset. Orchid had thought it was the woman's usual mismanagement of funds. The kind that had once cost Orchid half a million dollars before she'd put her mother on an allowance. "Why?"

"The note says at client's request."

She'd requested nothing of the sort. But she wasn't about to get into it in front of the headmaster.

After being assured they'd get to the bottom of this as soon as possible, Orchid hung up and flashed a smile at Headmaster Boddy. "Slight mix-up with the accounts. In the meantime, I'll just cover it . . ." She dug in her bag for her checkbook, and wrote out a tuition check.

A big one. Blackbrook was not cheap.

He stared at her. "Miss McKee, surely you don't have the funds in your personal account to cover your tuition. Students are just supposed to have spending money."

"And book fees," Orchid said, waving the check. "Daddy made sure I had a little extra this month. You know . . . because of the safari."

"Right." Headmaster Boddy hesitated another moment, then took the check. It *still* probably wasn't the craziest thing he'd dealt with all week. "You know, while I have you here, I must ask: why didn't you enter your biology project in the state science fair?"

Oh no.

"It was the best in the class. Your teacher and I were so disappointed. I know you don't need the scholarship"—he gestured to her check—"but the prestige of placing might be worth it. For your college applications, if nothing else."

"I'm not really one for competitions," said Orchid. *Or publicity*, she thought. "I just want to focus on my classes."

Headmaster Boddy considered this. "Yes, I looked at your grades earlier. You're one of the top ranked juniors in the school."

She'd definitely heard Scarlett mentioning that fact on occasion. "Ranks and awards and stuff aren't really my thing."

"A stealth scholar."

Her best role to date: introverted nerd. "Tell you what. I'll think about the whole state science fair thing for next year." She checked her watch. "Now, though, I have to run home and finish my history term paper."

She didn't, as it had been completed for almost a week. It was amazing how smoothly the lies still fell from her lips, even after all this time.

Headmaster Boddy sighed. "Very well. Send in my next appointment—Mr. Plum."

She headed out. Finn stood when he saw her.

"My turn?"

She nodded. "Good luck." He probably wasn't in trouble, either. Probably just being informed of the awards status of his latest chemistry experiment, which, of course, he'd be entering in all the competitions.

The weather had turned from frigid to positively arctic. They were supposed to get ice overnight. Orchid pulled on her thick knit cap with the earmuffs, buttoned her long, puffy coat up to her chin, and pulled up the fur-lined hood.

Some kids couldn't make it through their first winter

at Blackbrook. If the isolation didn't get you, the freezing darkness would. But for Orchid, the benefits of the former far outweighed any issues she might have with the latter. So what if the sun set soon after lunch, or it snowed from October until May? She was safe here. Invisible.

The sky was a wormy gray and the wind whipped through the bare branches of the trees as Orchid hurried across campus. The windows in all the buildings were dark and empty, as most of the students and faculty had already left for the holiday. Orchid was struck with the sudden realization that she could scream at the top of her lungs and no one would hear her.

Less a luxe boarding school movie, and more a thriller.

Her boardinghouse, Tudor House, was located on the very outskirts of the Blackbrook property, farther from the classroom quad than nearly any other building. It was a monument to crumbling glory. Once the property of a local logging heiress, it had served time as some kind of girls' reform school earlier in the century before being sold off to Blackbrook for use as one of its fanciest and most coveted girls' dorms. Orchid felt lucky to have been able to claim a room this year.

She kicked her boots off in the front hall and headed to the mail stand, where the residents' letters had been sorted into little cubbyholes.

"Hey!" Scarlett Mistry glimpsed her through the open door to the lounge and came dashing out, much to Orchid's chagrin. The petite Indian girl planted her feet wide and put her hands on her hips. "I heard you were just in Boddy's office."

Orchid shrugged and pulled out her mail. A catalog, a college brochure, a letter—who could be writing her? There was no return address, but the postmark was from the opposite coast.

"Finn texted me. He said Peacock went ballistic on Boddy." The resident queen bee of Blackbrook would not be ignored. She flicked the edges of her long, shiny black hair over her shoulder and raised her eyebrows. "So, what did she say?"

Orchid ripped open the letter, mostly to have something to do other than gossiping with Scarlett. It was bad enough she had to listen to the other girl hold court at dinner every night.

"Finn said he's lucky to be alive, the way she was screaming and throwing stuff around."

It was a single sheet of paper, with six typed lines.

Found you.
You didn't think you could hide from me forever, did you, Emily?
Then again, I guess there are still some holes in your security. Hope there's no issue with your finances. I was surprised to see how much they'd let me do.
I'm glad you're doing so well in school.
Be in touch soon.

Orchid heard Scarlett's voice as if from a great distance. "Come on, Orchid. You were there. What was it all about?"

Her mouth was dry. Her heart pounded.

"It—It seemed like Beth was in big trouble," Orchid said softly.

And she wasn't the only one.

2

Green

The snow went on for three days straight, which was not unusual for Rocky Point. All the locals had their salt and snow tires, their stocks of candles and canned food. When Vaughn Green was ten, a Christmas storm had knocked out the power for more than a week. Two days into this one, and Headmaster Boddy didn't so much as delay the nine A.M. exam start times. Which meant the maintenance workers—Vaughn included—were up at four A.M., shoveling walks so the rich students wouldn't get their toes wet on their way to class.

He probably should have found a way to get out of it, since he'd arrived at his own nine A.M. music theory exam with an aching back and sweaty pits. Still nailed it—which was why he had been the one to shovel the walks. His grades in music theory were way better than the ones in history, and the history term paper wasn't finished. Rich kids got things like extensions and excuses. The local scholarship kid had to maintain appearances.

By the third day of snow, even the locals were crying

foul, especially because the weather report promised that an even more severe ice storm was on its way over the weekend. The governor declared a state of emergency in the area, and half the town decided to evacuate, in case the storm surge made the two-lane road connecting Rocky Point to the mainland impassable. Headmaster Boddy looked at the situation and finally made the right call. In an email to the entire student body, he announced that all remaining exams would be postponed, and the few people left on campus would leave by noon the next day.

Only, the storm came one night early, and it was far, far worse than anyone had predicted.

Vaughn awoke to the sound of great cracks and booms. The power had gone out at some point in the night, and the chill was beginning to set in, especially around the windows. Vaughn remembered how it had gotten two winters ago, when the heat had gone off and ice formed several inches thick on the insides of the panes. He couldn't see much in the darkness through the driving sleet, but he guessed the sounds were made by trees tearing in two beneath the weight of ice.

He was half right. At six A.M., their neighbor dropped by to check in on them and reported that a few cottages down by the ravine had gotten stove up in the storm. All empty—thank goodness.

They probably should have evacuated sooner.

"Any news from Blackbrook?" he asked Vaughn. Everyone in town knew their golden boy.

Vaughn shook his head.

"Ayuh," said his neighbor. "Them from away don't know what they're in for."

Vaughn started packing on layers.

His brother looked amused by the plan. "Sure, kill yourself trying to get out there. Maybe they'll finally notice you when you're dead."

"Hard telling, not knowing," Vaughn replied. "If nothing else, they'll need an extra hand with the sandbags."

Oliver snorted. "Right. The only thing those Blackbrook kids respect more than a townie is a janitor."

Even after all this time, Oliver still hadn't kicked the habit of referring to the other students like that. *Those Blackbrook kids.* Rich, entitled, mostly useless, and shockingly bad at aiming into the urinals.

They were Blackbrook.

And that meant Vaughn was . . . Well, he didn't know exactly what he was. Not these days. But he'd never forget the day his life changed; the day he'd gotten his acceptance letter in the mail from Blackbrook Academy. He'd known it was his ticket to a new life.

Well, a new half life, at least.

Vaughn packed a bag while his brother sat in the old rocker, playing with his weapons collection and making snarky comments. Most folks in Rocky Point had at least one gun in their house, and Gemma had taught them both to shoot when they were kids, but Oliver's enthusiasm was as unbridled as it was unsettling.

Which was precisely how Oliver liked it.

Vaughn wasn't in the mood for his games. "Would it make you feel better to think I'm not going for *those Blackbrook kids?*"

"Then who?"

"Rusty Nayler," Vaughn said with a shrug. "Linda White."

"Whatever," Oliver sneered. "Give my love to Boddy. I know he's your favorite ass to kiss."

Vaughn finished packing and dressing, but before he headed out into the elements, he made a final appeal.

"Oliver, if I'm not back in two days—"

"You think we're keeping to the schedule in this storm?" His smile was nearly worse than his sneer. "Have fun. I've got my own plans."

That was never a happy thought. "Don't do anything stupid."

"Oh, like trying to cross the ravine in an ice storm?" He flipped a vintage tomahawk around in his hand. "Maybe they ought to rethink that scholarship."

Vaughn knew better than to reply. The scholarship was the best thing that had happened to Oliver in years, too, and he knew it.

But his brother wasn't done. He placed the weapon back on the coffee table. "Seriously, why do you bother?"

Vaughn swallowed. "Someone has to."

For a second, Vaughn thought he might get through. But, as always, it was wishful thinking. Oliver was silent.

"See you, then." Alone, he headed out into the storm.

It was a little more than a mile from his house to the Blackbrook campus, which stood at the very edge of the point. When the weather was nice, Vaughn would often ride to campus on his bike. But today, the roads would be greasy. He grabbed a pair of crampons for what he'd bet would be a painful hike.

There were two ways to get to Blackbrook: the long way, down the old shore road, across the ravine bridge by the old sawmill, and past Cartwright Park and the old Tudor House that marked the edge of the campus. Or, the shortcut across the wooded ravine. Both seemed treacherous in this weather.

When Vaughn set out, a wintry mix was falling from the sky, stinging his skin with every touch and crackling on the ground like breakfast cereal.

That was when Vaughn realized he'd forgotten breakfast. Nothing seemed to matter that morning more than not getting trapped with Oliver and his plots, which covered the house like a film of grime. His threats, which lay openly on every nightstand and behind every door.

He could stop for a snack now, and risk hypothermia before he reached Blackbrook. Or he could press on. Vaughn wrapped his scarf higher over his mouth, pulled his hood farther down around his face, and wished very hard that he'd remembered his balaclava. Gemma had never liked them. Said they made people look like criminals. Oliver had always made a point of wearing his after that. Vaughn only found it funny that people from away, like Gemma, grew up worried more about bank robbers than about their noses freezing off.

Between the drifts and the ice, it took Vaughn more than an hour to reach the bridge over the ravine on the main road—or rather, what was left of the bridge. English wasn't Vaughn's subject, but he was pretty sure there was a metaphor hidden somewhere in the cracked and broken tangle of lumber, rubble, and steel.

He should have packed more supplies. No one was getting on or off the Blackbrook campus anytime soon. On the other side of the ravine, he saw the old boathouse, already being buffeted by waves as the storm surge pushed the tide up the banks.

Vaughn turned inland, tracing the path of devastation toward the neighborhood overlooking the ravine. Several times, he heard thunderous crashes in the trees, echoing from rock to rock and drowning out the storm's crackling hush. Several times, he broke into a sprint as the branches above him creaked and moaned beneath the growing weight of ice.

This wasn't like the storms he'd grown up with. Snowstorms would muffle sounds, creating drifts of silence Vaughn had always thought you could get lost in. He'd once heard a song about a man who'd gone walking in a silent wood, only to slip into an enchanted world. But when Vaughn finally came to a break in the trees where the woods gave way to the ravine road, he realized this was no fairyland.

It was hell.

Once the home of lumber workers before the mill had shut down, the ravine cottages had seen better days. Porches tilted into the valley and paint was more of a suggestion than a promise.

Vaughn and his brother had been born in one of these cottages. That one, with the faded green door. The one that currently lay in a mangled wreck at the bottom of the ravine.

A few cottages got stove up! Typical Maine understatement. Half the homes here had been utterly obliterated. The road was a mess of roof tiles and splintered clapboard, and as Vaughn picked his way through the wreckage, he could barely differentiate between sheets of ice and the scattered shards of windowpanes.

He spared one last glance at the house with the faded green door. For just a moment, he remembered Gemma's face. Pale and sunken, as it had been the morning he'd found her.

Be glad she didn't live to see this. That was the echo of Oliver in his head. That house had ceased being a home long before Gemma's death, and she wouldn't even have remembered it, near the end. She'd remembered so little, after all.

Just her grievances.

He saw a flash of color against the gray and black of the storm. Another person out in this weather, picking her way through the rubble. Town this size, you knew everyone by their parkas. This was old Mrs. Douglass, from the post office. He waved and she gave him a Yankee nod.

"Vaughn?" The woman's voice echoed across the ravine.

"Ayuh." She'd had a fifty-fifty shot. He gestured up the slope. "Is the old footbridge still good?"

"For another few minutes, 'til the storm surge comes in. Don't tell me you're going to try to make it to Blackbrook! You'll get trapped out there! I'm sure they won't mind if you miss class just this once."

Better out there than in the house with his brother. "There's no class, ma'am," he explained. "I just want to make sure the flatlanders come through the storm all right."

Even through the layers of scarf over her features, he could see the face she made. "Well, good luck to you." She sounded like Oliver when she said it. As though, if he cast his lot with the Blackbrook folks, she'd wash her hands of the whole matter.

If he slipped on the bridge over the ravine and fell to his death, well, that was his choice, too.

That was how it went with those from Rocky Point and their fraught relationship with the school. Since the mill had closed, almost everyone in town made their living off Blackbrook one way or another. But that didn't mean they had to like it.

Vaughn had long ago gotten used to the contradiction. All his neighbors bursting with pride that he was a

Blackbrook kid, even as they spat the term at the other students at the school.

Near the top of the ravine was an old handmade footbridge sticking out from the side of the rock. The ice lay thick across its surface, and the drop down the bluff beneath its splintered boards was steep and slippery.

He could hear Oliver now. *Are you numb, risking your life for Blackbrook kids?*

But it wasn't for them. It had never been for *them.* It was for Vaughn. He put a foot on the bridge. It creaked and shuddered, but it always did that, even when they'd been kids and Oliver had dared him to cross that very first time.

Vaughn had never been the daredevil in the family. Every risk they'd ever taken, it had been Oliver forcing his hand. He took a step, and then another. The ice crackled and shattered beneath him. The woods tinkled around him.

He wondered if Mrs. Douglass was watching him. He wondered if they'd find his body at the base of the ravine. And then he wondered how things were at Blackbrook, and took another tentative step.

His boots slid out from under him. He grabbed for the rock as he went down, gloved fingers scraping uselessly against the stone. The crampons finally pierced the surface and stopped the slide, and he righted himself, his balance all askew beneath the weight of his pack. One more step, and he'd be safe.

There. He'd made it. He looked back across the ravine, seeking out the form of Mrs. Douglass in her bright coat, but she was gone. *Figured.* Vaughn pressed on.

It took another hour for the high gabled roofs of Tudor House marking the edge of the Blackbrook campus to come into view, and by that time, Vaughn had lost all feeling in his toes and fingers. He remembered learning that victims of hypothermia imagined they were too hot right before the end, and took that as a good sign, as he had never been so cold in his life.

Tudor House looked dark and empty from the outside, but the power was probably off here, too. He knew Mrs. White would not have left. Vaughn struggled up the marble steps to the porch, the spikes on his boots probably leaving nice long gashes in the stone, and knocked the lion's head knocker on the ornate front door.

After a moment, a girl answered. Her skin had the pale, nearly translucent cast most people got around here when the days grew short. Her hair was a muddy brown and aggressively brushed into a short, bushy bob. Her long bangs and square-rimmed glasses nearly hid her shockingly deep blue eyes, which widened as she saw him.

"Vaughn?" she asked. "You must be freezing. Get inside."

He obeyed.

"Though I don't know how warm it is in here," the girl went on, closing the door.

At once, the sound of the wind and the ice ceased. Vaughn nearly gasped from relief.

It was dim in the hall, but not dark, as light still came in from the tall window over the door. In the gloom, one might still imagine Tudor House looking as it had a century ago, in its glossy, Gilded Age glory.

"The power went out last night. Rusty's working on the generator." She looked up at him. "Are you okay? You're not frozen, are you?"

"It's a little nippy out there." She was very pretty, this girl in the nice warm hallway where he'd found himself. She wore an enormous sweater—one that looked like it had been knit for a linebacker—over a pair of fleece leggings and giant, puffy slippers. "Orchid?" he tried as he pulled off his gloves and hat. He was famously terrible with names, but that one had stuck.

"Yeah." She nodded. "From history class?"

"Sorry," he said, unwrapping his scarf. He was used to apologizing for forgetting people's names and letting people come up with their own reasons why. "I'm so cold."

"Of course!" She took him by the arm. "Come sit by the fire we've got going in the lounge. Mrs. White made a stew . . ."

He let himself be led into the lounge, where there was, as promised, a most marvelous fire. There was also another girl there, curled up under what he knew was one of Mrs. White's handmade crazy quilts. This girl he knew, too. Scarlett Mistry. Junior class president, all around superstar, rich witch.

As Oliver would say, the most *Blackbrook kid* in school.

Scarlett narrowed her eyes in his direction as he took off his coat and got closer to the flames.

"Vaughn Green?" she sneered. "What are *you* doing here?"

3

Scarlett

Scarlett Mistry supposed there were natural disasters everywhere. But it was all so very inconvenient.

When she was a child, her father had gone apoplectic over a hurricane that had flattened one of their multi-million-dollar high-rises in Miami Beach. A landslide in Vail had once collapsed the roof of a Mistry Hotels chalet. And her mother was constantly threatening to sell off the property in New Orleans before the levees gave way for good. Even in her family's native Gujarat, India, there were terrible floods when the monsoons came.

Property was a risky way to make a living, in Scarlett's opinion—not that she'd ever say as much to her parents. She'd long ago decided on an alternative route to fame and fortune, one free from the uncertainty of climate change and its unpredictable effect on the real estate market.

Unfortunately, she hadn't factored in power outages.

So instead of being able to check any of her feeds, she was stuck sitting in a wingback chair, her phone as dead as a brick in her hand, and listening to Orchid pepper the townie with questions about how bad the storm had gotten.

He wasn't big on details, that Vaughn Green.

Not that Scarlett needed Vaughn's opinion on how screwed they all were. After all, she was spending the afternoon sitting under a quilt by a fire like some sort of pioneer girl. Even the old crank radio the old, cranky janitor had dug out of some dusty storage shed wasn't tuning in to anything useful. The governor thought they should evacuate—but it was far beyond too late for that, according to Vaughn's report. The bridge to the mainland was in shambles, washed out by some kind of super-high tide called a storm surge—Scarlett had learned from the radio and everyone else's sage nods at the word—that had brought in massive chunks of sea ice, water, and debris.

"It's a good thing Tudor House is on a hill," said Orchid. "Or we might get flooded, too."

"We still might," said Mrs. White, coming in with a tray of food for the half-frozen Vaughn. What had he been thinking, tromping in here from the village in this weather? "The pipes burst once during weather like this. Rusty's done his best to winterize this place, but you never know with a house this old."

Vaughn jumped up to retrieve the tray from the dorm proctor. Scarlett had always liked Mrs. White, mainly because the old woman viewed any resident of Tudor House as under her immediate and all-consuming protection. She would even stand up to teachers and administrators on your behalf—a fact that Scarlett had not yet deployed for herself, but was glad to be aware of, should the need arise. Honestly, it was half the reason Tudor House had been Scarlett's top choice of dorm, despite being so far from the classrooms. Mrs. White might look like an aging hippie in her crocheted shawls and ever-present witchy broomstick skirt—even in the dead of winter!—but the old lady was entirely made of stone and fire.

"Thank you, dear," said Mrs. White. She lowered herself gingerly into a nearby chair. "This cold is getting to be too much for me, too. Maybe I'll retire and move to Florida."

Scarlett laughed. "Mrs. White, you'll never leave Tudor House." She was an institution at Blackbrook. People said she'd been here since Tudor housed a girls' reform school half a century ago.

"True." Mrs. White looked at Vaughn. "People come to Rocky Point and don't leave."

Somehow, Scarlett refrained from rolling her eyes. That would not be *her* problem. She'd already be gone, if it weren't for this stupid storm. She should have left days ago, but she'd had commitments as student body president. And she'd had plans that had seemed, at the moment, to take precedence over travel arrangements.

She hadn't counted on being cut off from all communication by this storm. What would her followers think?

Orchid, the only other straggler in the house, seemed overjoyed by their isolation. Scarlett's *actual* friends in Tudor House—Nisha and Atherton—had been able to leave campus early, along with Faith and Cadence, so Scarlett had resigned herself to sitting in awkward silence with their remaining housemate, Orchid McKee, until it was time for them, too, to return to civilization.

Orchid wasn't exactly talkative under the best conditions, and she'd spent the last two days in what could only be described as a deep funk. Scarlett had figured it was due to the weather, but weirdly, Orchid's spirits had lifted the moment they'd received the news that no one was getting in or out of town in this storm. She probably thought no one had noticed.

Scarlett was very good at noticing things. Like the way the townie still hadn't managed to explain what he was doing in his mismatched socks in their house, other than polishing off three bowls of stew and practically undressing right there in the lounge. Long underwear was still underwear, dude. It was right there in the name.

But Mrs. White had seemed pleased to see him. Mrs. White, who usually responded to boys breaching her inner sanctum as if it were an *actual* invasion. That was probably left over from the girls' reform school days, too. But for the townie, it was as if all bets were off.

"You can't go back now," Mrs. White was saying to Vaughn as he tucked into soup bowl number four. Scarlett wondered if they ought to ration food, especially since it didn't look like anyone was getting to a supermarket anytime soon. "The storm surge will have flooded the ravine by now. You can stay here."

"Where?" Scarlett asked. The other girls in Tudor House might have gone home for the holidays, but she doubted highly they'd want Vaughn and his stack of damp, musty coats and snow pants and things gunking up their rooms. She could imagine the fit Nisha would pull if he left ravine gravel on her cashmere rug. She pictured the passive-aggressive texts she'd get from Atherton if he used her face cream.

"He could stay here, in the lounge," Orchid offered, as if she had the right to do so. "That couch is super comfy. I've fallen asleep on it loads of times."

Mrs. White had a firm no-boys-past-nine rule, one which had ruined Scarlett and Finn's marathon study sessions loads of times. Her fingers itched to text him this latest outrage, but then she remembered that her phone was dead.

Finn might as well be dead. She hadn't heard from him since before the storm started, which was a little weird, now that she thought about it. He didn't usually go dark on her, even when he had his head in one of his experiments. The last she'd heard from him was three days ago, that flurry of messages about seeing Orchid in Headmaster Boddy's office, followed swiftly by the bombshell that Peacock had had some sort of nervous breakdown in front of everyone.

But he'd had to sign off before she'd gotten any of the really good gossip about what was happening, and, of course, Orchid hadn't been forthcoming with the info, either. Scarlett's most annoying housemate had just retreated to her room with the excuse that she had a history paper to finish.

She clutched her phone, thinking about Finn.

"Maybe Vaughn could go stay in one of the boys' dorms," she suggested. She may not want him *here,* but she couldn't deny he might have skills that could come in handy during a storm of this magnitude. Skills that Finn, for all his scientific genius, was utterly lacking.

But Vaughn didn't seem to like that idea. "I won't be any trouble, Mrs. White, really."

Yeah right. The townie had never been anything but trouble. Like last year, when they'd butted heads over her Campus Beautification Committee project. Vaughn was from the end of the freaking world. What did he know about how to put this school on the map? As if he were an expert on what Blackbrook needed, just because he grew up across the ravine.

In Scarlett's opinion, that was half the point of the ravine—to keep the Rocky Point people on their own side.

"You're never any trouble," Mrs. White replied, and it was possible she actually smiled. At a male. Scarlett blinked in astonishment. That had to be a first. Maybe there were more benefits to being a townie than she'd realized. "And you're not going anywhere. Not in this weather."

Great. So instead of riding out the storm and bingeing on TV and snacks with Nisha, she was stuck in Tudor House with the two people in the whole school she liked the least.

There was a bang as the front door opened, and the roar of wind went from dull and distant to deafening. Vaughn had really walked here from town? In this?

The new arrival looked like a hobo as he shoved the door shut. He wore a patched down coat and scuffed work boots, and scarves wrapped around his face to his eyelids. But the ancient plaid woolen hat the color of water stains was unmistakable. Rusty Nayler, the head of the Blackbrook custodial staff, had returned.

He didn't even bother unwinding his scarf before he addressed them.

"Pipes burst in Baylor House, and Boddy thinks the surge is going to flood out Dockery Hall and the chemistry lab."

"What do *you* think?" Mrs. White asked without missing a beat.

"I think it'll flood a lot more than that." He caught sight of Vaughn. "Green? What are you doing here?"

"Wanted to check on you and see if there was any way I could help."

Rusty harrumphed. "Mess isn't done getting made, and you want to work?"

Right. Vaughn Green worked with the janitors, too, when he wasn't acting holier-than-thou about every blade of grass on this campus. Or maybe that's the reason he was so unbearable about it.

"But I'll bet there's plenty to handle after," Rusty added. "Might even be some work for your brother."

Vaughn's grunted reply wasn't even decipherable as words this time.

"Boddy wants to move everyone left to higher ground."

"What does that mean?" Scarlett asked, suddenly suspicious.

Mrs. White sighed. "That means us."

4

Plum

The flood could only be a good thing. Finn Plum forced himself to cling to that notion as he packed up his computer, his important paperwork, and the digital scale he'd begged his parents to purchase for his birthday. No evidence meant no further inquiries, and Boddy would be so busy with whatever followed this disaster that their little conversation might be totally forgotten.

And if it wasn't . . . Well, Finn could cry, or mope, and pretend to be offended by the very idea that he might have done something wrong. Those tactics always worked before.

They had been instructed to evacuate straight to Tudor House on the hill at the edge of campus, but Finn had one stop to make first. The chemistry lab was down the hill, closer to the water, and he slipped on the ice three times before he got there.

The flood had already surrounded the building with an ankle-deep moat of slush and ice that Finn wasn't willing to risk his electronics to. Pulling out one of many garbage bags he'd brought for the purpose, he quickly shoved his backpack in one, stowed it somewhere safe, then swathed each leg in a garbage bag to protect his shoes and pants from the swirling eddies of the storm surge.

The move did nothing to help the bottom of his boots keep from slipping on the mud, however, and by the time he reached the lab, he wondered why he'd bothered. His feet were soaked through and numb with cold.

The door would be locked, of course, and Finn doubted he could open it with all the water there, anyway. But he wasn't going in the front way. He never did, except for official lab hours.

Around the right side of the building was the fire escape, and the long ladder Finn had climbed in rain and snow and the middle of the night. He kicked at the rungs, knocking loose the column of ice around every metal cross-bar, before he attempted to put his weight on them. *Clang!* He wrapped his arms up to his elbows around the higher rungs, ignoring the bite of the cold metal into the down of his coat, and prayed he didn't slip to his death. *Clang!* It was good the campus was all but abandoned. *Clang!* The sound was deafening, even against the howl of the storm.

This had never been the plan. There was a reason Finn studied chemistry and not geology or one of the other field sciences. He wasn't Indiana Jones. He liked labs, not oil rigs. He liked fluorescent lights and climate control.

But there was one thing he liked more, and it was hidden behind the air vent in room 203.

The lock in the window had never worked properly, not since Finn had first discovered it freshman year. Security at Blackbrook was a total joke, probably because the administration expected the remote location to do most of the work for them. And yet they encouraged him to do world-class science here; science that might be stolen by any idiot who also knew the third window to the left had a broken lock?

Yeah, right.

It took him less than five minutes, in and out. He eased himself through the window and carefully lowered himself onto the fire escape platform. If this scientist thing didn't work out, maybe he'd become a cat burglar.

CLANG! The sound of his boots hitting the metal grate echoed across the rising water.

Then again, maybe not. In the distance, on the raised path, he saw a lone figure in an unmistakably bright blue coat stop in her tracks and turn in the direction of the lab, as if searching for the source of the sound.

Finn froze. Of course! Of course *she* would be the one to catch him.

Maybe she wouldn't see him through all this sleet. Maybe if he stood perfectly still, she wouldn't see him at all. Like how dinosaurs or birds of prey were better at seeing movement. Peacock could catch a speeding tennis ball, but not Phineas Plum.

Behind her rose the walls of Dockery Hall, the girls' dorm most of them wanted because it looked out over the sea. They'd be paying for that choice now, Finn figured, what with the flood. From his perch he could see that the seaward floor of the building had been completely flooded out. She must have escaped via a back door up on the slope. Even now, he could see the waves crashing against the walls and sending massive cascades of water up onto the land with every breath.

He waited, still as stone, for her to move on.

But she didn't move. The water swirled about her powerful calves and she stood there as if she didn't even feel it, her legs spread in what he knew she thought of as her power stance. The one that made the opponents across the net quake in their pricey tennis shoes. It occurred to him that she probably didn't care at all about the sea view from her dorm. He'd bet money she only chose it because of its proximity to the tennis courts. She was the only girl he'd ever met with a firmer sense of purpose than himself.

Finn never had uncovered what she'd been in to see Headmaster Boddy about, back before the storm. He'd set Scarlett to the task, but had been too distracted to follow up, and then the power had gone out and there'd been no chance to find out.

He hoped it was nothing serious. More than that, he hoped it had nothing to do with him.

Just then, a gray wall of water rose up over the seawall, collided with the building, and crested its roof.

Finn didn't hesitate. "Beth!" he screamed, and pointed to the danger behind her.

But Beth didn't look at the wave. She looked at him. Their eyes met for a single second, and then the water hit her and she was knocked off her feet.

"No!" Finn half slid down the ladder. *Clangity-clang-clang-clang.* The water was almost up to his thighs now. No point in the garbage bags. He hissed in pain as the freezing water hit his most sensitive zones and he splashed toward where she'd fallen. She was already pushing herself to her feet. Her many bags and boxes were flung far and wide.

One was floating away with the undertow. Finn lunged for it and caught it before it headed out to sea.

"Are you okay?" he gasped when he reached her, holding out the sodden sports duffel in her signature blue.

She scowled at him and flung her wet hair over her shoulder. "Get your hands off my stuff," she growled.

"Excuse me?" He thrust the bag at her. "I saved your stupid gym shorts."

"No one asked for your help."

"Fine." He began to swing the bag back at the raging water, but she grabbed the strap and glared daggers at him.

"Don't be even more of a jerk than usual."

Last time he tried to do anything for her. He dropped the bag into the mud and tromped back up the hill toward where he'd stowed his backpack. "Get your own luggage."

"What a gentleman!" she screamed at him.

It was impossible to give someone the finger in thick

mittens. He clenched his jaw—mostly to keep from shivering—and thought seriously about returning to his dorm room, flooding or no. She was probably being evacuated to Tudor also, and he didn't exactly want to get stuck in that house with a fuming Peacock.

Finn knew well what a disaster that could be.

Another deafening crash of the waves, and icy shards of seawater pummeled down on him, almost knocking him off his feet. When the onslaught stopped, he steadied himself, slouching even deeper into the still-dry parts of his coat.

Don't look back.

He looked back.

Beth looked like a bright blue drowned rat. She still wore the backpack and carried the sodden box, but now dragged the watery duffel by a broken strap.

Finn sighed and trudged back down the icy path.

"I hate you," she said as she handed him the duffel.

"Back at you," he said, and together they headed up the hill toward Tudor House. The duffel was heavy and slapped wetly against Finn's soaking leg. Its repetitive *thwap* was the only way he knew he *had* a leg. Everything below the knee was numb, and the parts of his body he could still feel were screaming in pain. His glasses were spattered with chips of ice and mud.

Beth was wet through. He could see icicles forming on the ends of her wet, blue-streaked hair. Her lips had turned the same shade of blue.

"We should hurry before we freeze."

"I'm only waiting for you," she said, and starting walking quickly enough that Finn did indeed struggle to keep up.

Tudor House appeared before them, a dark mass in the stormy distance. Had it always been this far across campus? Ahead of them, a peal of laughter cut through the squall and the cold descending on Finn like a blanket. A girl in a metallic coat squealed as a figure in a dun-colored jacket swung her up over his shoulder like a sack of potatoes and dashed for the front steps of Tudor. Behind her, another girl in another metallic jacket waited for her turn.

"Don't even think about it," Beth drawled beside him.

"Carrying you?" It even hurt to talk.

"No, asking me to carry *you*."

The muscleman materialized in front of them, breathing hard. Up close, Finn could see he was almost painfully clean-cut, with neatly combed black hair and darkly tan skin. Also not much taller than Finn himself—the newcomer was built like the kind of football player who went to a school that spent its enormous budget on athletics instead of electron microscopes. He and Beth should get along great.

"Hey, you look like you got out just in time," the handsome football player person said in a booming voice. "Need a hand?"

"No," said Finn.

"Sure," said Beth, and before Finn could protest, the

new guy had swiped all their bags and was headed back to the porch of Tudor House. Then, faster than Finn would have thought possible, he rejoined them and, quick as a wink, swept Beth off her feet, too, and was jogging toward the house.

Finn jogged behind him, lest the new guy decide to pick him up next.

The Tudor House proctor was directing traffic in the shadowy hall, telling everyone to deposit their wet things in an enormous pile by the door and head in one direction for dry blankets and in another for warm soup.

All of Finn's things were wet, and he was not about to let them out of his sight.

"Mrs. White," he said, "can you just tell me where I'll be staying?"

He didn't understand how the tiny woman managed to look down her nose at him, but she did. Mrs. White had always had it in for him, for some reason. Every time he and Scarlett got together to drill flash cards, the second the clock struck nine, you'd think he'd turned into a pumpkin.

"Ah, yes, Mr. Plum. You'll be on the floor in the billiards room."

"Floor." Got it. At least he knew where he stood. Or lay, as it were.

"There are some spare blankets to make a bedroll. Please do not track all your wet things through my hall. The parquet dates to 1892."

"Yes, ma'am." But he didn't put anything down, and as soon as her attention was elsewhere, he headed to the billiards room, bags and all.

The new guy was already in there, shucking his foul-weather gear.

"Oh," said Finn, feeling uncharacteristically stupid. Of course they'd be sharing rooms. With strangers. And no private place to stash valuables.

"Hey," said the new guy, his white teeth flashing in his broad smile. "You must be Plum."

His handshake seemed strong enough to crush Finn's bones, but all Finn could feel through the frozen numbness was pins and needles. He couldn't call up enough sensation or control to squeeze back.

"I'm Samuel Maestor, but you can call me Mustard."

"Can I, though?" Finn couldn't stop himself from saying.

This guy was kidding, right?

Mustard?

5

Mustard

Samuel "Mustard" Maestor had slept in worse places. Two years ago, during freshman boot camp, they'd been dropped off in the middle of the high desert and given seventy-two hours to find their way back to the barracks through a wasteland of sinkhole-pocked tundra and deadly crevasses. The race had been concocted to form a sort of pecking order within the class. The boys would all know who was hard and smart and scary, and who . . . wasn't.

Mustard had come in first, of course. His father wouldn't have had it any other way.

By contrast, a soft, warm bedroll on the carpeted floor of one side of a fancy billiards room was a perfectly acceptable place to spend a few nights. By the grumbling of his new roommate, however, you'd think they'd been thrown into a gulag.

"How long do you think the hot water will last?" Plum asked. "If everyone is taking showers?"

Mustard shrugged. He'd been trained to keep his

showers to under two minutes. "Is there hot water at all? The power is out."

Plum, who was on the pasty side on a good day and quite blue with cold now, went almost translucent at the idea of no hot showers. He wouldn't have lasted a day at Farthing.

"There's a fire going in the lounge if you want to warm up," Mustard said. "But you'd better get in dry clothes first."

Plum's fingers were long and pale, and they fumbled helplessly with the buttons on his shirt. Probably numb. He needed that fire. Or even more radical treatments for possible hypothermia, like skin-to-skin contact.

Mustard averted his eyes.

The door burst open and in walked Scarlett Mistry, who had been in charge of his new student orientation last month. She'd seemed friendly enough, and had made quite a bit of noise about "students of color" like Mustard and herself needing to stick together on campus.

He hadn't seen her since.

She looked right at home among the polished floors and velvet curtains of this mansion. Her hair was as black and shiny as a raven's wing, and she was dressed in a pair of fleece-lined silk pajamas the color of her name. Everything shimmered in the light of the candelabra Plum had foolishly balanced on the surface of the pool table.

"Just look at you," Scarlett chided Plum, and rushed to his side, brushing off his hands and undoing the buttons of his shirt herself. "What were you even doing all the way down at Dockery? You could have been washed out to sea!" She cast a perfunctory look at Mustard. "Oh, hi, Samuel."

Plum stood there and let her undress him.

"You can call me Mustard," Mustard said, still trying his best not to watch whatever was going down on the other side of the pool table.

"Yeah, I already told you I wasn't doing that." She pushed the shirt off Plum's slim frame.

"Um, do you want me to leave you alone with your girl-friend?" Mustard asked Plum.

They both let out bursts of laughter.

"He's not my boyfriend!" Scarlett exclaimed. "We're a platonic power couple."

"A what?" Things certainly worked differently at civilian schools.

Scarlett had finished with Plum and leaned both hands on the table to talk to Mustard. "You're new here . . . *Mustard* . . . so allow me to explain. It's wall-to-wall romantic drama at Blackbrook. I don't have time for it. Neither does Finn." She jerked a thumb in his direction, but Plum was engaged in pulling off his pants, so Mustard kept his eyes on the girl.

"Oh."

"Not a lot of hookups at your backwards military academy?"

Not a *lot*, no. Just enough to cause problems. "Well, it was all boys, so . . . "

"So what?" Finn asked. He was down to his underwear.

Thankfully, Scarlett spared him from responding. "We're here to work hard and run this school. Our particular areas of interest are complementary, so there's no rivalry, and the lack of drama means there's little chance to get distracted from our ultimate goals. Similar goals, similar methodology. We're the perfect team."

Mustard blinked at her. Scarlett Mistry, despite being a girl, would have done fine at Farthing Military Institute. *Just fine.*

She clapped her hands, businesslike. "Okay, after you boys are all warmed up, we're making a vegetable-chopping assembly line in the kitchen. Mrs. White made a huge batch of soup last night, but Vaughn Green already ate half of it."

KP duty. Almost like old times. And, after a month of the kind of luxurious living Blackbrook provided, it would feel almost refreshing for Mustard to have to peel a few potatoes. It wasn't like he could give the pile of fuzzy pink blankets he was sleeping on tonight hospital corners.

He changed into a pair of dry socks and some house shoes and looked over at his new roommate, who appeared to be weighing his cold, damp options for a new outfit.

"Do you need to borrow some clothes?" he asked.

Plum frowned. "If you have anything, that would be great, thanks."

Mustard tossed him a new set of slacks and a waffle shirt. They'd be big on Plum, but not by much. He was tall, if slim. Plum examined the outfit carefully, swiping the damp curls out of his eyes and fingering the frayed cuffs of Mustard's shirt.

What? Weren't they preppy enough for him?

"You go on ahead," Plum said at last. "I'll catch up in a few minutes."

"Suit yourself," Mustard said, and departed.

The hall beside the grand central staircase was dark by now, the single candle burning in the front hall casting long shadows across the wallpaper. Mustard had never been in Tudor House before today. He'd never needed to be—it was mostly a dorm for a few lucky girls, though he'd learned in his new student orientation that there were study rooms and even a ballroom on the ground floor, used sometimes for school functions and other times for band rehearsal.

"Hey . . . Mustard?" He looked up the stairs to where two of the girls he'd met earlier were barreling toward him in unison.

"Hey."

"We wanted to thank you again for carrying us up here," gushed one.

"Those floodwaters are scary," said the other. The floodwaters hadn't been anywhere near where he'd carried them. There had been icy puddles, though.

"No problem . . ." He looked from one to the other.

"Karlee," said the first, pointing at herself. "Karlee Silverman."

"Kayla," said the other. "Kayla Gould."

"Gotcha," said Mustard. He definitely didn't. So they weren't twins, or even related. The matching glitter eyeshadow had thrown him off.

"So," said one of them. He can't believe he'd already forgotten. "You're new here."

"Yeah. Just started last month."

"Where are you from?" asked the other.

"I transferred in from a military academy in—"

"No!" she giggled and put her hand on his arm. "I mean, where's your *family* from?"

Oh. He wasn't yet used to the New England manner of getting to know someone. "Texas."

The one not touching him frowned. "Originally?"

He hated those kinds of questions. Did three hundred years count?

"Ah, Mr. Maestor," said another voice, keeping him from saying anything sarcastic. He turned to find the headmaster emerging from the lounge in sweatpants and a plaid bathrobe that he somehow still managed to make look like a three-piece suit.

"Sir." Mustard jerked to attention, then remembered it wasn't expected here.

The girls giggled. "So weird to see him in PJs," said Kayla—or was it Karlee?

"Like catching your gynecologist at the beach," whispered Karlee. Or maybe it was Kayla. Either way, the two of them vanished into the darkness, as if they'd been nothing more than creepy twin ghosts after all.

"At ease, soldier," Boddy joked. "I'm just glad to see you arrived. I gather you were bringing up the rear."

"There's no one else on campus?"

"We're the last stand," the headmaster said. "We're lucky it's so few, considering the severity of the storm damage. I wouldn't want to be finding beds for anyone else tonight. I'm trying not to think of all the calls I'll have to make to the insurance adjusters once the power is back on." He shook his head ruefully.

"How many of us are there here?"

"Ten. There's the three women already living in Tudor, a local student who got caught on the wrong side of the ravine when the bridge washed out, a member of our janitorial staff, three more female students from the flooded Dockery dorms, and you and another young man from Baylor."

"Eleven, sir," Mustard corrected. "Don't forget yourself."

Headmaster Boddy smiled. "And your father wouldn't let you go into advanced math."

Mustard didn't even blink. Reacting was the enemy. He may not have taken advanced math, but he'd had plenty of lessons in not letting instructors see you squirm. "Simple addition, sir."

The headmaster wasn't a military guy, but Mustard could tell that he was every bit as good at getting what he wanted out of the grunts. "Come now, Mr. Maestor, you've been here for over a month. More than enough time to settle in and see that the workload you arrived with is not suited to your talents."

"My father likes my curriculum the way it is." Research didn't have advancement potential. He could sense his father's sneer from here. He didn't raise a son to get stuck in a lab or be a pencil pusher. "And he's the one paying the bills."

Headmaster Boddy seemed to think for a moment. "What if I called your father? Perhaps he doesn't know all the opportunities our school offers."

Mustard didn't know how to tell the headmaster that the thing his father admired most about Blackbrook is that they'd taken Mustard mid-semester without asking too many questions.

"Think it over," the headmaster said to him. "I see potential in you. Your test scores are off the charts, but your old school never let you explore your own dreams."

Mustard grimaced. Exploring his own dreams is what landed him here to start.

They'd arrived at the kitchen, where there were a fair number of lanterns burning, and several other students already hard at work making soup under the supervision of the Tudor House proctor, Mrs. White. Mustard recognized one of them from his early-morning runs through campus. Vaughn Green was one of the only kids who ever seemed to get up earlier than Mustard did.

At Vaughn's side, mangling a carrot as if she'd never peeled one before, was a skinny girl with a mousy-brown bob and long bangs that kept falling over square-rimmed glasses. Beside her, making quick, neat dices out of a pile of potatoes, was the tall blond girl he'd met when she was walking up to Tudor House with Plum. She'd been every bit as soaked from the storm surge, but had already changed into a dry outfit, scraped her long blond hair into a high, tight ponytail, and was hard at work. Mustard appreciated that. He understood she was some kind of big tennis star, and mostly went by her nickname, Peacock.

Mustard appreciated that, too.

Headmaster Boddy turned toward the proctor, an elderly woman in a colorful crocheted shawl with wild, graying hair. "I brought you a new volunteer, Mrs. White. He's eager for a little exercise in school spirit." He gestured to the table, and his gaze fell on Peacock.

"Miss Picach, how lovely to see you here. Perhaps we can finish our little chat this evening."

Peacock clenched her jaw and started obliterating the potatoes.

When Boddy was gone, Mustard took up a position at the end of the table, but didn't see any more knives or peelers. "Hey, do you have another knife?" he asked Peacock.

No answer.

He tapped her on the shoulder. "Do you have another—"

"What!" She whirled on him, blade out.

Mustard jumped back, and they both stared at each other, breathing hard. Peacock seemed to catch herself and considered the knife in her hand for a long moment.

"Take mine," she said at last. "I've had enough of Boddy's school spirit."

Then, Blackbrook's best athlete plunged the knife into the heart of the nearest butternut squash.

6

Peacock

— EP WORKOUT LOG —

DATE: *December 5*

TIME WOKE: *7:19 a.m. (see notes)*

MORNING WEIGH-IN: *146 lbs*

BREAKFAST: *2 vanilla-shortbread-flavored nutrition bars (420 calories, 12g protein), cold water*

LUNCH: *Blueberry-date nutrition bar (210 calories, 12g protein), 4 dried figs (84 calories), 1 bag salted popcorn (100 calories), cold water*

AFTERNOON SNACK: *Hot tea with lemon, one chocolate bar (360 calories, 6g protein, see notes)*

DINNER: *Vegetable soup (nutritional info unknown), 4 slices of bread with butter (400 calories)*

ADDITIONAL: *Hot cocoa? (???)*

MORNING WORKOUT: *N/A (see notes)*

AFTERNOON WORKOUT: *Waded uphill .5 mile carrying 50 pounds of weight. More after the wave hit me.*

EVENING WORKOUT: *N/A (see notes)*

NOTES: *There's a blizzard AND a flood. We were supposed to evacuate for the mainland today, but missed our chance or something. All I know is the power is still out, so I slept late, and no machines today, which doesn't even matter because apparently the gym is underwater, just like my dorm room. This is so stupid. They moved us all to high ground, but there's no gym in Tudor. There's not even a set of free weights here, and my new roommate looked appalled when I asked, like how dare they move their stupid old pool table and put in a treadmill. I took all my awards when I left my dorm, but a wave hit me on the way and now the box they're in is disintegrating. Do trophies rust?*

And of course, HE'S here.

We're all having cocoa around the fire tonight, which is fine, but hardly enough food, and I'm going to run out of protein bars soon. DON'T FORGET TO LOOK UP HOT COCOA NUTRITIONAL INFO WHEN POWER COMES BACK ON.

I'll make up for it tomorrow, if any of us get out of this storm alive.

7

Green

Vaughn wondered if this was what it was like all the time for the live-in students on campus. Like the stories he used to hear from Gemma when he was growing up. Kids curled up before massive roaring fireplaces, chatting about books and science with their professors and each other.

Everything was so cozy, with the stacks of old blankets and the flickering firelight. One could almost ignore the howling wind beyond the walls, and the horrible cracks and booms that kept echoing up the hill from the campus. Every crash brought winces from the assembled group, and worried glances between Headmaster Boddy and Rusty. The two men were in hushed conversation about the conditions outside. Mustard was sitting nearby, nodding sagely at descriptions of downed trees and floating debris, but Vaughn felt no temptation to join in. He and the rest of the custodial staff would have enough to do once the storm passed.

"Can you actually die of boredom?" asked Scarlett to no one in particular.

Well, maybe they usually all spent their evenings with their faces buried in their phones.

"This cocoa is amazing, Mrs. White," said Finn Plum as he polished off his mug. "How do you do it?"

"It's an old Tudor special," she replied, her tone brusque but proud. Vaughn knew this cocoa well. Mrs. White might have claimed it for Tudor House, but Gemma had been the original inventor.

"Dash of vanilla extract," broke in Scarlett, to Mrs. White's obvious dismay. She didn't want to share her secrets.

"That makes sense," Finn said. "The alcohol in the extract might have an effect in the way the lipids interact on the palate—"

"There's no alcohol in my cocoa!" Mrs. White cried indignantly. She cast a worried glance at Headmaster Boddy, as if he might get the impression she was helping her charges catch a buzz on.

Vaughn got the impression the folks here thought Mrs. White was an aging hippie, which was pretty accurate. Oh, and that she had once been married, which was decidedly less so. He wasn't sure where the "Mrs." part of her name had come from, but it certainly wasn't a husband. Men had never been part of the picture, with Linda White or with his grandmother. But at Tudor House she was Mrs. White, so Vaughn just went with the flow.

"No, Mrs. White," Scarlett said quickly. "He just means the extract. It's made with alcohol. Not the drinking kind."

The furrow that had sprouted on Mrs. White's wrinkled brow wilted and she sat back in the chair, smoothing her long broomstick skirt over her legs. "Oh, yes. I knew that."

Vaughn watched Finn make a face he thought only Scarlett could see, and caught sight of Scarlett, in response, giggling and kicking Finn under the blanket they shared on the couch. Fortunately, Mrs. White didn't seem to notice any of it.

Those two were a real piece of work. If someone told him that they knew where all the bodies were hidden, Vaughn would believe it in a heartbeat. Sucking up to all the teachers' faces, then rolling their eyes and ridiculing the adults behind their backs. Two-faced jerks. He hated people who pretended to be who they weren't.

And what about hypocrites, Vaughn? he couldn't help but think. *You hate hypocrites, too?*

That snide little inner voice was Oliver's, as usual. But it wasn't correct. *He'd* never pretended to be anyone he wasn't. Not really.

"Well," said Orchid charitably, "the cocoa's amazing, no matter what's in it." She looked at Vaughn. "Didn't you have some?"

"No," said Vaughn. "But I'm okay." He'd never been into sweets. Not like his brother. Also, he'd been gorging himself on soup all afternoon. At home, he mostly subsisted on frozen burritos and ramen noodles. Mrs. White's fresh vegetable soup had been a real treat. Or, he supposed, it had been all of their vegetable soup, since the chopping had been a group effort. Maybe the other students got together and cooked every night, too.

He wondered how things were going back in the village. The storm surge would have overflowed the ravine by now, leaving most houses waist-deep in water.

On the rug, Karlee had finished twisting Kayla's hair into some kind of elaborate braid-knot thing, and was now casting around for someone else to bug.

"Can I braid your hair?" she asked Scarlett. "It's so pretty and shiny."

"Absolutely not," Scarlett replied. Vaughn couldn't blame her.

Karlee tried Orchid. "How about you?"

Orchid also looked skeptical. "Um, it's pretty short."

"Karlee can handle short," chirped Kaylee from the rug.

"I don't think—" she tried again.

"Come on, please!" Karlee whined. "I'm so bored!"

Vaughn knew the look on Orchid's face. The one that said it was easier to relent than keep fighting. He wore it often.

Karlee got to work. "Oh, I hadn't realized you colored your hair."

"You color your hair?" Scarlett asked from the couch, incredulous. "*That* color?"

Orchid's lips pursed, but she said nothing, only yelped a bit as Karlee tugged on another strand. "It didn't turn out the way I'd wanted. Kind of muddy, I guess. I got it out of a box."

Karlee clucked her tongue. "Going brown can be tricky."

"You know," said Kayla, "you'd look really good as a redhead."

She would. Orchid's skin was pale, and the fire had heightened the color on her cheeks. A girl this pretty in his history class should probably be someone he'd noticed before now.

He just wasn't always his best self lately.

Vaughn looked away. At the table in the corner, Rusty and the new kid were talking sandbag strategy. Better this Mustard character than him, was all he could think.

"Next time you want to color your hair," Karlee was saying as she tortured every lock on Orchid's head, "you come to me."

"Um . . ." said Orchid, looking scared.

"Peacock did for those blue tips," Karlee said. "And don't they look great?"

Beth Peacock was no longer in the lounge, and couldn't weigh in on whether or not she liked her dyed blue tips. The tennis star had been mostly quiet throughout dinner, and when they'd all come in here, she'd claimed her mug of hot chocolate and vanished.

"Wow," said Kayla, who was watching the progress with Orchid's hair. "You have amazing cheekbones. Has anyone ever told you that?"

"Not recently," said Orchid, wincing a bit as Karlee tugged the hair at her temples.

"Well, how could they with your hair in your face all the time!" Kayla reached up and pulled off Orchid's glasses. "Ooh, can I do your makeup next?"

Orchid reached for the glasses. Her eyes were kind of a ridiculous blue. Vaughn had noticed that earlier. "Please give those back."

"Oh, you're already wearing makeup," Kayla said to Orchid. "Girl, your contouring is all wrong. You're supposed to enhance your features, not hide them."

Orchid snatched back the glasses, blushing furiously. "We're done here."

"Geez," said Kayla. "We were only trying to help."

Orchid's half-finished braid tumbled down around her face as she scooted well out of the range of Karlee and Kayla's impromptu salon and over to Vaughn's side of the fire.

She plopped down beside him. "Hi."

"Hi," he replied, pleasantly surprised. He just hoped she wouldn't want to talk about their history class.

"Hey," said Scarlett to Finn. "Do you think we'd get cell service? You know, if we could use a battery charger or something?"

"Not likely," Finn said. "Especially not a high-speed connection. That's ultra-high frequency, which is more affected by water in the atmosphere . . ."

Scarlett sighed. "What about satellite?"

"Satellites are *above* the clouds. Sorry, Scar." Finn patted her knee. "You are officially *unplugged*."

"I'm bored, is what I am," she whined. "Do we have any games or anything here?"

"There's billiards," said the transfer student, who insisted everyone call him Mustard. "As long as Finn doesn't mind everyone tromping through our bedrolls."

Finn looked appalled by the suggestion. "Aren't there board games or something in the library?"

"I can go check," Vaughn found himself saying.

"I can go with you," Orchid broke in. It was half suggestion, half plea. "I know where they are."

They exited into the dark hall, whose soaring ceilings and grand marble staircase formed an excellent acoustic backdrop for the roar of the wind beyond the mansion's walls. It should have been terrifying, but Vaughn felt safer tonight than he had in months.

"So, you've been assigned to the library tonight?" Orchid asked.

"At least." Maybe the storm would last for a while, and Vaughn wouldn't have to go home for days. They arrived at the door of the library. Beyond lay dark shelves crammed with dusty books. "You said you knew where the games were kept?"

She gave a little half laugh. "Um . . . Well, I think there might be an old Monopoly set in here . . . somewhere. I mostly didn't want Karlee's makeover."

"I take it you don't play a lot of board games."

"With Scarlett?" she scoffed. "She'd play for blood." She swept the beam of her flashlight over the shelves, looking for any games.

"You know, I always picture the residential students sitting around here at night, playing games and singing songs . . ."

"Like a scout troop?"

Okay, it sounded cheesy when she put it like that. "Come on. Don't wreck all my illusions at once."

"Sorry, dude. I don't think anyone has sat around the lounge singing songs since I've lived in this house."

Vaughn considered this. Maybe it was the soup, or the storm, but he was feeling impulsive tonight. He usually didn't have the option of being impulsive. School and custodial shifts and studying and traveling back and forth between the campus and home—everything had to adhere to the schedule, or it wouldn't work at all. "Maybe now's the time."

He left the library and headed farther down the hall, into the ballroom at the back of Tudor House. The cavernous room was occasionally used for exams or student assemblies, and, more often than either—for band practice. He peered into its dim recesses.

"Aha." An acoustic guitar leaned against the chair rail.

"You play?" Orchid asked as he retrieved it.

"Yeah." He pulled the strap over his chest. "When I have the chance."

Back in the lounge, only Mrs. White looked up when

they returned. Kayla was now attempting to braid Karlee's hair. It wasn't going well.

"Didn't have much luck with games," said Orchid brightly, "but Vaughn's promised to play for us."

"Oh, goody," mumbled Scarlett.

"What a lovely idea," said Mrs. White. "Thank you, Vaughn. It'll be like old times."

He sat down and began to tune the instrument. "Mrs. White, will you sing for us?"

"You can sing?" Orchid asked her.

"Vaughn's telling tales."

He chuckled and bent over the instrument, feeling out a melody.

"Oh, come on, Mrs. White," coaxed Scarlett. "If you have a hidden talent, we want to hear it."

Mrs. White shrugged one bony shoulder. "I can't sing any of your new songs."

Vaughn thought about the times he'd heard Mrs. White singing. Nursery rhymes, mostly, and old folk songs. There were times, when he'd been young and his parents had been home from tours, that her voice would echo up and down the ravine along with Gemma's. "I won't play a new one, then." His fingers began to work out the chords of an old English folk tune. "Here's one for this cold, haily, windy night."

He began to sing. His voice would never compete with the trained efforts of some of his heavily coached classmates in the music department. There was only so much you could do practicing at home, and his parents had never had the opportunity to teach him. But he knew he could hold his own, and at least he could be sure his playing was second to none.

By the second verse, Mrs. White chimed in, her voice as strong and clear as ever.

"Let me in," the soldier cried,
Cold, haily, windy night.
"Oh, let me in," the soldier cried,
"For I'll not go back again, no."

Wasn't that the truth?

Like always, he got lost in the tune, in the heartbreaking story of deception and betrayal. Around him, the conversations dimmed, or maybe they had ceased entirely. By the second repeat of the chorus, Vaughn had even gotten Rusty, Orchid, Karlee, and Kayla to join in. But then the verses took a turn for the risqué, because after the poor girl did let that freezing soldier in her house, he had some pretty interesting ideas on how to get warm.

Headmaster Boddy clapped his hands. "Okay, okay, that's enough."

Vaughn's fingers fumbled over the strings. "But, sir, it's a folk song. We studied it in music history this term."

"Did you?" The headmaster looked genuinely baffled. Blackbrook teachers got to design their own courses, and the humanities teachers had more latitude than most, as the administration didn't keep careful watch over anything that wasn't science.

"It's a night visiting song," Vaughn explained. "That's the whole point of the genre. The man comes in, seduces the woman, and abandons her to ruin."

"Well!" he replied. "I guess if it's schoolwork . . . "

"It's incredibly sexist," Scarlett pointed out.

"No different than everything we study in English," Orchid pointed out. "Documenting how sexist society is."

"You mean how sexist it *was*?" Mustard asked. "Sexism is basically over."

Every woman in the room stared at him in shock.

"Did they keep you in a *box* in your old school?" Scarlett asked, appalled.

"Easy there," said Finn to his friend.

Orchid glanced at Vaughn. "I was listening. The girl and the guy spent the night together, but it only ruined one of their lives. *Hers.* Sounds familiar to me. Boys never get in trouble for things like that."

"No," said Mrs. White, and sipped her cocoa.

Mustard was staring down at his hands, saying nothing.

Headmaster Boddy cleared his throat. "Perhaps this is a good time to go over the rules for our current circumstances. The regular dorm policies apply, despite the unusual circumstances. No closed doors in mixed company, and no inappropriate activities. Mrs. White and I have purposefully stationed ourselves in the study and the lounge because they are the rooms at the foot of the stairs.

Boys on the first floor, girls on the second. No one will be going up or down without our knowledge."

The students exchanged amused glances. They all knew the strict codes of conduct when it came to co-ed relations at Blackbrook. They also all knew exactly how many students broke those rules.

"And I think maybe no songs about seductions on cold winter nights, Mr. Green." Headmaster Boddy gave him a knowing glance. Beside him, Orchid smiled and played with the tassels at the edge of the carpet.

"I think maybe give us a little credit," he blurted. "I could have easily picked a murder ballad, and it doesn't mean someone's going to get killed tonight, either."

Just then, there was a horrible crash right outside the door, and suddenly the sound of the storm got a whole lot louder.

8

Scarlett

It was a horrible jumble, all of them trying at once to get to the door. Mrs. White managed it first, and flinging it wide, revealed utter chaos beyond.

The large stained-glass window over the transom had shattered, and in the firelight spilling out from the lounge, the floor of the hall glittered with a mix of glass, ice, and freezing rain. Wind roared through the hole above the front door, bringing water and wet leaves.

"What was it?" Boddy asked from somewhere in the crush.

"Out of my way!" Rusty pushed through all of them. "Tree branch," he reported, shining his flashlight on the offending piece of wood. "Looks to be from the maple out front."

"Will we lose any more?" Boddy asked as they spilled through the bottleneck into the hall.

"The Lily Window," Mrs. White wailed. She leaned against the hallway wall and looked at the destruction with her hand pressed to her chest.

"It's okay," said Scarlett, touching her proctor's shoulder. "They can fix it."

Maybe. Or maybe it was a priceless piece of history. The stained-glass window had been original to Tudor House, well before its reform school days, when the resident heiress and her glamorous furnishings matched the luxe wood paneling and rich details. Dorm room beds and couches subjected to decades of students' butts weren't quite the same.

Mrs. White did not appear remotely comforted, and Scarlett couldn't blame her. The old woman reached down and picked up a long shard of beautifully painted amber glass. "The Lily Window," she said again, forlorn.

The window had depicted a field of bright orange tiger lilies and had been one of the most glamorous reminders of how gorgeous the mansion must once have been. Scarlett herself had taken many photos bathed in the kaleidoscope of light that shone through it on sunny afternoons.

Now it lay in ruins on the floor.

They'd been such good pictures, too. She'd gotten loads of comments from people about what kind of lighting she'd used, and even some detractors who insisted her shots must be some kind of professional trickery, as the tiger lilies made her brown skin shine like gold.

Now what was she supposed to do?

Scarlett carefully picked her way over the shattered bits of colored glass. What a shame. Just then, she remembered that her room upstairs faced the same direction—and the same tree—as the Lily Window. If her window had broken, too, her stuff could be blowing away in the storm right this very minute!

"I need to close my shutters," she said at once.

"You haven't closed your shutters?" Vaughn asked. He had somehow already found a broom and had started to sweep up bits of glass.

"No!" she snapped at him. "I thought that was the *janitor's* job." And with that, she turned on her heel and headed up the stairs.

She found Peacock lurking at the top of the landing.

"Where have you been?" Scarlett asked. She hadn't seen Peacock since Mrs. White and Headmaster Boddy had shown up in the lounge with the hot cocoa. Scarlett couldn't blame her. Sitting alone in the cold and the dark was probably preferable to whatever had been going on downstairs. Though, if someone held a gun to her head, Scarlett would be forced to admit that the townie was halfway decent with that guitar. Certainly as good as some of the people she'd seen online, even those with bigger followings than she had. Of course, they also had better fashion sense than Vaughn Green. Packaging was such an art.

"I was working out," Peacock replied, though she didn't seem to have even broken a sweat. Guess that was what happened when you were at peak physical condition like Peacock was. Now, there was a girl who knew how to package herself! "What was that noise?"

"Tree branch through the window," said Scarlett.

"What?!" Peacock craned her neck down the stairs, but looked in no hurry to join the group in cleanup.

"I want to make sure my shutters are closed, in case we lose any more branches."

"You haven't closed your shutters?" Peacock asked.

Scarlett did not deign to answer that as she hurried into her bedroom and shut the door behind her.

Sweet silence. And darkness. She turned on the battery-powered lantern Rusty had assigned her. Her computer, camera, and recording equipment lay like so many cold, useless bricks on her desk. Her window, fortunately, was still intact. She crossed to it and looked out, but saw little other than snowdrifts, rain, and the dark shadows of tree branches beyond the glass. The storm was still pretty strong, to judge by the waving branches. More might fall before the night was through.

The window screeched in protest as she opened it, and papers ruffled all over her room. Wet wind assaulted her from the outside, and she shivered, scrabbling at the clasps holding the shutters in place. They may not have been moved for years.

Scarlett soon found herself leaning halfway out the window, trying to figure out how to get the shutters closed. If she killed herself trying to close these darn things, she was going to be super annoyed.

Over the storm, she heard a knock at the door.

"Scarlett?" Finn. Thank goodness.

She hauled her body back inside, then ran and opened the door for him.

He grinned, his hair flopping over his eye in that way he knew drove the girls crazy. "So much for Boddy watching the stairs, huh?"

She rolled her eyes at him. "Give me a hand, will you? I'm trying to close the shutters."

"You haven't closed your shutters?"

"Ugh!" Scarlett yanked him inside. She didn't need a lecture from Finn, too.

Together, they managed to coax movement out of the rusty shutter hinges, then close and secure them from the inside. Scarlett slammed the window closed, and they flopped down onto her bed, side by side.

Scarlett looked down at her silk pajama shirt, which was now streaked with rain and who knew what else. "This had better come out."

"At least you have your own clothes. I'm stuck in these until my stuff dries." Finn held out his arms, revealing the frayed, turned-up cuffs and waffle pattern of a khaki-colored shirt she did not recognize from his wardrobe. Finn tended toward the super-preppy end of the sartorial spectrum. He was the only boy Scarlett knew who could actually make a cardigan look good.

"Whose rags are those?" she asked.

"The new kid. What's his deal, anyway?" Finn knew that Scarlett could be counted on to get the goods on any new student at Blackbrook.

"I haven't had a chance to figure it out yet. He started right before I went home for Diwali, remember?"

"Oh, right."

"Transferred from some military school out west, though he's kind of cagey about the reason he left. Doesn't seem like a threat." He wasn't taking a single honors class, according to Scarlett's intel from Boddy prior to Mustard's orientation meeting. That reminded her. "Hey, you never told me what Boddy wanted you for the other day."

"When?"

"Um, when Peacock tried to brain him in his office?" She hadn't gotten an answer out of Orchid, either, and the storm had come in right after.

"Oh, right—He wants me to tutor someone. By the way," he added quickly, "did you get any info about what Beth—what Peacock—was in for?"

"Not yet," said Scarlett, "but now that she's in the house, we'll worm it out of her."

"*You* will," he corrected her. "You know she won't speak to me."

Scarlett waved off his concern. "Of course. You know I have my ways."

Finn looked around at her setup. "So, this is the inner sanctum."

Scarlett spread her arms wide. "Voilà! None who have seen it may live."

"You'll make an exception for me though, right?" He batted his unfairly long eyelashes at her.

She pretended to consider this. "Fine. But I'll have to take a toll. You can drop your eyeballs in the dish on the way out."

He laughed. "How did you keep Boddy from making you bunk with the terrible twosome?"

"Karlee and Kayla are staying in Mrs. White's room."

"And Peacock?"

"I made sure to stick her with Orchid." Scarlett's secrets were safe. At least for tonight.

"You arranged that pretty well," said Finn.

"Yeah, unlike you. Trapped on the floor with that drill sergeant."

"True." He frowned. "It's too bad we aren't really up here making out."

She shoved at him. "Eww, stop." Her speech to Mustard hadn't been a lie. It wasn't only her parents who believed Scarlett had better things to do in high school than waste time dating. Romance was a hassle. Who needed it?

"I'm sorry," he said in a tone that meant he was definitely not. "Would you rather be up here with *Vaughn*?"

"Hardly."

"No?" he asked, skeptical. Finn found the idea much more difficult than she did. "I figured every girl in that room was about to swoon at his rugged pioneer-with-a-fiddle routine earlier."

"A fiddle is a violin, not a guitar."

"Really?" Finn looked confused. Anything that didn't go into a test tube always confused him. There were many things she liked about her best friend, and Scarlett would even call his singular passion for science one of them. But it did occasionally render him clueless.

"Honestly, I thought that song was creepy."

Finn shrugged. "It's a folk song. He's right, by the way, there are way creepier ones. Have you heard that one about the guy who hanged his girlfriend and then went back to bed?"

Must be one of the "murder ballads" Vaughn had mentioned. "What a lovely musical genre he's into. Hasn't he heard of pop? Or anything written this century?"

"Not up here in the wilderness."

The shutters rattled under the onslaught of another gust of wind. Scarlett supposed they would have to rejoin the group soon enough. She didn't care what the others thought, but it wouldn't do to break the rules.

"Leave it to Vaughn Green to actually come to school in a blizzard," she said. "He's a bigger suck-up than you are."

"I'm . . . trying to take that as a compliment."

"You should take it as a challenge."

Now Finn's interest had been piqued. "Really?"

"Haven't you noticed him everywhere?"

"You mean . . . cleaning?" Finn asked. "I thought that was his job."

"No, I mean, it's like he's in every humanities class in the catalog. Who takes music history?" She hadn't even known that was an option, but apparently Mr. Green was acing it. "How does he even have time to work janitorial with his course load?"

Finn fixed her with a look. "What's your real fear, Scar?"

She sighed. "I'm afraid he's gaining on me for the humanities honors." Blackbrook, with its laser focus on scientific achievement, didn't have a single valedictorian. A lot of STEM geniuses were hopeless at humanities, and the school recognized that by splitting the top honors in two. And she and Finn had a pact. Science honors for him. Humanities for her.

Obliterate the competition together.

Behind his glasses, Finn's eyes narrowed. "Well. We can't have that."

"Exactly." Let Vaughn Green play all the folk guitar he wanted. He could join an army of coffeehouse musicians. As long as their turf was maintained.

Finn thought for a minute. "Okay, well, there's not much I can do until the power's back on, but I'll look into it."

She put her head on his shoulder. "I knew you would."

Finn straightened. He loved being reminded of his special talents. "At least I don't have to worry about him competing for your affections."

"Never, baby," she said with a smile. "You know I only have Machiavellian schemes for you."

9

Orchid

After they'd finished sweeping up the hall and Rusty and Vaughn tacked up a tarpaulin over the broken window, everyone headed to the kitchen for refills on their cocoa. Everyone but Orchid, who slipped silently back into the lounge.

The fire had died down to embers, and the room was dim, though still warmer than it had been in the hall. The last she'd seen her glasses, she'd been sitting on the carpet, drinking cocoa and listening to Vaughn play the guitar, like something out of a music video or a cologne ad. She'd felt safe, even with the storm raging outside.

Ironic. The campus getting wrecked by this flood was the only thing protecting her from certain doom. When the evacuation began, and then just as quickly stopped due to worsening conditions, the other students got frustrated, but Orchid just breathed a sigh of relief. She didn't even care that the power outage meant her accountant couldn't call her back. The important thing was this: If no one could get off Rocky Point, then no one could get *on* it, either.

There. Orchid caught sight of her chunky black frames near the corner of the carpet. One arm of the glasses was bent upward at an awkward angle. She swiped them off the floor to examine the extent of the damage. At least the glass lenses hadn't broken. A large mirror with an ornate gilded frame hung next to the mantel, and Orchid crossed to it to check out how bad they looked when she had them on.

Just as she'd feared, the glasses sat crookedly on her nose. They'd be annoying to wear, but she supposed it would be expected, even so. *Actual* glasses wearers wore bent and broken glasses anyway, because it was better than walking around half-blind. She removed them and examined her reflection in the mirror.

Her hair hid half her face, which was little more than a pale oval in the dying light. The bright blue of her eyes, however, was clear, even in the gloom. Maybe she should consider colored contacts.

And what difference did it make, really? Her hiding place had been discovered. If her secret was about to come out, maybe she should just enjoy what little time she had left. Throw caution to the raging nor'easter winds.

Be in touch soon.

That's what the letter had said. The lack of specificity seemed perfectly pitched to cause her peak terror. No indication of time, or explanation of what it meant to "be in touch." More mischief with her finances? Actually coming out to Maine? What did the monster have planned?

Orchid took a deep breath and leveled with her reflection.

He'd better not come out here. And you know what to do if he tries it.

She'd been strong once. She could do it again.

Orchid sighed. She just really, really didn't want to. She wanted to go to class, and take tests, and yes—sit in the lounge and discuss folk songs and sexist literature with other students. Even if it was with Scarlett Mistry. To be normal, for once in her entire freaking life.

Not that it had ever really been *that* normal, she was forced to admit. Normal teenagers had friends, didn't they? Friends who had slumber parties or did each other's hair, like Karlee had tried to do. But Orchid McKee could barely get within arm's reach of her fellow students without them seeing through her supposedly brilliant disguise. On some level, she had always known that, which was why she'd managed to spend more than two years at the school without letting anyone in.

"Hey."

She whirled around to see Vaughn Green standing on the carpet, guitar in hand. Orchid fumbled to put on her glasses for a short, awkward moment, and then gave up entirely. "I broke my glasses."

Vaughn raised an eyebrow. "Uh-oh. How well can you see without them?"

Say you're farsighted. Say they're a mild prescription. But she didn't do either of those things. There was no point in lying anymore.

So instead, she smiled sheepishly. "Actually, they're mostly for show. I confess, I'm a tragic hipster."

Vaughn shouldered the instrument. "If you say so. I don't really know anything about fashion. People mostly wear flannel in this town."

"Then it's good the nineties are coming back," she said. "Were you born here?"

"Right across the ravine," he said. Weird. She hadn't known there was so much as a clinic in Rocky Point, let alone a hospital. "Where are you from?"

"California."

"Oh, so then you're used to blizzards."

She laughed. She'd never before realized he was so funny. Or so cute. The Vaughn from history class was slumpy and mostly silent. The only times she remembered him speaking up at all was to get into bizarre devil's advocate–style debates about whatever historical atrocity they were studying. She still recalled his opinion that they should not have handed out life jackets on the *Titanic*.

They were going to freeze in those icy waters, anyway. Better drowning than hypothermia. At least it's quick, and you don't have to deal with floating bodies afterward.

Spoken, she supposed, like a Maine native. A super creepy one.

Between that and the talk of murder ballads, Vaughn definitely had a dark side. Still, Orchid never would have guessed it, looking at the boy standing across from her, smiling like a puppy with a treat, his amber-brown eyes sparkling even in the dying light from the fire.

His performance tonight had been . . . something else. Back in her old life, Orchid had known a few pop stars, and, to be frank, most of them didn't even know how to hold a guitar. Vaughn, hidden away at the edge of the world, was the real deal.

Maybe she would have learned that long ago if she'd dared to set foot near any of the performing arts kids at Blackbrook. But she'd always deemed that far too dangerous.

She gestured to the instrument. "You're a really good musician."

"Thanks," he said, running his hand through his hair. But then he frowned. "You don't think we're going to come back next term and find out we can only sing G-rated nursery rhymes, do you?"

"Nah. I think Headmaster Boddy's just stressed because of the storm. He's usually pretty cool." She thought about their conversation in his office the other day. "You know, unless he's trying to pressure you to use your scientific talents to 'make the world a better place.'" She made little air quotes with her fingers.

Vaughn looked relieved. "I haven't really dealt with him. I try to stay invisible around here."

"Me too," she said before she could stop herself.

"I can tell."

"You can? I must be doing a bad job of it, then." Under normal circumstances, Orchid would have freaked.

"No," he said awkwardly, gesturing at the frames in her hand. "I mean . . . the fake glasses."

"Oh." She looked away and twirled the frames in a circle by the broken arm. "Yeah. Well, what can I say, it worked for Clark Kent."

Only difference was, she turned into a superhero when she had the glasses *on*. Orchid McKee had all kinds of special abilities. She was invisible—usually. She was a genius—just ask Headmaster Boddy. And, until she'd received that letter, she kind of thought she was a master of disguise.

Vaughn was still examining her, though, and she didn't like it when people watched her too closely. It reminded her of the old days. She hadn't liked Karlee and Kayla buzzing around her like makeup artists, either. Or maybe it wasn't so much that she didn't like that they were looking, but that she feared what it was they might see.

All this effort to make a new life for herself, and Orchid McKee was as much a role as any other.

"Don't you ever want to look like someone different?" she asked Vaughn.

He laughed mirthlessly. "Every single day." He added quickly, "You know, small towns are like a fishbowl."

She wondered if it was tough, being one of the few locals at the school. That was a type of celebrity, too, in its own way. "It's hard to turn invisible when everyone is looking at you."

"You should get better at finding phone booths." His smile flashed in the darkness.

"What's a phone booth?" she asked coyly.

His smile grew wider, and for the first time since the power went out, Orchid felt a little too warm.

She cleared her throat and folded up the glasses. "Well, um, I should get to bed. Thanks again for the music tonight."

"You're welcome, Orchid. Thanks for giving me a place to stay in the storm."

Ha. Nice try, buddy. But Orchid blushed anyway. As she exited into the hall, she saw Headmaster Boddy again.

"Going to bed?" he asked.

"Yeah. Thought I'd read for a bit, as long as the batteries in my flashlight last."

Headmaster Boddy made a grunting sound in his throat. "Might want to save those. We don't know when the power will come back on."

Orchid looked up at the tarp fastened over the hole above the door. "Such a shame about the window. Do you think you'll be able to get it replaced?"

She imagined a stained-glass window was pretty expensive, and a fancy historical one was probably doubly so. Still, the window seemed as fundamental to Tudor House's charm as the carved wood mantles and bannister. Imagining the entrance hall without the dancing colored lights the panes provided seemed as unthinkable as losing the whistling radiator in the library, or . . . or Mrs. White as the house proctor.

The headmaster pursed his lips. "This whole place is a

relic. It should be the first to go, but who knows how plans might have to change once we get a look at the damage on the lower side of campus."

As she was from California, floods weren't something Orchid thought about much. Earthquakes, sure. Forest fires. But once the water was gone, couldn't everyone just mop up? Or would they have to replace the buildings entirely? Would insurance cover that? "You don't think the other buildings are permanently ruined, do you?"

He straightened. "I wouldn't want to speculate. Have a good night, Miss McKee, and do give some thought to our conversation from last week. You expressed yourself so well earlier this evening. I have no fear that you would be able to defend your research with the same degree of clarity and intelligence."

Orchid ducked her head. "I just—"

"You're worth too much to keep your light hidden under a bushel. Just promise me you will consider it."

She sighed again. He did want the best for her—for all the students at the school. Deep down, Orchid knew that. "I promise."

Mr. Boddy smiled at her, and she headed to bed, shaking her head as she passed Scarlett's room and caught sight of Scarlett and Finn with their heads together, whispering and giggling, and went inside her own room, where Peacock was scribbling in a journal by the light of her headlamp.

Orchid thought about how lucky she was, to be here

at Blackbrook Academy, where you might not love all the people around you, but at least you felt safe.

It was the last time such a thought would ever cross her mind.

—————

By morning, the worst of the storm seemed to have passed. The wind outside had all but vanished, and when Orchid ventured to open the protective shutters over her windows, it was to a field of gray ice and slush covering the flooded campus, but no more coming from the sky.

To most people in the house, she was sure this was a welcome sight. But all Orchid saw was the beginning of the end.

At least the power was still out. There was no way the travel routes would be restored before the power was, right?

Orchid was alone. Peacock's sleeping bag was empty, though the other girl had warned her last night that she tended to get up early for her morning workout. Orchid was relieved that Peacock had managed to do so silently. She wasn't used to having other people in her room, and she was already jumpy enough.

After a quick trip to the bathroom, Orchid sat down to see if the broken arm on her glasses might be repairable, but despite tightening the screws, it seemed that the frames had been permanently damaged. She taped the arm back in place and tried on the result, but her handiwork was unstable and the edges of the tape caught on her hair. She frowned at her reflection. Did she dare go without her glasses? Would makeup be enough to hide her features?

She glared down at her well-worn contouring brush. And what if she skipped even that? For once, what if she just let people draw their own conclusions about the resemblance between Clark Kent and Superman? After all, Headmaster Boddy had been right. She couldn't keep hiding for the rest of her life. She was seventeen now. Nearly an adult. An adult who might bear some coincidental resemblance to a little girl a lot of people recognized—but, hey, stranger things had happened, right?

Besides, as far as anyone knew, that girl was long gone. Orchid had made sure of it.

She put away her makeup and got dressed.

Peacock met her at the door, a towel wrapped around her tall frame.

"Oh, hey!" Orchid said. "How was your workout?"

Peacock scowled. "I tried, but it's so gross and slippery out there, and you still can't get anywhere near the gym . . ." She flopped dramatically on the bed. "This sucks. I'm about to crawl out of my skin. Do you think Mrs. White will flip out if I do some stair work in the hall?"

Orchid blinked. "Um . . ."

"Actually, it's gross out there, too. The stupid tarp came down overnight and the floor's all wet. I practically slipped and broke my neck already today."

"The hall is flooded?" Orchid asked. Way to bury the lede, Peacock.

The other girl sat up, looking contrite. "Oh yeah. It's pretty bad."

"We need to mop it up before the water damages the wood!" cried Orchid. "That parquet floor is original to the house. Mrs. White freaks out if we so much as walk on it with high heels."

"Mop?" Beth shot her a look. "Don't we have, like, two janitorial staff people already in the house?"

Orchid's mouth snapped shut. Okay, she'd take care of it herself. She was one of the actual residents of Tudor. If anyone could be expected to respect the house, it was the people who lived here when it *wasn't* a storm shelter. Tudor may not be the shimmering jewel it was back in the timber baron days, but the mansion still had its charms.

Besides, Orchid knew who else might appreciate it too. She pulled on an oversized sweater, fleece leggings, and a pair of fingerless gloves, slipped her feet into a pair of boots, and headed out.

Even from the top of the stairs, Orchid could see the extent of the damage. The tarp lay crumbled in a heap on the hall floor, and freezing air whistled in through the shattered window. The floor shimmered with puddles of icy water, some of which showed signs of crystallizing from the low temperature. She wrapped her arms around herself for warmth and carefully headed down the wet staircase, afraid that the marble beneath her feet might have frozen over, too. From the look of the floor below, the tarp must have been down half the night.

She should wake Mrs. White. Then again, the old woman had already been so upset to see what had happened to the window. Maybe, if Orchid got the floor cleaned up quickly, Mrs. White would never need to know. Before she could stop herself, Orchid took a quick left toward the library, and knocked softly.

It took a minute for Vaughn to answer. He was dressed in flannel pants and a grungy, long-sleeve thermal shirt missing buttons nearly to the waist. He still looked . . . pretty good. Maybe she'd been in Maine too long.

He rubbed his fist groggily across his eyes. "What's wrong?"

"Hey, I hate to bother you, but the tarp came down in the hall—"

"Oh no, is it still raining? Do you need help rehanging it?"

"No . . ." She bit her lip as she realized what she must look like. "You know what? Go back to bed. I know where the mops are."

Already he looked more awake, but his voice still creaked. "You sure?"

She started backing away. "Positive."

"Okay."

She turned away, cursing herself. She was no better than Scarlett or Peacock, waking up the poor scholarship student to mop her floor after a blizzard. She could mop. She knew where they kept the cleaning supplies.

Probably.

In the far back corner of the house was the conservatory, a sort of quasi-greenhouse where Mrs. White cultivated a bunch of ferns, some orchids, and a trio of dwarf citrus trees much beloved by all the girls in Tudor. Orchid had helped Mrs. White with watering and pruning loads of times, and she recalled that some mops, brooms, and brushes had been stashed in the utility closet where Mrs. White kept the gardening tools. She'd find what she needed in there.

The hall was dim, back behind the stairs, and the puddles of water dotted about the floor hinted at how long the tarp over the window must have been down. She couldn't believe the rain had made it all the way back here. The door to the conservatory was shut, and at first the handle didn't even turn. Was it locked? Orchid had never seen it locked the entire time she'd lived in Tudor. She pulled harder.

No . . . It was only stuck. Probably the cold, or the dampness or something, which had caused the wood to expand. She threw her shoulder against the door, and it popped as it opened. Cold, gray light hit her eyes from the massive windows at the back of the house. She blinked at the brightness, shielding her eyes as she stepped into the room.

She'd hardly gotten past the threshold when she tripped over something and fell. Orchid threw out her arms to catch herself before she slammed into the hard, tiled floor, but instead she hit a soft, bulky mass, then rolled into yet another frigid puddle.

The windows must have broken in here, too was her first hazy thought. And then she looked at her arms, which were bathed in red.

And two feet away lay a crumpled form. His skin was gray. His mouth was slack. His pale fingers still clutched the handle of the knife jutting out of his chest. But it was his eyes that terrified her the most. Flat, unblinking, and staring right at her.

"Orchid?" came a voice behind her, and she tried to inhale, but there was no air. There was no air anywhere. She was covered in blood and she couldn't breathe. Just like before. Just like before.

"What did you need help with—"

And then Vaughn, too, lost the ability to speak. Or at least, she no longer heard it over the thunderous rush in her ears. She felt his hands on her shoulders, pulling her up and back out of the room, and he seemed to be shouting her name.

Dark spots appeared in the corners of her vision. She choked and spluttered and stared into Vaughn's light brown eyes, until they were the only things she could see.

"Breathe," he ordered, and she did.

Her lungs inflated, and she gasped, "Mr. Boddy! He's dead!"

10

Mustard

The wind whistled through the hole in the hall window. The tarp was being used for other purposes.

It was Mustard who had covered the headmaster in the tarp, with the assistance of Rusty Nayler. They'd debated about whether or not they should attempt to move him, or even roll him over from where he'd apparently fallen on that knife. Mustard was afraid if they didn't get the corpse somewhere cold, at least while they were all still trapped in the house, they'd soon regret it.

"Where would you put the headmaster of Blackbrook Academy?" asked Rusty. "In the shed, where he could get flooded out and float away?"

"It's not the headmaster anymore," Vaughn had said, nearly under his breath.

It might not have been Boddy, but it looked like him. Headmaster Boddy, with his neatly trimmed white beard and fancy pajamas. Boddy, only with skin the color no skin should be, and eyes as dead as glass, and the giant hole in his chest.

They'd compromised and opened one of the big conservatory windows, letting in the cold air. Hopefully it would be enough to slow the progress of—whatever it was that happened to a body in death.

The girls were taking it well. Mustard had half expected hysterics—screaming, fainting, maybe some vomit. Girls in movies always did stuff like that. Girls in real life, though . . . well, it wasn't like he really knew any.

Orchid had looked a bit green around the gills when he'd first come into the conservatory, but Mustard chalked that up more to shock than anything else. Boddy's blood still stained her clothes from where she'd fallen on top of the body. Vaughn had brought her wet rags to wash with, but she'd taken only a few perfunctory swipes at her skin before giving up. Now she sat on a chair in the corner of the hall, knees drawn up to her chest, her face drawn and pale, but calm.

Everyone was quiet. Beth Picach hadn't spoken three words since coming downstairs. Karlee and Kayla, both in pastel fleece pajama sets, were holding each other, sobbing with their heads down on each other's shoulders. Mrs. White was standing, her back against the wall as if for support, and watching the proceedings with red-rimmed eyes. He supposed that was the storied stiff upper lip all the locals were famous for. Nothing ruffled them, even finding a corpse next to their potted Phalaenopsis.

At last she seemed to realize how ghoulish it was for everyone to be standing around, watching them wrap the headmaster up.

"Come to the dining room," she ordered the rest of the students in a voice few would be willing to disobey. "I'll make tea."

"I—I need to change," said Orchid softly, and excused herself.

Mustard and Rusty washed their hands, then joined the others.

Scarlett, predictably, had taken charge of the conversation in the dining room.

"I don't know why he would have done such a thing," she was saying as they entered. "He didn't seem that upset last night. I mean, concerned about the damage, to be sure . . . But suicide?"

"Maybe Blackbrook doesn't have insurance," said Peacock. "And the damage is going to be extensive."

"That can't be right," said Plum. "A school like this, with the endowment we have . . ."

"Not everyone gets flood insurance," Scarlett pointed out. "If you're not in a flood zone—"

"Blackbrook *is* in a flood zone," said Vaughn. "We're right on the sea."

Mustard couldn't believe he was listening to this. Weren't these kids supposed to be geniuses? "Excuse me," he said. The others all looked at him. "Are you saying— Do you think this was a suicide?"

"Of course," said Scarlett, as if he were the one being unreasonable. "His hands were on the knife."

"That doesn't mean—" He looked helplessly at

Rusty, whose expression was as closed off as if it were every day he came upon the bloody corpse of his boss. Rusty just shook his head and went to take a seat in the corner.

Mustard frowned. He'd work that bit out later. "All that means is he grabbed it, which could have happened after he'd been stabbed. Think about it, if you get even a splinter, what's the first thing you do?"

Scarlett glared at him for several long seconds, then slumped in her seat. "Well, I guess I grab it to try and pull it out."

Shaking his head, Mustard slid into an empty seat.

"But that doesn't mean we should rule it out."

Mrs. White entered the room with a steaming teakettle. "That's enough of this kind of talk. No one is going to speculate about anything until the authorities get here. The fact is, we don't know what happened to poor Mr. Boddy. Maybe it *was* a suicide."

Mustard rolled his eyes. "If you're going to kill yourself, there are a lot easier ways to go about it than a knife in the heart."

Everyone's heads turned in his direction, and their expressions were all a mix of shock and disgust. He raised his hands defensively. "I said *if.*"

Way to make friends at your new school, Mustard.

But seriously. That Scarlett had obviously watched too many samurai movies or something. Who killed themselves like that? It seemed like such an . . . inconvenient way to do it. Why hadn't he just gone out into the flood, or thrown himself off the side of the ravine, or—

"How *are* we going to contact the authorities?" asked Karlee. "The power's still out."

"Are there police in Rocky Point?" Finn asked. "Or . . . um . . . deputies?"

Vaughn looked amused. "You've never gone to the village, have you?"

"Why would we do that, townie?" Scarlett snapped.

"Well then, we'll have to contact the mainland." Mustard looked at Rusty. "Do you have a ham radio or a scanner or something?"

"Not out here," said Rusty gruffly.

"They'll have one in Rocky Point," Vaughn offered. "When the waters recede a bit more I can try to get over the ravine to the village and see what the situation is. The road to the mainland is washed out, but the cops have boats."

Orchid arrived in the hall. She must have showered, despite the cold. Mustard supposed he would do the same, if the alternative was having a dead man's blood on his hands. Her hair was wet, scraped back from her face, and her glasses were back on, crookedly hanging off her nose. Wordlessly, she took a seat at the table and crossed her arms, staring unseeingly at some spot in her lap. Her hands were buried inside the cuffs of her giant sweater, and her lips were pressed into a thin line.

Rusty spoke up at last. "My money's on the authorities being up to their ears in rescue missions." His tone was low and even-keeled, which would have struck Mustard as strange if he hadn't been every bit as monotone last night, talking with Headmaster Boddy about the devastation the flood had wrought on the campus. Mustard remembered listening as the two men discussed the rising waters to the tune of Vaughn's guitar strumming. They'd gone over gas lines and electrical issues dispassionately—Rusty a soldier reporting a reconnaissance, and Boddy a calculating general, able to keep calm in the face of a brutal attack. A scientist reviewing difficulties within the parameters of an experiment.

Mustard had found it soothing actually. The adults seemed to have everything under control.

Only, it had all somehow been a lie.

Rusty clucked his tongue. "A lot of people spent the nights in their attics, with this flood. Not everyone's got their cushy little mansions."

"Yeah, but we're the ones with a dead body on our hands," Scarlett insisted.

"It's not an emergency, though," said Plum, patting his girlfriend's hand.

She snatched it away. "Not an emergency for *whom?* The headmaster of one of the most elite schools on the Eastern Seaboard was just found *dead*, in a *blizzard*, in a house filled with his *own students*. This is going on the nightly news."

Orchid's head shot up. "No. You don't really think that?"

"Oh, I definitely think that," said Scarlett. "It's going

to be a huge scandal. And that's why we need to not only get in touch with the authorities, but we're also going to need to call our parents. With any luck, they can keep our names out of this mess."

Karlee started crying again. Or maybe it was Kayla. Mustard still wasn't entirely sure who was who.

Mrs. White cleared her throat. "All right. Enough of this speculation. Does anyone want more tea?"

No one did. One of the Karlee-or-Kaylas burst into tears and ran from the room, and the other one followed. Now, there was the girly response all the movies he'd ever seen had trained him to look out for. Still, it was only one out of the six of them. Maybe she was also trying to live up to movie expectations.

Peacock, for comparison, had barely looked up from her little blue notebook the whole time.

Also, if Mustard was honest with himself, he kind of felt like crying, too, and he'd barely known the man.

Mustard remembered the last conversation he'd ever had with the headmaster, in which Boddy had promised to contact Mustard's father and convince him to allow changes to Mustard's curriculum. At the time, Mustard had hoped for anything that might prevent that from happening. He hadn't anticipated it would be death.

All of a sudden, he understood why Scarlett might want to believe it had been a suicide, as unlikely as it sounded. Because . . . What was the alternative?

A murder, that was what.

Mustard looked around the table at the others as if with fresh eyes. Just last night, they'd all been eating vegetable soup, drinking hot cocoa, laughing and chatting and singing before the fire. At ease, despite the storm raging all around them.

Just last night, he and the headmaster had been standing together in the hall, talking about Mustard's class schedule, as if Boddy expected everything to be back to normal by the time the school opened next term, flood or no flood. But nothing would be normal, no matter how much tea Mrs. White poured.

He looked at Vaughn. "If you think you can make it back to the village, it's worth a try."

Vaughn nodded sagely.

"No you don't, young man," said Mrs. White. "The last thing we need is another accident on our hands."

"An accident?" Mustard echoed.

"A *death*," Mrs. White clarified. "It's dangerous out there. How is he going to manage to get across the ravine?"

"I have a boat," Rusty cut in. "I brought it up yesterday, 'case the flooding got worse than we could manage. Thought it might come in handy. It's out back."

"Can you navigate the ravine?" Scarlett asked.

Rusty shrugged. "Ayuh. Safe as being here."

Another hush stole over the table. Mustard couldn't help but think it was the smartest thing anyone had said all morning. If Headmaster Boddy had been killed, then someone had killed him.

Someone sitting at this very table.

"There, Mrs. White," said Vaughn. "Rusty and I will take the boat to the village and try to contact the police on the mainland."

Mrs. White pursed her lips. "I'm not sure we should have people leaving the house."

Mustard had to agree. After all, they were all suspects in a homicide.

"The storm is still very dangerous."

Right. That, too. Besides, how would the cops even know there was a homicide to investigate unless someone went to contact them?

"I don't know what other options we have," Mrs. White said at last, and since he supposed she was the one in charge now, that seemed to put an end to the matter. "Though I wouldn't get your hopes up, Vaughn. Like Rusty said, they've got a lot of real emergencies on their hands."

A murder, thought Mustard, definitely ranked as an emergency.

Soon after, Vaughn and Rusty set out in the rowboat to see if they could cross the ravine and get into the village. No one else wanted to brave the elements, but that left all of them in the house with nothing to do. Whatever easy camaraderie had coalesced the previous evening was completely gone. It wasn't as if they could sing songs or braid hair with a dead body wrapped up in the conservatory and suspicion and fear hanging heavier than the clouds in the sky.

Mustard wished he knew anyone in this house well enough to share his thoughts with. Frankly, any of them might be a killer, and how would he know? Or maybe they'd sent the killers off already, scot-free in their get-away rowboat.

Not much comfort in that thought.

Orchid helped Mrs. White clean up the tea things, and Peacock opted to burn off some energy by jogging up and down the stairs in the hall. Scarlett and Plum disappeared to do—well, whatever it was they did alone together. Mustard still wasn't entirely sure what was meant by a platonic power couple. Co-ed schools were weird.

Which left him alone in the hall, staring at the hole in the window and the water freezing into ice sheets on the floor.

"Someone should clean that up," Beth said as she jogged in place on the landing. "It's dangerous."

Someone, huh? "Do you know where they keep the mops?" Might as well do something useful with all this nervous energy.

She shrugged and started another lap. She seemed to be taking the death of the headmaster in stride. Literally.

He headed into the kitchen to ask the women who actually lived in the house.

"In the closet in the conservatory," Orchid said in a small voice. "I was trying to get a mop for the hall when . . ." She hesitated, then swallowed. "That's how I found the body."

Mustard nodded. "I'll take care of it."

As he entered the conservatory, his eyes went immediately to the large, still lump in the center of the room. It shouldn't have an effect on him. Dead bodies were a part of combat, after all. An essential fact of military life.

But he'd never seen one. Not a human one. Any second now, he expected the mass of tarp to rise and fall, as if Headmaster Boddy were only sleeping. But it never happened, and the longer he stood there, the more hairs rose on the nape of his neck. Swiftly, he opened the closet, grabbed a mop and bucket, and slammed the door closed, checking again to make sure the corpse hadn't moved.

It hadn't.

In the hall he discovered the mop was stiff and frozen, as if any moisture that had remained trapped in the fibers of its head from previous use had crystallized in the conservatory broom closet. Maybe *that* would be a good place to store the body.

But he'd worry about that later. For now, he wanted to get the water off the floor. It seemed like an awful lot to have come through the window, but maybe it had been raining harder in the night. The puddles of water extended all the way down the hallway, nearly to the conservatory, and Mustard had already emptied out the bucket once in the bathroom sink by the time he reached the front hall, beneath the broken window.

Just a little more KP duty. There was nothing else for them to do at this point. Rusty and Vaughn were trying to get help. No one seemed in immediate danger. Mustard wanted to help, too, and the most immediate thing he could think of was to mop the floor.

The cold wind kept him moving fast. He'd have to find something to cover up that window with. If they were out of tarps, maybe he could try trash bags, or cling film. He looked around the hall. Rusty must have moved the ladder sometime in the night.

Another chill went down his spine. No. *Headmaster Boddy* had been the one to move the ladder. He remembered that now. The two men had carried it together out onto the front porch. It might have been one of the last things the man had done in his life. Or maybe it had been brushing his teeth, or reading a chapter in some musty old book, or making sure everyone was tucked into their beds, where they were supposed to be.

And what if someone wasn't? Would that be reason enough to kill the headmaster?

Mustard didn't want to dwell on all the possibilities. He pushed the mop even faster across the parquet floor as scenarios ricocheted disturbingly through his mind.

There was Scarlett and Plum, always sneaking off together. And Scarlett, so determined to argue it was a suicide.

There was Rusty, who'd hardly said a word when the body was found. Who hadn't seemed remotely upset, and who also had been quick to volunteer to leave the scene. Vaughn had volunteered, too. He also deserved a spot on the suspect list, especially after Boddy had scolded him for his racy song.

And Peacock! He remembered her behavior in the kitchen yesterday, chopping vegetables and staring at the headmaster as if she wanted him dead. Maybe she'd had the chance.

He wondered if the others were making lists. Probably not. They'd all been in school together for years. They were probably great friends.

Mustard was the only outsider. They probably all thought *he* did it.

Mrs. White was right: it did no good to speculate. The police would be here eventually, and they were trained for this kind of thing. He'd learned at Farthing that the quickest way to get in trouble was to operate beyond the mission. He wasn't a detective. His father thought police work was only one step above desk duty.

Combat or bust.

After several more minutes of hard mopping, the floor still shone with moisture, but all the puddles had been sopped up. He stuck the mop head back in the bucket and headed for the conservatory. He'd check the closet for another tarp for the window. They'd need something.

The body remained where he'd left it, still and creepy and somehow smaller than Mustard had remembered the headmaster being. But it hadn't moved. It wouldn't move. It was a corpse.

It was like his father always said: he needed to stop acting like such a pansy. Mustard swallowed and opened the closet door, setting the mop and bucket back in their corner. A bare bulb hung from the ceiling, and Mustard instinctively pulled the cord before remembering there was no power and no light. He fetched a flashlight from the hall, then returned to peer through the shadows at the closet's contents, stacked neatly on the shelves and clustered in stacks against the far wall.

There were old watering cans and pottery in a box labeled *Decorations*, another marked *1972*, some brooms, a few old rags and gardening tools, a box of lightbulbs, another of paper towels, an ancient shoe box that seemed to house old seed packets, and—

There. A tarp, neatly folded, but smeared with markings that might have been dirt or paint. Either way, it was better than leaving the hall exposed to the elements. He tucked it under his arm, backed out of the closet, shut the door—and saw the man standing in the corner of the room.

Mustard nearly jumped out of his skin and yelped.

A second later, he realized it wasn't Boddy at all, but Finn Plum, standing by the back wall of the conservatory and looking at him, one eyebrow lifted.

Mustard's jaw clenched. "How did you get in here?"

"The usual way. I didn't see you in the closet."

"You have a reason to be here?" Mustard replied.

"Who died and made you—" Plum cut himself off. His gaze darted to the corpse under the tarp. "I mean—Mrs. White sent me to see if you needed help with the cleanup." He nodded at the tarp under Mustard's arm. "Covering up that window is going to be a two-man job."

"Yeah," Mustard conceded. "Do you want to go get the ladder?"

Plum did not look as though he did. He was back in his usual preppy clothes. Mustard had found the things he'd lent the boy neatly folded on his side of the billiards table that morning.

Now Plum was staring at the tarp-covered corpse, his expression drawn. "Scarlett still thinks it might be a suicide."

"Do you?" Mustard ventured to ask.

"No." Plum shook his head. "I don't get why he would have done it like this. You didn't know him. He was a scientist. Everything always planned to perfection. And he was a chemist, too, which meant he should have been able to think of a thousand ways to poison himself, if he'd wanted. But . . . stabbing? It's not precise. It can be incredibly slow and painful."

That's exactly what Mustard had been wondering. He almost said something to Plum along those lines, but the words died in his throat when he saw the other boy walking toward the tarp.

"What are you doing?" Mustard cried, but it was too late. Plum pulled back the covering over the headmaster's face.

"Do we have to leave him on the floor like this?" Finn asked, his voice choked with some kind of emotion.

"I don't know. I think until we can get the police here . . ." said Mustard, shaking his head.

"What difference could it make?"

"Evidence. Clues. DNA . . ."

"We already messed with the crime scene." Finn gestured to the tarp.

"I don't know," Mustard said, frustrated. "Do I look like a cop?"

Plum turned his way. "Honestly? Yeah."

Mustard wondered if the boy's hair did that floppy curly thing naturally, or if Plum spent an hour in the mirror every morning, perfecting it. He averted his eyes, but that only meant he was looking at the dead body instead. Suddenly, he couldn't stop from staring at it, couldn't stop his brain from cataloging all the gruesome details. The skin, the blood, the fingers that still hadn't loosened their hold on the handle of the—

Mustard's brow furrowed. "That's a Fairbairn-Sykes."

"What?" Plum asked.

"That's an F-S stiletto," said Mustard. "A World War Two fighting knife."

"A *fighting* knife?" Finn drawled. "And you know it on sight?"

Mustard shrugged. At the military academy, they memorized weaponry like other students learned different poetry meters. "It's a famous weapon. My father thinks it's important to study military history." He had a whole collection.

Plum was unimpressed. "A knife? That's old-school, at least in the military. Wouldn't your time be better spent learning how to program a drone or something?"

Desk job, said his father's voice. Mustard scowled and returned his attention to the knife. "I wonder if it's an original or a replica." Maybe the weapon held a clue as to who might have wielded it. Though it's not as if he could picture anyone in this house liking antique military daggers. It wasn't as if Karlee or Kayla kept daggers in their glitter purses.

But when he looked closer, he noticed something else. There were several long, shallow slashes on Boddy's hands, not near his wrists, but rather across his knuckles and alongside his palms.

As if, prior to plunging the knife into his own chest he'd been . . . fighting it off.

11

Peacock

— EP WORKOUT LOG —

DATE: *December 6*
TIME WOKE: *6:00 a.m. (back on schedule!)*
MORNING WEIGH-IN: *They don't keep scales here, apparently*
BREAKFAST: *2 lemon-custard-flavored nutrition bars (420 calories, 12g protein), green tea*
MORNING WORKOUT: *500 stair reps*

NOTES: *They found the corpse of Headmaster Boddy in the conservatory. There have already been two meetings about what to do. The power is still out and the flooding is still too bad to run outside. Will probably do more stairs this afternoon.*

12

Orchid

O rchid felt like, somehow, Tudor House had gotten submerged in the flood, only no one else noticed. How else to explain this strange floating sensation, or the way that everyone's voices came out muffled, as if they were calling back and forth under the water? She tried to concentrate, but everything became lost in the roar of the tide.

Vaughn and Rusty had gone for the police.

He's back he's back he's back he's back.

Scarlett thought it might be suicide.

He's here he's here he's here he's here.

And now Mustard had gathered her and the four other girls in the hall, clustered on the marble stairs, and was explaining in great detail the particular qualities of the particular antique military knife that was sticking out of the particular chest of their dead headmaster.

Did he like antique fighting knives? Orchid could not recall. At least not here, at the bottom of the sea.

Besides, she told herself, if the knife was still in

Headmaster Boddy's chest, it wasn't exactly a danger anymore.

Not like the person who had used it.

Orchid fought back the tide of terror enveloping her and tried to concentrate on what the others were saying. She'd never met the new kid before yesterday, and didn't know if he was given to wild flights of fancy, like Scarlett and her nonsense suicide theory. Orchid hadn't been so out of it that she'd missed her housemate's notion.

At least Mustard didn't buy it, either. And he'd been the one doing the talking. Finn Plum had nodded in confirmation of the revelation that there were injuries on Headmaster Boddy's hands "inconsistent with a suicide," but otherwise had added no extra information.

Once, in another life, Orchid had done a three-episode arc on a famous crime show. She'd played the murder victim, which had been fun during the flashback scenes, but had also required a lot of lying around half naked on fake mortuary slabs while actors pretending to be detectives stood above her and said things just like that.

It had sounded every bit as incomprehensible then.

"So . . ." said Scarlett. "What you're saying is, someone stabbed Headmaster Boddy, then put his hands around the old knife?"

"I'm saying I don't know why he would have slashed up his own hands before stabbing himself in the heart."

"Maybe he was trying to . . . slash his wrists or something. Did you check out his wrists?"

"I didn't touch the body," said Mustard. "I don't want to mess up any fingerprints for when the police get here. It's a crime scene."

"Just let it go already, Scarlett," Orchid found herself snapping. "He didn't commit suicide."

Not that she blamed Scarlett for clinging to any option—no matter how horrible—that kept her safe.

After all, didn't Orchid make the same kinds of choices herself? The chill had nothing to do with the falling temperature in the hall.

You didn't think you could hide from me forever, did you?

How stupid to think she could. Even more moronic to think that the storm would protect her. All it did was strand her here, with no help of defense or escape.

"It's too bad Rusty and Vaughn already left," said Karlee. "The police need this info, too."

"Where's Mrs. White?" Mustard asked.

"Wasn't she in the kitchen?" asked Finn.

"She was," said Orchid. "We were cleaning up in there. I think she went to change." Or collect herself, or something. There was a dead body in her house. That would rattle anyone.

Orchid knew that for a fact.

"She wasn't in her room upstairs," said Karlee. "That's where we were."

"Maybe she's in the bathroom," said Kayla.

Finn knocked on the study door. "Mrs. White?"

No answer.

He knocked again, harder. "Mrs. White?" A frantic note had entered his tone.

Behind them, the door to the lounge opened and they all jumped.

Mrs. White stood on the threshold. Her eyes looked tired. She seemed to have aged ten years in the last several hours. Orchid wondered if they all looked like that. "Yes? Did you need something?"

Mustard stepped forward. "Mrs. White, Finn and I were just in the conservatory looking at the corpse and—"

Her eyes widened in horror. "Why would you do that? Can't the man get a single moment of peace, even in death?"

"Well, ma'am, it seems that Mr. Boddy—"

"Headmaster Boddy," Mrs. White corrected, her tone clipped, her gaze as cold as ice.

Mustard was undeterred. "—had slash marks all over his hands. As if he was fighting off an attacker with the knife, before he was stabbed."

Mrs. White took this in. "What do you mean?"

"I saw them, on his body. I don't know why a man committing suicide would take the time to cut up his hands first."

"Or why he'd use a knife to start with," Plum said. "That doesn't feel like the headmaster."

"You are not the coroner," she said harshly to Mustard. "And you," she added, turning to Plum, "are not the police. I suggest you leave an investigation—if one is necessary—to those trained to do one. We're in a bad enough situation as it is."

"You think?" Scarlett asked, her voice frantic. "If it wasn't a suicide, then there's a murderer in this house! How can you just expect us to stay here? Any of us might be next!"

"Scarlett!" Mrs. White cried, astonished. "What did I just say? My goodness, what a fantasy you've cooked up. As if one of your fellow students could have murdered a man! On what grounds?"

Because, of course, a murderer needed a motive. Orchid could tell when that same thought occurred to the other people in the hall. The flickering gazes, the changes in posture, the expressions that morphed from horrified to suspicious. They were each making their own mental list.

Karlee and Kayla: Clueless.
Mustard: But then why would he be the one tipping them all off?
Scarlett and Finn: Devious enough to try anything, for sure, but they were total teachers' pets.
Peacock: There had been that fight with the headmaster, and Finn had told Scarlett, which meant half the school knew.

She wondered what they were thinking about her. What motive they imagined that was one hundred percent wrong, but also right in the only way that mattered.

She *was* to blame.

Only . . . If the person who wrote her that letter had wanted to get to her—if he'd killed Headmaster Boddy to do it—what possible reason would he have for not finishing the job?

Lost in thought, Orchid didn't even realize that she was still staring at Peacock, until the other girl snapped at her.

"What?" Peacock cried. "Do I stink or something?"

Orchid quickly returned her attention to her hands in her lap.

Mrs. White clucked her tongue. "No. I'm afraid if Headmaster Boddy met a bad end, it was something else entirely. But that won't be for us to say. We must remain calm until Rusty gets back with the police."

"I don't understand," Mustard said to her. "Who do you think is responsible?"

Mrs. White looked grave. "I've just been in the lounge, looking at the headmaster's belongings and trying to get a sense of why he'd even be in the conservatory so late at night."

"And?" Scarlett nearly pounced.

"Yesterday, he brought over boxes from the school office," Mrs. White said. "In case he couldn't reach it during the flood. Important files and such. I saw them when he arrived. And now—well, several are missing."

"What's missing?" asked Mustard.

"His personal laptop, for one," said Mrs. White. "And

the lockbox with all the petty cash. Several thousand dollars, easily." She shook her head.

"A thief?" asked Finn.

"A looter!" exclaimed Scarlett.

Orchid lifted her head. *A looter?*

"After a disaster like this, there are always looters," said Mrs. White. "And with the campus nearly empty for the holidays, and the evacuation order in place, it might be reasonable for a thief to expect that Tudor House was abandoned, too. I think Boddy was in the wrong place at the wrong time."

The rushing sound that had been filling Orchid's head ever since she'd discovered the body began to fade, just the tiniest bit.

Mrs. White's eyes went glassy, but no tears fell. "We had an agreement, he and I. We would sleep downstairs, by the doors and the stairs, so we could hear anything. But I was so tired last night—the storm had kept me up the previous evening. I must have been more deeply asleep than I thought. If some looter broke into the house, he might have woken the headmaster when he was in his room, robbing him."

If nothing else, it would explain why no one else had been harmed. Orchid couldn't imagine any other reason.

"And he chased the thief into the conservatory?" Scarlett asked.

"And faced him alone," said Mrs. White. "And lost his life for it." She seemed to waver on her feet.

Orchid and Scarlett jumped up to help the old woman.

"Really, Mrs. White," said Scarlett, "it wasn't your fault."

And maybe—just maybe, it wasn't Orchid's, either. She'd never felt quite so warmly toward Scarlett in her whole life.

But Mrs. White merely put a hand over her eyes and sobbed.

"Come sit down in the study," said Orchid, her mind reeling. Together, she and Scarlett helped their proctor into the study, where she'd spent the previous evening. She sat on the couch she must have slept on last night. A pile of blankets and sheets were neatly stacked to one side.

Orchid thought of her own unmade bed, upstairs. Even with all this disaster, Mrs. White had still found a way to take care of her house. Her precious Tudor House that she'd watched over all these years.

"Can we get you anything?" Scarlett asked. "Tea?"

"Since when do you know how to boil water, dear?" Mrs. White asked her. At least she hadn't damaged her sense of humor.

Scarlett's lips pursed. "Your stove is tricky."

"Not that tricky," said Orchid. You just had to know how to strike a match.

"Orchid," Scarlett declared. "Go put the kettle on."

Figured. The second anyone gave Scarlett half a chance, she would put herself in charge.

Karlee and Kayla appeared at the door.

"Kayla and I want to know if there's anything we can

do," Karlee said, wringing her hands. "Like, maybe we can give Mrs. White her room back?"

"And sleep where?" Scarlett asked.

Karlee blinked. "Oh, you don't think we'll be spending another night in this house, do you? The police are coming now."

That remained to be seen. Orchid unfolded a quilt and tucked it around Mrs. White's knees.

"And . . . the body, in the conservatory," Karlee went on, looking a bit pale. "That's right under our room. If I look out the window, I can see into it."

"Or we *could*," chimed in Kayla, "if it weren't for the snow."

They could move to her room, but Orchid didn't imagine they would feel any more comfortable being up the stairs and down the hall from a dead body than they would be directly above it. And if there was even a slight possibility that her own fears were true, they'd be even less safe.

On the flip side, there was safety in numbers. Maybe she should pack her room full of guests.

Like a human shield.

Orchid fluffed a lacy pillow and set it behind Mrs. White on the sofa. "They have a point, ma'am. You might be more comfortable in your own room."

"No," she said firmly. "Headmaster Boddy wanted staff to—to—" She buried her face in her hands. "To protect you children."

That hadn't turned out too well for him, had it? Orchid

wrapped her arms around herself and shivered. It was getting colder in here every minute. "Are the guys putting another tarp over the window?"

"They're arguing about the best way to do it," Karlee replied.

Scarlett pushed past them both. "I'll take care of it."

Orchid raised her hands and stepped back. "You want to be the boss?"

"Of course." Scarlett gave her an incredulous look. She and the other girls left to supervise the tarp hanging.

Alone with Mrs. White, Orchid finished tucking the woman in. "Don't blame yourself, Mrs. White. I don't think the looter would have known anyone was here. He won't be back. We're all safe now." How much she wished she could believe it!

"Safe?" Mrs. White echoed. "We're never really safe. I have lived in this house since I was your age, and now . . ." She shook her head.

Orchid understood exactly what she meant. Tudor House was now a murder house, and nothing would ever be the same again. She'd thought Blackbrook was her sanctuary, but even here she'd been discovered. She'd felt at home in Tudor House, but even here there was tragedy and violence.

Nowhere was really safe. Orchid should have realized that a long time ago.

"Let me heat you up some soup," she insisted. She had to keep busy, or she might jump out of her skin.

Outside in the hall, Scarlett was barking orders at the boys struggling with the tarp. Orchid left the scene as soon as possible, before Scarlett could boss her around, too. In the kitchen, she found the remains of yesterday's soup in the cooler. She pulled out the container and the broken glasses slipped off her nose. She folded them up and stuck them in the pocket of her sweater. They were turning into too much of a hassle to deal with, anyway. Orchid poured some soup in a pot to heat on the gas stove. At least they still had the gas for heating and cooking. Once the window was covered again, the house would warm up.

She was lighting the pilot when a rap on the window made her heart leap into her throat.

Vaughn stood at the window. There was ice crusted on his skin and head, and his down coat hung heavy with water.

She rushed to the kitchen door. It stuck, and shards of ice shattered all around her when she was finally able to yank it open.

"What happened!" she cried. "Where's Rusty? Were you able to contact the police?"

He was slow to respond and she wondered for a second if he had hypothermia.

"Rusty," he said, blinking. "We got separated."

"Did you fall off the boat?"

"The boat sank. Scraped over some kind of debris in the floodwaters . . ."

She pulled him inside. "Take off that coat. You're

going to freeze. Come sit by the oven." The soup for Mrs. White could wait. Vaughn needed it now.

"So it's bad out there?" She turned the burners all the way up and set a kettle on for good measure.

"Like the end of the world." Vaughn took off his boots. One of his socks had a hole in the toe and the other was missing its heel. His sweater had seen better days, too. "The flood is starting to recede in places, but all land beneath the water is ruined. Downed trees and dead animals."

"That sounds terrible. Do you think Rusty is okay?"

"Last I saw him, he'd made it to the far side of the ravine." He sat with his back against the side of the oven, while Orchid found an old fleece blanket and gave it to him to wrap around his body.

"That's good. It means he'll get to the police. Someone will come and get us."

"I wouldn't hold your breath. It's a disaster out there."

"But they've got to prioritize us!" Orchid insisted. "With the headmaster being dead? Isn't that enough of an emergency?"

Vaughn said nothing. Maybe he was frozen solid. She stopped pestering him. When the broth steamed, she ladled some into a mug and handed it to him.

"Drink up."

He obeyed.

Dread began to rise within her again. Somehow, she'd convinced herself that it would be all right once the police came, but even Rusty sounded skeptical that they'd be able to make it here anytime soon. And if they couldn't count on rescue from the authorities . . .

She put her hands on the edge of the counter and closed her eyes. It wasn't so bad. Like Mrs. White had said, it was probably a looter—a robbery gone wrong. And if so, the killer was long gone and unlikely to return. They had heat, and water, and a roof over their heads. She checked the pantry. "At least we've got plenty of provisions."

Vaughn snorted. "Right. We won't have to resort to cannibalism, like the Donner party."

"Huh?" Her eyes narrowed. "Cannibals?"

"Yes, remember? From history class? They got snowed in for months and had to eat their dead?" He stared out the window. "Sometimes I wonder if I could do that. If I had to."

Orchid vaguely recalled that story from class. Strange, Vaughn had seemed so much more charming last night, by firelight. When he hadn't been discussing eating people.

After half the mug was gone, she thought he'd probably been sufficiently warmed to hear more updates. "After you left, Finn and Mustard took a look at the body. They identified the knife, and they saw cuts and scrapes on his hands—the hands holding the dagger. Definitely not a suicide."

Vaughn just stared at her, unblinking. "What do you mean by that?"

"We think the headmaster might have been murdered," said a voice by the door. Orchid looked up to see

Scarlett standing there with Finn. "We came by to see if you were heating the kettle by the light of a candle."

"Vaughn said the boat sunk," she explained to them. "He and Rusty were separated. And just look at him! He's nearly frozen through."

"I'm not so bad now," he said. "There are dozens of rabbits and foxes and deer floating around out there who are way worse off than me."

"Gross," said Scarlett. "I think we've all had enough of corpses for one day."

"Is Rusty okay?" Finn asked.

Vaughn lifted one shoulder. "He made it to the other side of the ravine. I'm sure he's in the village by now."

Or dead of hypothermia, Orchid thought.

"You said you think the headmaster was murdered?" Vaughn asked. He peered at each of them in turn, his gaze intent but unreadable.

"Yes," said Scarlett. "Probably a looter. There's cash and Boddy's computer missing from his room. We think someone came in here last night trying to rob the house, had a run-in with Headmaster Boddy, and escaped."

Vaughn nodded thoughtfully. "Would a looter just steal from Boddy and leave?"

Orchid caught her breath. "What do you mean?"

Vaughn shrugged. "Blackbrook kids have nice stuff. I imagine a thief would think there's plenty to take."

"Well," said Scarlett, "we think maybe he didn't know anyone was here and was just getting started when the headmaster surprised him, and after he killed him, he just grabbed what he could and ran."

Vaughn took another long sip of his soup, as if considering this scenario. "A looter, huh? I don't know."

"What do you mean, you don't know?" Scarlett put her hands on her hips.

"Well, it's just this, Scarlett." He stood, and the blanket unfurled over his shoulders like Dracula's cape. "I've been out there, and I know how bad it is, even this morning, when the tide's gone down some. I don't think it's possible that anyone got in here last night, and even if they did, there's no way they got out."

It didn't matter how close she stood to the stove, Orchid felt cold all over.

Vaughn went on. "So I don't *think* it was a looter who murdered Boddy. But this I *know*: whoever killed him is still here."

13

Scarlett

Scarlett looked down at the list she'd been surreptitiously keeping in her notebook as they all sat in the dining room, eating a mostly silent lunch of "whatever they thought might spoil first." According to Karlee, Mrs. White was still asleep on the couch in the study. Scarlett figured this was a good thing. The poor woman had to be close to hysterics, between the way her precious home had been turned into an emergency shelter, the destruction of the window, and the whole murder-in-the-conservatory thing.

It was probably best that she wasn't the one in charge right now.

As far as Scarlett could tell, within the realm of possibility, Headmaster Boddy's death could be contributed to one of four factors:

1. Some kind of terrible knife accident

2. Suicide

3. A stranger/thief/looter

4. A person and/or people in this house

Was she missing anything? She'd been considering the issue ever since they'd found the body, and she thought she had the bases covered. The rest was merely a matter of probability.

Number one: An accident. Unlikely. Like, vanishingly so. Scarlett was sure in all the infinite multiverses that there had been or would be people who accidentally, in the middle of the night, sliced up their hands with an antique military knife, then followed up by accidentally plunging it into their own chests . . . But come on.

Number two: Suicide. As much as she hated to admit it—since this had been her theory to begin with—suicide was looking pretty unlikely, too. Even if the scientist headmaster had for some reason chosen this dramatic and messy method, she doubted he would have slashed the backs of his hands first. No, he'd been fending off an attack.

See? She could admit when she was wrong.

And why would he have wanted to do such a thing, anyway? Scarlett had never been able to make that part make sense. Blackbrook certainly had flood insurance. No one on the school's advisory board would be able to lay this disaster on the headmaster's doorstep. Besides, that wasn't the man she had known. As a member of student council and the head of the Campus Beautification Committee, Scarlett had worked with him on many school projects. She'd taken his chemistry class freshman year. They'd always gotten along famously. He'd been brilliant and kind, strict, but fair, willing to listen to student input and inspire student excellence.

And now he was gone. Scarlett blinked, but no tears came. What a relief it might be, just once, to be able to cry. The others had done it. She'd watched Orchid downstairs in the hall after she'd discovered the headmaster, symmetrical tracks of tears running over her porcelain skin. Karlee and Kayla had done it. Mrs. White had all but broken down in the study after Mustard described the murder weapon.

But Scarlett had never been a crier. She'd been a fixer. If there were problems, there was no point crying over them when you could solve them. And if the police weren't coming, then someone else would have to solve this particular problem. She took a deep breath. Onward.

Number three: A looter. A stranger. A person who had broken in to Tudor, killed Headmaster Boddy, and absconded with his money and computer. When the idea had been put forth, it made the most sense of all. Of course there would be looters in this disaster, and of course they would target a mansion like Tudor House. Maybe it was all as Mrs. White had surmised. Boddy just got caught up in a robbery gone terribly wrong. But that didn't make them safe now.

First of all, there was a chance the thief would return. Scarlett had tens of thousands of dollars of computer equipment in her bedroom at this moment, not to mention jewelry. This thief had proved himself willing to kill to get what he wanted.

Or she! Scarlett didn't want to be sexist. Women were totally capable of robbing houses, murdering headmasters, and coming back for more. And that's assuming the thief really did leave the scene of the crime.

As much as Scarlett hated to admit that Vaughn Green was right about anything, he had a point about how hard it would be for the thief to escape. And the looter, whoever he or she was, would have had to escape by boat, if they escaped at all. Otherwise . . . they were still here.

On the campus, at the very least, and possibly even hidden somewhere in the house right now.

This was a big house. Scarlett had lived here all year, and she had yet to venture into the attic. And as far as she knew, no one had checked the locked-up rooms belonging to the other girls who called Tudor House home. Faith and Cadence and Nisha and Atherton had all gone home before the storm hit, and last night, Mrs. White had not wanted to open their rooms for the newcomers without permission. But now, all bets had to be off. They needed to find out if anything had been stolen. They needed to find out if anyone else was in the house.

It was enough to make her never want to go upstairs again. To never be alone again in Tudor House, period.

Number four: Someone here did it. Scarlett sneaked a glance at the people sitting around her. This thought had been the constant drumbeat in her head, ever since Orchid had found the body in the conservatory. That someone here, in this room, was a murderer.

Now she looked at Orchid, who was only toying with her soup. Scarlett never had learned what Orchid had been to the headmaster's office about, back before the storm. She turned to Peacock, who was also scribbling in a little bright blue notebook. Nor had she gotten the story on what Peacock had been fighting with the headmaster about. Finn would be no help with the latter, of course, but she could probably deploy him for the former . . .

She turned to Finn. While the rest of them had raided the kitchen, he'd been restless as anything, wandering the halls between the conservatory and the lounge, as if retracing Boddy's final steps would somehow help him solve the equation of the man's death.

He glanced at her sheet of possibilities, then up at her, his brow furrowed.

Seriously? he mouthed at her.

Scarlett cleared her throat to get the room's attention. "I think we should search the house."

A chorus of murmured gasps went around the table. They mostly came from the side where Karlee and Kayla were sitting.

"Okay," said Mustard, putting down his fork, as if he were ready to leave that minute.

"Wait," said Finn. "No. Why?"

"To make sure there's nobody here."

"But there *is* a body here," said Kayla. "In the conservatory."

Scarlett rolled her eyes.

Vaughn, who had been shoveling down cake as if he hadn't already eaten half the provisions yesterday, sat back in his seat and crossed his arms over his chest.

Scarlett went on. "With the state the campus is in, there's a reasonable possibility that whoever attacked Headmaster Boddy is still here."

Another set of gasps.

"A murderer?" asked Karlee. "In the house with us?"

"Look," said Finn. "Let's not get ahead of ourselves. There are a dozen buildings on this campus that the looter could be hiding out in."

"So don't we owe it to ourselves to make sure there's not a killer in this one?" Mustard replied.

"Would *you* stick around here after you stabbed someone?" Finn asked.

"Having never stabbed anyone, I couldn't tell you," said Mustard.

Vaughn shrugged. "It makes sense. Of course the killer would want to leave the scene of the crime—if they could. But with the storm . . . that may not have been an option."

Finn frowned. "Rusty left."

"True," said Vaughn, his tone even. "Maybe it was Rusty, and he purposefully sunk our boat so he could escape to the mainland." He leaned forward, and his voice dropped a register. "Or maybe Rusty never made it to the village alive at all."

"Eww," said Scarlett. Was he about to start in with his dreadful murder ballads again? "Don't joke about that when we have an *actual* dead body in the conservatory."

"That's what I said." Kayla pouted.

"I'm not joking." Vaughn looked affronted. "I nearly froze on my way back to the house, and I'm not an old man like Rusty. You Blackbrook kids can't imagine how bad it's gotten out there. Anything could have happened to him before he reached safety."

Number four: Someone here did it. Vaughn was right. Anything could have happened, including that he was the killer and had murdered the janitor, too. Scarlett couldn't rule it out.

Though, of course, it was unlikely that he'd be bragging about it now, macabre taste in music or not.

"Can we please stop talking about this?" Karlee asked.

"No," said Orchid. "If there's a chance that there's a murderer in this house, we need to know about it." She turned to Scarlett and nodded. At least for once, she was planning on being helpful.

Finn shook his head. "No—it was a *looter*, like Mrs. White said. They took the headmaster's valuables and ran."

"Swam, you mean," said Mustard.

"In which case, they're drowned under all those floodwaters," Finn insisted, his voice rising. "There's no one in the house! There's no need to search."

"I don't want to take that chance!" Scarlett cried. "I'm shocked that you would be willing to risk it."

"I agree," said Orchid. "I'll sleep a lot better knowing there's no one else here."

"But that does leave another possibility," said Vaughn

ominously. "If there's no one else in the house, then maybe it wasn't some looter at all. One of *us* did it."

Exactly what Scarlett was afraid of, no matter how Mrs. White had scolded her for considering it. Maybe she should start a suspect list, counting down from least likely to most. She already had a pretty good idea of how it would go.

6. *Kayla Gould: Uh, no.*

5. *Karlee Silverman: Ditto.*

4. *Mustard: Seemed to have the skinny on military fighting knives, but from all evidence barely knew the headmaster. Although, no one knew why he'd left that military academy . . .*

3. *Orchid: Wimp, though she had gone to that mysterious meeting in the headmaster's office last week . . .*

2. *Vaughn: Goth AF. Quite possibly a secret serial killer who writes songs about his victims.*

1. *Beth: By Finn's account, had actually tried to kill the headmaster in her mysterious meeting in his office last week.*

That was everyone. Oh, wait. Finn. Scarlett looked at her friend. *Nah.* He'd liked the headmaster as much as she had. He'd been so upset all morning.

"Are you calling us suspects?" Finn shouted across the table at Vaughn.

See? Wild with grief.

Vaughn raised his hands in defense. "I'm just discussing possibilities. Playing 'what if?' You're the scientist, Plum. Isn't that how you come up with theories?"

"That is so different," Finn said.

"Maybe," Vaughn said, "we should ask ourselves who in this house might have a reason to want the headmaster dead?" His eyes slid in Peacock's direction, and it was as if everyone at the table suddenly seemed to remember the gossip about what had happened in Boddy's office before the storm.

Mustard broke in. "Okay, let's not jump down each other's throats. Remember, we're all on the same team here."

"The murderer isn't," Vaughn pointed out, smirking. Wow, he was insufferable. She wished Mrs. White were here to see how he behaved when she wasn't around. She watched him take yet another brownie from the plate and swallow it in two bites. All this talk of murder certainly wasn't having an effect on his sweet tooth.

Mustard, too, was unamused. "Let's just concentrate on making sure there's no one else in the house."

"By searching in groups of two?" asked Orchid, her tone that soft, light kind that somehow still managed to make everyone in the room stop and pay attention. Scarlett didn't know how Orchid managed it. She herself had never been able to get people's attention except by volume. "After we've just raised the question of whether or not someone sitting at this table killed the headmaster?"

"Very good point, Orchid," Vaughn said. "I for one would not want to be left alone with a psychopath."

Judging from the nervous glances shooting across the table, no one else did, either.

Karlee looked at Kayla. "Dibs on Kayla as my partner."

"What?" said Kayla, staring at her friend. "Why?"

"Because, dummy," said Karlee, "I know neither of us did it."

"Yeah," said Kayla, "but if we're together and we come upon the killer, hiding somewhere, how are we going to stop him from getting us, too? I want to be with Mustard." She turned to the new kid. "You have, like, military training and stuff, right?"

"Well," said Mustard haltingly. "I . . ."

Looked like Mustard didn't want to be on the hook for single-handedly taking down a murderer with only those two for backup.

"Okay," Scarlett said, slicing her hand across the table. "Maybe splitting up isn't such a great idea."

"Or maybe we could split into teams," Orchid suggested. "Three-person teams. There are nine of us, if you include Mrs. White, and three floors to search—this one, upstairs, and the attic."

"Dibs on *not* the attic," said Karlee.

"That sounds like a fair compromise," said Mustard.

"Do you really want to disturb Mrs. White?" Finn asked. "In her fragile condition?"

"To catch a murderer?" asked Orchid. "Yes. I think she'd be fine with that."

"She's hardly fragile," Scarlett pointed out. She'd just been through a lot that morning. Finding a corpse in your house wasn't exactly a stress-free event. And Tudor House was *her* house, more than it belonged to any of the students who lived here.

Finn considered this. "Okay, then I volunteer that you and I take the ground floor with Mrs. White. That way, we won't have to disturb her too much while we look around."

"Thank you," said Scarlett.

"Of course, dummy," he replied. "I know neither of us did it."

Scarlett bit her lip to hide her smile. "That leaves . . . Orchid, Vaughn, and Beth for the attic."

Beth looked up from her notebook, possibly for the first time during the entire conversation. "What?"

How very odd. The obvious suspect, if it was someone in this house, was the only person anyone had witnessed threatening the headmaster.

Could the tennis star be a killer off the courts?

"We're teaming up to search the attic," Vaughn explained to Peacock, as if to a child. "Hopefully none of us is a murderer."

Orchid shot Vaughn an incredulous, disapproving look, and he returned what Scarlett guessed was supposed to be a reassuring smile, but seemed, somehow, more like a baring of teeth.

At least it would be Orchid dealing with Vaughn and Peacock, and not Scarlett or Finn. She didn't envy her housemate, heading off to search some dank, dreary attic with the two people on the top of Scarlett's suspect list.

On the flip side, if Orchid wound up dead, at least they'd be able to narrow their list down.

Outside, the wind buffeted the house, and the windows rattled in their panes. Scarlett was quite glad to be staying on the ground floor. Though, of course, that was the only floor where someone had actually died.

Scarlett shut the door to the study behind her and held her finger up to her lips. "Mrs. White is still asleep," she said softly to the other students. "I say we get started on the rest of the house."

Everyone else agreed and headed up the stairs to the other floors. She turned to Finn. "Where do you want to get started?"

"Well, there's obviously no one but Mrs. White in the study," he said, "and we were just in the dining room and kitchen, so no one is likely to be in there . . ."

"Whatever we do," Scarlett said, "one of us should stay near the door at all times, to make sure a killer isn't sneaking around from room to room ahead of us while we search."

"Good idea," said Finn. "With our back to one side of the doorjamb, so no one can sneak up on us."

Scarlett nodded. In the long term of their friendship, they'd been involved in many schemes, but none had been quite so physically dangerous. Together, they headed down the hall toward the library.

This was where Vaughn had spent the night, and indeed, his bedroll lay mussed on the floor, with the guitar he'd used yesterday, his backpack, and what must have been yesterday's clothes piled in a neat stack nearby. She nodded at the belongings. "He looks like he plans to stay for a week with that pack," she said. "I wonder what's inside."

Finn, who had entered the room while Scarlett manned the doorway, toed the backpack. "We'll probably never get another chance to check it out."

They looked at each other for a long moment, each waiting to see who would be the first to decide that their noble aims trumped any claim Vaughn Green might have to privacy.

As usual, Finn blinked first. He knelt and opened the flaps on the pack. Scarlett forgot to keep an eye on the hall as she watched him excavate Vaughn's things.

There were boxers, and socks, and a few extra shirts. Gross and boring. Everything that boy wore was some variation on the color *drab*. She would swear one of the sweaters in there was an identical duplicate of the one he was already wearing. Next, Finn took out packages of batteries and little plastic bags of what looked like home-made trail mix.

"No wonder he's been eating like he does here," said Scarlett.

"Hey." Finn glanced up at her. "Are you watching the hall, or analyzing his stuff?"

She shrugged. "Can't I do both?"

Finn sat back on his heels. "There's no school stuff in here. No planner, no textbooks or folders."

"Oh well," said Scarlett. "It was worth a try. Don't worry, we'll get him somehow. Look on the bright side. Maybe he's the killer and they'll have to kick him out of school."

"*That's* the bright side?" Finn asked incredulously. "That he stabbed Headmaster Boddy?"

"*Someone* stabbed him," Scarlett pointed out.

"Yeah, but why would it be Vaughn?"

"I don't know. Maybe Headmaster Boddy threatened to pull his scholarship for singing songs about sex and murder."

Finn laughed.

"Don't worry," Scarlett said. "He's a distant second on my list."

Finn eyed her with an intent gaze. "Who is first?"

"Um, who do you think?" She lowered her voice to a whisper. "Peacock, of course. Trying to finish the job she started in his office last week."

"Oh." Finn frowned.

"Or, you know, a looter." She shrugged.

Finn stood and brushed Vaughn's townie grime off his hands. "Well, there's no one here."

"Did you check behind the curtains?" She pointed at the long velvet curtains framing the window at the far end of the room. They hung perfectly still in thick, deep, cranberry folds. "That's where they always hide in movies."

"Well, that's pretty clichéd, then." But Finn rattled the curtains, just to make sure. No murderers fell out.

Bored, Scarlett surveyed the hallway. No movement there. The wind rustled the tarp tacked up over the broken window. She could hear the murmured voices and footfalls of the other teams upstairs.

It was probably a looter, right? A looter who was long gone, no matter what Vaughn said about conditions outside.

When she glanced back in the room, it was to see Finn tilting out the spines of the books on the shelves, one by one. "What are you doing?"

"Checking for secret passages."

She rolled her eyes. There'd always been rumors at Blackbrook that Tudor House was chock-full of secret passages that had once been used for liquor running from Canada during prohibition, and then later, when the house had served as a reform school, to let boys sneak in and out to see the girls who lived there.

But they were nothing more than that: rumors. She'd asked Mrs. White about these secret passages the week they'd all moved in.

Mrs. White had merely laughed. "Are you kidding?"

she'd said. "I've lived here for fifty years, and I've never seen anything like what you are describing."

"Well, Mrs. White would know best," said Finn. But he kept pulling at book spines.

"If there were more rooms in the house, Blackbrook would probably find a way to turn them into student dorms," Scarlett said. "Or, you know, more lab space."

Finn shoved a book back into place. "This is probably futile, right? Let's try the next room."

The next room was the billiards room, where Finn and Mustard had slept the previous night.

"This is a room they should have turned into lab space," Scarlett said. "Who plays billiards anymore?"

Finn checked behind the curtains, underneath the table, and in the narrow gaming cabinets. All empty, of course. "I bet the people searching the attic are going to be done any minute," he said. "That is, if they didn't all murder each other first. If it's not a looter, my money's on Beth. We should figure out what went down with her and Boddy."

Scarlett smiled and shook her head. "Wait . . . Where's all your stuff?"

"My stuff?" Finn glanced at his bedroll and small pile of belongings. "It's all here."

"Didn't you have a bunch of bags yesterday?" She took two steps into the room. "I saw them when I was helping you change your clothes."

"No . . . Just the one backpack."

"Uh, no," she replied. "You had that leather satchel. The one I got you for your birthday that you keep your lab notes and that precious digital scale in. And your computer bag, too."

And then, as if catching himself, he nodded furiously. "Yes. Yes, I did. You're right."

Of course she was right. Finn wouldn't have evacuated without his laptop, or that stupid scale of his. He loved his work more than life itself.

"Oh no," he said, his pretty eyes wide, his pretty eyelashes fluttering. She knew that look. They'd practiced that look together. "My stuff has been stolen, too! Just like Headmaster Boddy. It must have been the looter!"

Scarlett stared at him, confused. No, *baffled*. Because she knew that Finn leaned hard into the whole absent-minded professor act. She joked about him not caring about anything that didn't fit into a test tube.

But she knew also that it meant he would notice if he woke up and his work was gone. Which meant . . .

Phineas Plum was *lying*. To *her*.

14

Plum

She bought it. Of course she bought it.

She probably bought it.

Right?

Finn stood for two full seconds in utter agony before Scarlett said, "We should report this to the others. It's not like finding the actual killer, but at least if more things are going missing, it corroborates the theory that there was a looter in here."

Yeah, she bought it.

"When do you think your stuff went missing?" she asked him. "Maybe when we were at lunch?"

"Um . . ."

"I mean, obviously you would have noticed if it was gone when you got up this morning," said Scarlett. Her stare never wavered from his face.

"Yes." He was nodding again. Agreeing with Scarlett was never a bad strategy. "I think it must have been while we were at lunch."

Her eyes went wide. "Oh my God. That means the looter must still be in the house!"

Should he act terrified? Should he act relieved he wasn't murdered, too? Finn wasn't sure.

This was almost as bad as his meeting with Headmaster Boddy, back before the storm. Finn had never been able to perform on his feet. If he was given time to prepare, he'd do fine. To study, as if for a test. But he hadn't had time to make up a story. Not then, and not now. Scarlett was so much better at this kind of thing than he was.

Already he could see his error. It was like she always told him—the best lies were served up with pieces of the truth. He should have told her that he'd hidden his valuables. She'd understand that. With all these strangers in the house, with no ability to lock his door—it would have made perfect sense to her. Why hadn't he said that?

Was it too late to change his mind now?

"Oh, man, Finn, I'm so sorry!" Scarlett exclaimed. She put a comforting hand on his shoulder. "To lose all your work like that."

He nodded miserably. "I—I don't know what I'm going to do."

"Well," she said, squeezing his shoulder, "the first thing we should do is make sure no one else has had anything stolen, and that this guy has fled the premises. Right?"

Yes, probably. Wait, was it? This was where things began to get twisted in Finn's mind.

If he were a looter, say, who'd already scored thousands

of dollars from the headmaster's lockbox, and had accidentally murdered a guy to boot, would he honestly stick around to swipe a student's laptop and a digital scale?

"It's so strange," Scarlett said. She still hadn't removed her hand from his shoulder. It was starting to feel heavy. "That a looter, having already gotten all that money from Headmaster Boddy, would endanger himself by waiting around here on the off chance he could fence a digital scale."

A chill stole over his body as she looked at him. Her gaze was steady and intent.

They'd always had this talent, like they knew what the other person was thinking. They could anticipate each other's needs. It's what made them such an unbeatable pair.

He should have known it would get him into trouble.

"Well," he said lamely, "it cost about three thousand dollars."

"Could a thief sell it for that much?" Scarlett asked him. "Would he even *know* what it was?"

Finn was pretty sure that if he did have his digital scale with him in this moment, they'd find that Scarlett's hand on his shoulder weighed at least half a ton.

He squirmed out of her grip. "We should search the rest of the house. If he hasn't gone, there's a chance we could get all our stuff back."

There, that seemed to work. At the very least, Scarlett didn't say anything else as they left the billiards room and headed for the conservatory.

The room was still very cold, which was probably a good thing, given that they were storing a dead body in it. Scarlett again manned the door while Finn made a show of checking behind potted plants and under the shelves where Mrs. White kept her orchid collection.

"Don't forget the closet!" Scarlett called.

Finn checked the closet.

"Anything in there that looks like it could be your stuff?" she asked.

No. He hadn't hidden it in the closet. He stood there, just inside, peering into the darkness and looking for clarity. Scarlett was his best friend. They'd trusted each other with so many schemes in the last few years. Things that could have gotten each of them in a world of trouble. Maybe, just maybe . . . he could trust her with this?

"Hey, Scar?" he began.

"There you are, Scarlett." Beth's voice. Every muscle in Finn's body pulled tight. Not Beth. Not now. "We're done with the attic. There was nothing there but boxes and old dress forms and some broken furniture."

"Oh, Peacock!" Scarlett called merrily. "It's so *good* to see you."

Finn melted farther into the closet, relieved. Scarlett had a new target. After all, Beth was her number one suspect.

Or at least, she had been five minutes ago.

He crouched in the shadows and peeked out through the gap between the door and the frame. Beth was standing next to Scarlett in the doorway, towering over her, as usual. In her hands, she held some type of long metal object.

"You know," Scarlett went on, "I've been meaning to ask you . . . Word on the street is that you had a bit of a run-in with Headmaster Boddy the other day, before the storm."

Okay. This was according to plan. Scarlett would get the intel they needed on Beth.

"*Word on the street?*" Beth echoed sardonically. She turned the metal thing over and over in her hands. Finn peered closer. It was a lead pipe. "You mean, Finn told you?"

"Um," said Scarlett. "I don't know. Might have been Orchid."

Beth snorted. "Whatever. Doesn't really seem to matter now, in light of everything."

"Did you get in a fight with him?" Scarlett pressed. "Did you . . . Did you throw something at him?"

"Do you think I *killed* him?" she shot back, as if it were one of her lethal volleys. "Man, you two really are something. There is no low you won't sink to, is there? Even accusing me of *murder.*"

Finn didn't know what he did then. He wasn't sure if his knees gave out, or his heels dropped, or his hand on the door slipped, but he must have made a sound, because suddenly both girls turned his way.

"Finn?" Beth called. "Is that you? Get out of there!"

Finn hesitated.

"*NOW.*"

He emerged from the closet, head hung sheepishly.

"Go ahead," Beth said, her chin raised. She pointed the lead pipe at him like she was a queen with a scepter. "Call me a murderer to my face. I dare you."

"Beth," he started, "all I said is that you're the only one who seemed to be on bad terms with the headmaster—"

"His corpse is lying right behind you," Beth cut in with a sneer. The pipe sliced through the air as she gestured wildly with it. "Do you think I stabbed him? Are you going to stand here and tell me I *plunged a knife into his heart*?"

Finn shrank away from her. He looked to Scarlett for help, but she stood with her arms crossed, looking at him smugly.

And that's when he realized: She had never bought it. Not once.

"Maybe I shouldn't believe what Finn tells me," said Scarlett.

"You definitely shouldn't. He's a liar."

"*Is* he." Scarlett clucked her tongue.

"Oh, please!" Beth said. "You know how he is. Don't pretend."

"Yeah," Scarlett said. "I know. But I never thought he'd lie to *me*."

"Been there," Beth said. "You two deserve each other. Excuse me, I think I'll go *murder* a few more people this afternoon. I hear it's aerobic."

She stomped off down the hall. For a long moment, Finn and Scarlett just stared at each other.

"Scar—"

"Maybe she's right," Scarlett said. "Maybe we do deserve each other. Because, in all honesty, Finn, I can't tell right now if you're lying to me about something stupid or if you killed that man under that tarp."

Uh-oh. And to think he'd imagined he could rely on her.

"But you're lying about something."

Okay, she *was* serious.

"No—" he tried.

"No, you didn't kill him, or no, you aren't lying?"

"No, it's not something stupid." He looked down at the floor. But maybe he was just being stupid *about* it. After all, he may not be in the clear yet. Not even with the flood. Not even with the headmaster being dead.

She looked at him and shook her head, a deep sadness overcoming her face. "I've told you everything."

"Yeah." He wanted the floor to swallow him up. He didn't know if Beth had killed Headmaster Boddy, but he kind of hoped she'd come back and kill him.

"*Everything*," she repeated. "You could destroy me with the stuff I've told you."

He knew all of that.

"Does it have to do with why you were in the office that day?"

"Yes."

"Are you in trouble?"

He raised his head and met her eyes. "Yes."

Her arms were still crossed tight over her chest. "You stupid boy. Whatever it was, we could have fixed it. That's what we *do*."

"Okay!" He held his hands out. "Let's fix it. I'll tell you everything, and then you tell me how to fix it, because I've already screwed up on my own."

"No way," Scarlett said. "Fix it yourself. I have a killer to catch."

"Please, Scar?"

"No! You don't get to treat me like this. We're supposed to be a team, Finn. But you blew it. Just like you blew it with Beth."

"Beth was different." Beth had been his girlfriend. His *real* girlfriend.

"Not that different."

He clenched his jaw. "You'll be sorry, Scarlett. You'll be sorry if you don't help me and I have to do this on my own."

She laughed. "Yeah, right. Like you'll be able to manage anything without me. Good luck with that. I'm off to finish searching the house. I assume I don't have to worry about your missing items?"

"You don't have to worry about anything of mine," he snapped.

"Fine!" She turned on her heel and marched off.

He watched her disappear down the hall. It was empty now, with no sign of Mrs. White or the other students, but Finn closed the door anyway.

"Just in case," he explained to the corpse under the tarp.

Headmaster Boddy had wanted to see what he was up to, after all. Poor man. Now he never would. Finn supposed he should be relieved, but he wasn't. Not yet, anyway. Relief would probably come later. He was still in shock.

One thing he would never deny: he owed so much to Headmaster Boddy—all those hours in the chem lab freshman and sophomore year, all that careful attention to and encouragement of Finn's work.

Finn's work. That's what he had to keep in mind, every time he started feeling a twinge of guilt. *His.*

He turned to the row of orchids lined up against the far wall, and with a flick of his fingers against the underside of a shelf, released the latch to the secret passage.

They'd been rumors, but only Finn had cared enough to track them down, to perform the meticulous trial and error on every book in the library, every brick in the wall. Not even Scarlett had bothered. Anything that wasn't a threat to her fell completely off her radar.

Pity, really. Then again, her lack of curiosity had helped him in his quest, just like Mrs. White's strict curfew rules. He'd only *pretended* to leave the house after their study sessions. It had taken many nights in Tudor House to learn its secrets, but it had paid off. After a few moments in the passage, his eyes adjusted to the dimness, and he saw his masterpiece. Still there. Still safe.

Still all his.

15

Mustard

The biggest thing Mustard had discovered in their search of the second floor of Tudor House is that he really needed to up his game when it came to decorating his dorm room. Back at Farthing Military Academy, they were each given a two-foot-by-two-foot bulletin board upon which they were allowed to put photos from home or other personal items. Here, every room in Tudor House was wall-to-wall posters, gauzy curtains, knickknacks, basket chairs, throw pillows, and stuffed animals.

Not that Mustard was about to cover his spartan dorm room with a collection of teddy bears. But he wouldn't mind one of those down comforters. It was freezing here.

The second thing he discovered was that his partners in this search, Karlee and Kayla, were basically useless.

"Ooh, look at all this electronic equipment!" Karlee exclaimed when they checked Scarlett's room. Mustard noted that Scarlett, at least, had not been subject to any looting, and swiftly looked in her closet, behind her desk, and under her bed for any intruders. All clear.

"Does she podcast or something?" Kayla asked, examining a microphone on her desk. "Have you heard her podcast?"

"No!" exclaimed Karlee. "What is it, school gossip?"

"Probably, knowing Scarlett."

"Let's try the next room," Mustard said brusquely as he ushered them out. Scarlett also had a top-of-the-line gaming computer. It would be worth good money to a thief.

This looting theory didn't hold water.

The other rooms on the floor—to which they'd been granted access, care of Mrs. White's "borrowed" skeleton key—were similarly filled with luxuries large and small, and also similarly devoid of unexpected persons or any signs of theft. The bathroom was a bathroom, and Mrs. White's room, where the two girls had spent the night, was neat as a pin, except for the items he instantly tagged as belonging to Karlee and Kayla—he didn't think Mrs. White went in for glittery lip gloss. There was a small, old-fashioned television, a sewing basket, some antiques, and, on the far wall, several rows of framed photographs in grainy, faded colors.

"Who are these people?" Mustard tapped a frame.

"Probably reform school ladies," Kayla said. "But they don't look that rough."

"No," Karlee said. "They weren't gang members or anything. Mostly girls who partied too much, sent here by their parents who didn't want to deal anymore."

Mustard nodded in understanding. Sometimes the kids at military academies had been sent away for troublemaking, too—for values of troublemaking that included such high crimes as graffiti, or taking the car without permission, or dating the wrong person.

"What happened to the reform school when Blackbrook bought Tudor?" he asked.

"I think it was shut down by then," said Karlee.

"Or maybe they just enrolled the girls at Blackbrook," said Kayla. "Isn't that when it went co-ed? Mrs. White would know."

They moved on to a storage closet and the second bathroom. No sign of an intruder. Which was what Mustard was afraid of.

He couldn't stop thinking about the look Peacock had been giving the headmaster last night in the kitchen while she'd been chopping vegetables. As if she'd love it if the headmaster were a head of cabbage. And then this morning, all that stair running, even as the rest of them wiped the headmaster's blood off their shoes. As if she hadn't been as shocked and appalled as the rest of them.

"Did you guys notice any strange behavior with the others this morning?"

"Aside from one of them being murdered?" Karlee asked. "No. I mean, that kid Vaughn is always strange . . ."

"He's cute, though," said Kayla. "I liked his song last night."

"And Orchid," Karlee added. "Like, if the police ever asked about her, everyone would go, 'Quiet loner, keeps to herself . . .'" She snickered.

"It's just that I was thinking that Peacock didn't seem too upset about the headmaster," said Mustard. She'd been more interested in her workout than a man's death.

"Duh," said Karlee. "Word is she tried to brain him last week with a candlestick in his office." She gasped and clapped a hand over her mouth. "Wait, do you think she tried again, and actually did it this time? Oh. Em. Gee."

Kayla looked doubtful. "Headmaster Boddy was killed with a knife, not a candlestick."

"That's not what I mean!" Karlee rolled her eyes at her friend.

Mustard leaned in. "What do mean she tried to brain him last week?"

"Oh, it was the hot gossip on campus before the storm. Finn Plum saw Peacock in Boddy's office, shouting at him and throwing anything that wasn't tied down."

"What for?"

"Well, she wasn't practicing her serve, that's for sure. What did she say to him?" Karlee thought for a moment. "'You'll live to regret this.' That's what they said she said."

"See?" said Kayla. "She said, he'll *live*."

"Yeah," said Karlee. "To. Regret. It."

"And you said Finn saw this?" asked Mustard. He'd rather get a firsthand account than—well, than whatever one might choose to call this conversation.

"Yeah, and Orchid," said Karlee. "But good luck getting her to talk. She wouldn't even let us do her hair."

As they exited into the hall, he saw Orchid, Vaughn,

and Peacock descending the pullout stairs that led into the attic.

"All clear up there," said Vaughn. "Unless you think Boddy was murdered by a mannequin."

Mustard did not.

"I think I need to wash up, though," Vaughn added blithely. "You guys have hot water, right?"

"Not really," said Orchid. "You'll have to use the kettle on the stove."

"Great. Excuse me."

Peacock flipped a short length of lead pipe from one hand to the other, with the ease that came of spending half your life playing with a racquet. She, Karlee, and Kayla followed Vaughn down the stairs, but before Orchid could follow them, Mustard got her attention.

"What's up?" she asked when he pulled her aside.

"Karlee told me a story that Peacock got in a fight with the headmaster in his office last week. And that you were there."

"Oh yeah, that." Orchid sighed. She looked down the landing to make sure Peacock and the others were out of earshot. "I keep thinking about that, too."

"Did she really try to hit him with a candlestick?"

Orchid pursed her lips. "I don't know. The door was shut. We heard a thump, and then, when I went inside, the headmaster was picking a candlestick up off the floor. It's possible it just fell over."

"But they were screaming at each other?"

"Well, Peacock was screaming," Orchid said. "She looked really upset. Headmaster Boddy was trying to calm her down, and then she said—"

"'You'll live to regret this'?"

Orchid flinched. "That sounds really bad, doesn't it?"

Mustard had to agree.

"If it helps, it was like a response, you know?" Orchid added. "'*You* will regret' whatever." She smiled weakly. "Delivery matters, right?"

"Do you think she killed him?"

Orchid hesitated a long moment. "I don't know. I don't know what the fight was about."

What did it matter what the fight was about, if she was angry enough to get violent? People had been killed over parking spaces.

"Hey," said Peacock, and Orchid jumped a mile. Interesting. She may not be able to say whether she thought the athlete had killed the headmaster, but she wasn't comfortable with having her back to Peacock, either.

Especially the Peacock who came toward them, still brandishing the lead pipe. "Are we done with this whole search thing yet? I want to get an afternoon workout in if I can."

"Go check with Scarlett," Mustard said. "If she's done downstairs, then I think we've covered our bases." But as she turned to leave, he said, "Wait."

She looked at him.

Best get this from the horse's mouth. "Why were you arguing with the headmaster in his office last week?"

"None of your business," she snapped. "Wait . . . What are you asking me?" She glared at them both.

"We were just wondering," Orchid said, "because—"

"*None* of your *business!*" Peacock seethed. She shook her head, and the electric-blue ends of her ponytail whipped back and forth like live wires. "What were *you* in his office for?"

"There was a problem with my tuition check," Orchid responded instantly. "But we got it resolved."

She looked pointedly at Peacock, who pursed her lips.

"Okay, if you must know, he was denying my request to go watch the Grand Slam in Australia next month. I got an invite and needed to be excused from school."

Orchid frowned. "Why would you need to keep that a secret?"

"Whatever, we're done, right?" Beth whirled around and marched back down the stairs.

Orchid looked at Mustard. "Do you buy that?"

"No." But he wasn't sure he bought the looter story, either. "I'm going to see what's going on downstairs."

"Me too," said Orchid. "We should also let Mrs. White know that Vaughn came back, and that Rusty probably made it to the village. She'll be worried."

Downstairs, Orchid went off to check on Mrs. White, and Mustard found Karlee and Kayla snacking in the dining room.

"Have you seen Scarlett?" he asked.

They had not, which meant they had not checked with her before ceasing their search, like he'd asked them to. The chain of command had completely broken down. This kind of thing would never fly at Farthing.

He checked the kitchen next, but it, too, was empty. Nothing in the larder but food, and nowhere to hide behind the cabinets or the stove or the fridge. Through the window set in the door he caught sight of Vaughn on the back stoop, looking out into the flooded woods and park that surrounded Tudor House. Weird. Hadn't he come downstairs to wash up?

Mustard tapped on the window. "Everything all right?"

Vaughn crossed the porch to the door and cracked it open. His coat was still soaked and muddy from his failed attempt to reach the mainland this morning, but he'd clearly put it all back on and gone outside anyway. Mustard quickly revised his assessment of the boy. He was definitely Farthing boot camp material.

"Hey," he said. "I was thinking maybe we should gather some firewood and get it inside—in case the furnace runs low on oil."

"Might be a good idea." Mustard doubted there was much in the way of dry wood. "Think there's any chance Rusty will be able to get back here soon with the cops?"

Vaughn was silent as he handed over some logs from under the tarp on the porch. "I don't know. The currents over the ravine are still wild. I don't know how anyone could get out here."

"We didn't see any sign of a looter upstairs or in the attic. I still have to talk to Scarlett about the downstairs, though."

"Of course Scarlett thinks there's a looter," Vaughn said with a rueful shake of his head. "First a suicide, now a looter . . ."

"Hey, it's easier than believing your theory," Mustard said. "That someone in this house is a murderer."

Vaughn straightened with another log in his arms. "*My* theory?"

"Yeah, you know, the one you almost started a war over at lunch?" Vaughn had been the one to start pitting them against one another.

But Vaughn didn't respond, and then Mustard noticed blood dripping down the boy's nose.

"You're bleeding."

Vaughn rubbed the back of his glove against his face, then looked at the red smeared across the fabric. "Oh."

"Probably the cold," Mustard said. "Let's get you a rag."

They carried the few logs they could find inside, then Vaughn got himself set up at the kitchen table with some paper towels to let his nose drain, and Mustard heard voices outside the door. He looked to see Scarlett standing with Peacock outside the ballroom, and went to have words with her.

"All clear on the lower level?" he asked.

Peacock glared at him. Scarlett didn't exactly look happy, either.

"I don't know," she said. "Finn and I didn't finish checking."

Mustard bit back his frustration. Sure, order them all over the house, but then don't do your own work. "Which rooms are left?"

Scarlett gestured in the direction he'd come. "That side."

"So the kitchen, dining room, and lounge?"

"And the *secret passages*," Scarlett said, rolling her eyes. "Which don't exist."

"Yes they do," argued Peacock. "I had a friend living here when I was a freshman, and she said they were real."

"Did she say where they were?" Scarlett asked.

"Well . . . No."

Scarlett gave Mustard a look which said, *See?* She was standing close to Peacock, clearly unconcerned that the taller girl might smack her with the lead pipe she was still carrying, despite the gossip from Finn about Peacock's fight with the headmaster.

So Scarlett, at least, didn't think Peacock was a murderer. To own the truth, Mustard wasn't sure he thought it either, though as far as he could tell, she was the only one with an established motive.

So much for leaving the investigation up to the cops. From Vaughn's description of conditions outside, it might be a while before any police arrived at all.

"Okay," said Mustard. "Do you want to help me finish?"

"Not really," said Scarlett. "I've had a rough morning."

"Me too," chimed in Peacock.

They both stared pointedly at Mustard, who raised his hands defensively.

A millisecond later, Peacock had turned back to Scarlett. "Anyway, we'd been together for about two months, and I told him I was first on the wait list for honors chem." Peacock whirled. "Excuse me, did I invite you to this conversation?"

Mustard had heard enough. The kitchen and the dining room were covered, so he headed down the hall to the lounge. If he'd been in charge of surveying this level, he would have started with the room that had actually been looted, but whatever, Scarlett.

The lounge door opened with a strange little pop, as if there were a pressure differential between the hall and the room. Strange. Might be because of whatever air was leaking in around the edges of the tarp in the hall. Might be because this house was ancient and creaky.

So many questions and almost no answers.

The sofa in the lounge was still made up with sheets and pillows for the headmaster's bed. The covers were rumpled and thrown back, as if he'd only gotten up to go to the bathroom.

Go to the bathroom, get surprised by a looter, and get stabbed.

Or maybe someone had knocked at the door. Or maybe he'd heard a sound and gone to investigate.

The headmaster's things were piled in a corner of the room, just as they had been last night. There was a suitcase and several boxes filled with file folders. On the end table next to the sofa sat a pair of eyeglasses—the headmaster's—resting upside down, their arms not even folded. He'd never need them again.

Mustard shook off the gloom and got to work. He checked behind every stick of furniture and poked at the curtains to make sure they weren't hiding anything either. Nada.

There was a thump from somewhere behind him. Mustard spun around, but the room was still empty. Still, he knew he hadn't imagined it. He walked to the center of the room, turning slowly. Nothing appeared out of place, but after a moment he could smell wood ash. He looked at the fireplace, where the charred remains of last night's fire still lay in the grate. Maybe one of the burnt logs had crumbled.

He bent over to examine inside the fireplace. It wasn't the world's largest hearth, though the mantel above it was big and ornate, practically encrusted with carvings of ladies in skimpy togas and cherubs in even less. Along one side stood a lone male figure, his muscular physique garbed only in a single fig leaf.

He peered closer. No, not a fig leaf. A maple leaf. How appropriate for Maine. He wondered if the reform school girls pictured in Mrs. White's framed photos had found this poor gentleman amusing.

His finger brushed the leaf, and it flipped open, revealing . . .

Mustard's eyes widened, and then, when he realized what he was actually looking at, they widened even more.

Yeah. The reform school girls definitely knew about this dude.

It was not an engraving of the figure's anatomy—not an *accurate* one, anyway. But it was, unmistakably, a switch. Currently, it was pointing down. He didn't even hesitate before flipping it up.

A panel opened in the back of the grate.

It was a flue. Just a flue. Or an ash trap, he told himself.

Or a secret passage.

Mustard took a deep breath, crouched, and squeezed his way inside. Stone walls rose up around him, and there was a short set of stairs, curving around a corner and underground, following the architecture of the house.

He should go get someone. If there was a looter—a murderer—hiding here, Mustard shouldn't confront the guy alone.

He took another step down into the passage. The light from the lounge behind him was almost gone down here. He could barely see his hand in front of his face. But as he took another step down the curving staircase, he noticed there also seemed to be some kind of glow up ahead.

Emboldened, he continued. Five more steps, and the floor evened out into a long, narrow passageway, with a sickly, dim-looking light coming from some unnamed source. The stone walls were freezing to the touch, and the floor was littered with dirt, dust, and small crunchy bits that Mustard did not want to examine too closely. The passage seemed to dead-end up ahead, but after another few steps, he saw the glow only got brighter.

It was a corner. He caught his breath.

Back in military school, they'd do drills like this all the time. MOUT drills, they'd called them. Dust, close quarters, flashlight beam at the end of your muzzle your only source of light. They'd practice being Green Berets or SEAL teams. Mustard had been very good at them.

He'd hated it, every time. Even when he knew that there were only flash bombs and blank adapters to fear. He didn't like that moment when he turned the inevitable corner and stared down the barrel of the inevitable enemy combatant. He was trained never to hesitate. To shoot first.

Like now.

One more step brought him in full view of the tiny chamber around the corner. The sickly light, the bags and equipment on the table, and the person standing before it.

Plum spun to face him, his expression a mask of terror.

"Oh," he gasped. "It's you."

16

Peacock

— EP WORKOUT LOG —

DATE: *December 6*

LUNCH: *PBJ on wheat (450 calories, 15g protein), chicken drumstick (70 calories, 10g protein), 5 carrot sticks (25 calories, 1g protein), see notes*

NOTES: *Very concerned about losing muscle mass unless I get a real meal and workout in. They think it's possible Boddy was murdered by a looter last night. Now Scarlett and Mustard actually want us to go SEARCH for the looter, if there is one. Scary stuff.*

I HATE HIM
I HATE HIM
I HATE HIM
I HATE HIM
I HATE HIM

DOES EVERYONE IN THIS FREAKING HOUSE THINK I'M A MURDERER????
P.S. Found a bar weight in the attic while we searched for clues. That'll come in handy.

17

Green

The kitchen chairs in Tudor House were old and rickety, with frayed caning and hard backs, but Vaughn thought he might never get up anyway. His nose had stopped bleeding, but a deep weariness seemed to suffuse his bones, despite his having fully enjoyed the rare opportunity to sleep in past sunrise that morning.

You know, before they'd found the dead body. Before he'd gone off on an hours-long failure of a quest to reach the mainland.

Before he'd battled his twin brother in the flooded-out yard.

According to that new Mustard kid, Vaughn had had a very busy morning, starting fights. It figured Oliver would find a way to cause trouble. As if anyone here needed any more, after what had happened to Boddy.

Murder. It fit so well with everything else he had come to understand—about this house, this school . . . about the way life always seemed to go. What was that line? Nasty, brutish, and short.

Anything else was just an illusion. He should learn to accept that.

Seventeen years, and it had just been crash after crash. Left with Gemma for long stretches when his parents went on tour, then permanently a few years later, after they died. When Gemma died, too, and everything looked like it was falling apart, he could see Rocky Point closing in around him—the noose pulling tight.

And then he'd gotten the scholarship to Blackbrook. A way out.

Only, maybe it had been nothing but another illusion. The idea that if he just played along for a few more years, he could be free forever. Free from Rocky Point, free from his family's sad history, free from his brother's machinations. If he kept his head down and worked his butt off and never listened to Oliver's vicious little whispers in his ear that it was a waste of time, and that no one would ever give them a chance, so they had to steal it, no matter what the cost.

He'd loved it at Blackbrook. But he had no idea what would happen now. The storm wouldn't break them, but a murder might.

And that was supposing it didn't get any worse from here.

As far as Vaughn could tell, everyone in this house had spent the morning running in circles. Searching for a looter who probably didn't exist, and turning on one another as that became more and more obvious. And meanwhile, as far as he had been able to ascertain, not getting one step closer to discovering the real culprit.

He was in danger of falling asleep on the chair. Also, he was starving. He could probably scrounge for some food here in the kitchen. Surely they'd all eaten lunch. No one was in the kitchen now. No one would be suspicious if they caught him foraging for food.

But he should go see Mrs. White. She was probably having a nervous breakdown, between all the people tromping over her house and the corpse in her conservatory. She'd also be the only one in Tudor who would recognize Oliver. Vaughn would be able to get the full story of what had transpired the last few hours from her.

Vaughn hauled his body off the chair and lumbered down the hall, pausing only to shed some layers in his makeshift room, the library. His clothes weren't where he remembered leaving them, but his brother was probably responsible for that. He changed into a drier, less-blood-stained sweater. His ribs hurt. They'd probably bruise tomorrow. Vaughn may have won their fight just now, but Oliver had certainly left his mark. He caught sight of his face in a mirror. The blood had been wiped away, but his nose was a bit swollen, and his cheeks were raw from the biting cold.

His twin would be worse off, though. Vaughn figured he'd given his brother a black eye at least. Oliver wouldn't be back anytime soon. Couldn't be.

He left the library, headed down the hall, and knocked on the door to the study.

Orchid opened it.

"Oh," she said flatly. "It's you." Uh-oh. Something had changed. It always changed when Oliver got involved.

"Hey, is Mrs. White in there?"

"Vaughn?" The woman's voice floated out. Orchid held the door open for him and he stepped inside.

"Hey. I wanted to check in and see how you were doing." Mrs. White smiled, but Orchid's expression remained closed off and suspicious. He hated it when he got those looks.

"You're always so sweet," Mrs. White said. Orchid's eyebrows hit her hairline. He refused to react. "I'm sorry I slept through all the commotion. I think, between the storm and the shock of Brian Boddy's death, it was all too much. I certainly would not have allowed you all to search the house like this. It's far too dangerous. What if the looter was hiding somewhere?"

So Mrs. White was on board with the looter theory, too. Vaughn's head hurt. "If there's an intruder in this house, we'd be in danger anyway."

"It was fine," said Orchid. "We didn't find signs of any intruders."

"Well, at least we've determined that. He must be long gone by now."

Orchid glanced at him. "Vaughn thinks there's no way any looter, if he got onto the campus, would have been able to get out."

Vaughn didn't confirm or deny this, though he had to agree with Oliver that a "looter"—or anyone else who made it out here—would not be able to cross the ravine again. Vaughn and Rusty's attempt had only been half-successful, and he still had no idea how Oliver had made it across without a boat.

Which meant his brother was probably still skulking around somewhere on the Blackbrook campus, looking for mischief. Still, he wasn't sure what Oliver had been up to, making that point to the others.

Other than causing them to fight amongst themselves. That was his brother's signature move. He looked at Mrs. White, but she gave no indication that she knew Oliver had even been here. Maybe she really had slept through his entire visit.

"Maybe not," said Mrs. White, "but I don't think the person is going to stick around the scene of a crime, either. No, the looter is either long gone or hiding out in some other building on campus. There would be plenty to choose from, even with the flood." She looked rueful. "But my bet is on gone, and with the headmaster's things, too. Such a shame. Hopefully, when the police get here, they'll be able to get to the bottom of the matter."

Vaughn looked out the window at the devastation on the street. When he and Rusty had left that morning, they had considered the headmaster's death to be a suicide. Would the police come running under such circumstances, when there were probably life-and-death scenarios occurring all over from the storm? "I wouldn't hold your breath."

"And what about your other theory?" Orchid pressed Vaughn.

"Other theory?" Mrs. White asked. She peered at him, her eyes narrowed.

Orchid supplied the details. "That if it's not a looter, it's one of us."

Right. Well, he'd had a busy day, it seemed. "I can't be the only one to think it's a possibility." It's not as if everyone in this house were BFFs.

Orchid crossed her arms over her chest.

Mrs. White sighed. "What did I say about that? It's not going to do any good to incite a panic."

"I'm sorry, Mrs. White," said Orchid. "It can't be easy, watching your home become the site of violence like this."

Mrs. White's gaze slid in Orchid's direction. "Oh, girl, have you forgotten what this place once was? If this house has a soul, it's been begging for more excitement than the yearly hair-pulling fight between whichever two students get the highest SAT scores."

"A murder is hardly a party like the old days," said Vaughn.

"Party?" asked Orchid. "I thought Tudor House was a reform school."

Mrs. White's smile might have given Mona Lisa a run for her money. "Vaughn, dear, run and get me the album from the bottom shelf over there. The one marked '1970 to 1975.'"

Did he have to? Obediently, Vaughn trotted over and grabbed the big leather-bound book from the shelf. His muscles ached as he moved.

Mrs. White sat forward on the couch and patted the spaces to either side of her. "Let me show you what Tudor was really like, back when I first came here."

Vaughn couldn't do anything else but look. The pictures were mostly meaningless to him. The usual grainy, colored shots of teenage girls in wide-legged pants and patterned minidresses. They had long shiny hair or big puffy bouffants. They sat in front of the fire reading, or posed with mugs around a dining table laden with roasts, or lined up in winter coats and long scarves against a field white with snow. He recognized a face in the crowd.

"Oh, wow, Mrs. White, is this you?" Orchid pointed at one of the photos.

She nodded. "Want to know what I was in for?"

Orchid laughed nervously. She was probably picturing fistfights or stealing cars. "Okay."

"I went to Woodstock."

Orchid's laugh turned genuine. Almost musical. "You're joking. A concert gets you sent to reform school?"

"According to my parents. It was also the third or fourth time I'd run away from home." Mrs. White smiled, remembering. "They were at their wits' end trying to figure out what to do with me."

"So they sent you from a rural farming village to a rural logging town," Vaughn joked. Man, he'd have loved to have been at Woodstock. He'd never heard this story of Mrs. White's before.

"I didn't come straight from Woodstock," said Mrs. White.

"But yes, my first night here, I thought it was a prison. We didn't even have the bridge over the ravine yet. You could only get here by boat."

"If you thought it was a prison," said Vaughn, "why did you never leave? You were so good at running away."

Mrs. White was silent for a long moment. "It was never what I was running *to*, Vaughn. It was what I was running *from*."

"Home wasn't safe," Orchid said suddenly. "So safety—*here*—became home."

Mrs. White patted Orchid's hand. Vaughn considered this. Wasn't it why he had come to Blackbrook yesterday? Because he felt safer here than in his own house, alone with a brother who rarely even tried to understand why the school was so important to him.

Except it wasn't safe here, either, anymore. There was a corpse in the conservatory that proved it.

He watched as Mrs. White turned another page, her fingers flitting lightly over long-past images of herself and her friends and their antics during Tudor's glory days. There were boys in some of the photos, of course. Blackbrook boys who either didn't mind the reputation that Tudor girls had, or thought of it as a bonus. He looked into the smarmy faces and wondered if anything had really changed. A Tudor girl might be one step up from a townie, but it was a small one.

"I can't believe I never looked at these before!" Orchid exclaimed. "All this time, the whole history of the house was sitting there on the shelf, getting dusty."

"Well," said Mrs. White. "How can it compete with scrolling through your phone?"

Mrs. White paused on a close-up of herself sitting on a stone wall, the peaks of Tudor House rising in the distance. Her arm was slung over the shoulder of a bright-eyed girl. They both wore kerchiefs wrapped across their hair, and kicked their sandaled feet in the direction of the camera.

Vaughn had never seen that one before.

"Who is that?" Orchid asked.

"My best friend, Olivia Vaughn," said Mrs. White pointedly.

"Vaughn!" exclaimed Orchid, and glanced at him, smiling. "That's funny."

"Yep," he agreed politely, and looked away. With any luck, they'd change the subject soon.

But Mrs. White went on. "Now, *she* was brilliant. She'd have fit right in here with you Blackbrook geniuses. Never seen a mind like hers in my life."

Vaughn swallowed.

"What happened to her?" asked Orchid.

"Same thing that happened to all of them," Mrs. White said. "Moved out, had a family, got a life. All the things I never really managed."

"No, I mean, did she become a scientist or anything?" Orchid asked.

"She was a scientist, yes." Now Mrs. White did look at Vaughn, but he didn't know what he was supposed to say. It was Oliver who concerned himself with the legacy of

Gemma's scientific achievements. She closed the book. "I suppose I should start thinking about dinner . . ."

"Don't trouble yourself, Mrs. White," Orchid insisted, jumping up. Vaughn followed suit. "We can fend for ourselves, honestly."

"But it's my *job*," she replied. "Please. If I'm not taking care of Tudor and the people here, then what is the point of any of it?" She gave Vaughn her hand to help her up. "Isn't that right, dear?"

"Yes, ma'am." He didn't have the energy to contradict any of Mrs. White's stories. Not this afternoon. But "moved away" might have been an overstatement. No one escaped Rocky Point.

"Are you sure we can't help?" Orchid asked as Mrs. White moved to the door. "There are so many people here."

"Please," said Mrs. White with a dismissive wave of her hand. "I'm barely recovered from all the 'help' the headmaster insisted you kids provide yesterday. It'll be easiest if I'm on my own. Why don't *you* relax? Take a nap! Vaughn here looks like he's been run ragged."

"Thanks," he grumbled as Mrs. White departed.

Orchid returned the album to its shelf. Her expression was thoughtful. "You know, you hear rumors about the reform school or whatever, but I guess I got this weird idea in my head about strict curfews and stiff rulers."

"I don't know if the idea at Tudor was ever to truly *reform* the people they sent here," said Vaughn. "Mostly, I think it was just to make them disappear. Do you know the number one reason a girl wound up in this house, back during the glory days Mrs. White was just talking about?"

Orchid frowned. "Well, from the pictures, I'd say pregnancy."

"Bingo." Vaughn tapped his nose. "Out of sight, out of mind. Nine months at Tudor, and she could go back to her own life and pretend nothing had ever happened."

"And what about the babies?"

"Adopted, mostly," he replied. "Sometimes the people in the village took them. Growing up in Rocky Point, everyone knew someone whose bio-mom had passed through this house."

"When did it all end?" Orchid examined the shelf. There was one more album, after the one they'd taken out. It was marked *1976.* She opened it. In the beginning, there were lots of pictures, but they grew sparser and sparser, and in the end, it was nothing but blank pages.

"When Blackbrook started getting big," Vaughn said. "When they got all that money from Dick Fain's glue and bought out half of Rocky Point. The school went co-ed, and bought Tudor to house the new female students." That was a story Oliver would never let him forget.

"And Mrs. White stayed on as proctor," Orchid said, nodding. "Sounds like a movie."

"Well, you heard her," said Vaughn. "Without Tudor, what's the point?"

It must be nice, to belong to something that much.

Vaughn had never in his life felt that way. He was born here, but he'd always been an outsider. He was a Blackbrook kid, but as his brother reveled in reminding him, he would never fully live the life the other students enjoyed. He'd never had anything that was really his.

Maybe that's why he never got on board with his brother's plans. Vaughn just wanted to let the past die. It was the only way to make a future of his own.

"Are you okay?" Orchid asked. Her hand rested on his arm.

He blinked down at her. Had he been wavering on his feet? "I think Mrs. White is right. I should take a nap."

"Naps can't hurt," Orchid said.

He chuckled. "I don't think I've had one since I was a toddler." Not with his schedule. Not with his habit of sleeping with one eye open.

She gave him a curious look, but maybe it wasn't all that curious. "You know, you don't have to show off all the time."

"Show off?"

"I mean, like last night with the guitar, or today when you were spouting all those creepy theories about who might have killed the headmaster. I like you just the way you are."

The guitar performance he'd cop to, but he couldn't be blamed for today. So she thought Oliver had been acting *creepy*! Good to know he wasn't the only one. But then again, everyone in the house was on edge thanks to his brother's little performance this afternoon.

Vaughn wouldn't let that bother him. He'd long ago learned not to hold himself responsible for Oliver's antics. But the other comment stung. He thought they'd had a connection last night. "You don't like my music?"

She had such a pretty smile. "I actually loved it. You're extremely talented."

He didn't need soups or hearth fires or hot stove backs to keep warm. He could just remember her words. "Thanks." He almost didn't want to ask the next part. That was another lesson he'd learned—don't search for clarification; just fill in the version you like best. But he couldn't do it with Orchid. He had to know. "But you think it was showing off."

"Well . . ." She ducked her chin and her bangs fell into her eyes, but they didn't hide her smile. "Wasn't it?"

He smiled back. Okay, she had him there. "A little."

"*A little?*" she repeated.

Now he grinned wide. "Oh, Orchid, when I really want to show off, you'll know it."

18

Plum

Finn raised up his hands. "You scared the life out of me! I thought you were the murderer."

The way Mustard was standing there, Finn wasn't entirely sure he would survive this encounter anyway. The other boy was big. His frame filled the narrow passageway. There'd be no getting around him.

"You— You thought *I*—" Mustard tripped over his words. He gestured wildly toward the table at Finn's back. "What are you doing in here? Is that Boddy's computer? Where did you put his money?"

"Hold on, hold on—"

"Answer me!" Mustard roared.

For a second, it was all silence. The low hum of the instruments on the table, a distant drip from somewhere in the passageway. Mustard standing, feet planted apart, across Finn's only exit.

When you had no defense, your only option was an offense. Scarlett had taught him that.

"Well, what are *you* doing here?" he shot back.

"Finishing searching the ground floor," cried Mustard. Finn thought about pointing out that this was *not* the ground floor. "Since you and your girlfriend can't be bothered to do your jobs."

"She's not my girlfriend," Finn snapped.

"Whatever is going on with you two. Now, what are you doing with the school's files?" He didn't look ready to drop it.

"I don't know what you're talking about."

Mustard made an incredulous face. "Those things, behind you on the table."

"I'm not sure what any of this has to do with the house search."

Mustard looked astonished. "Because you seem to have the things we're *looking for.*"

Finn couldn't think of anything. He couldn't say the things were Boddy's and he had just found them. He'd lose them anyway.

His gaze traveled over Mustard's shoulder, as if he could somehow magically transport himself away.

"Forget it," Mustard said, seeing the direction of his gaze. "You're not going anywhere until you've answered my questions."

Finn straightened. "Excuse me? Kidnapping? Maybe *you're* the murderer."

"Do you have any idea how delusional you sound right now?" Mustard shook his head in disbelief. "I thought you were supposed to be the genius of the school, and you sound like a total moron. Do people actually *buy* your crap?"

Finn blinked, and it was like all the air left his body in a rush. He'd been berated by Beth. Abandoned by Scarlett. Chased down into a dungeon and confronted by this soldier, this stranger who had decided to put himself in charge and didn't care at all who Finn Plum was at Blackbrook.

"Yeah," he admitted. "Usually."

Mustard didn't move a muscle. He didn't smile. He didn't seem to think it was cute.

"Okay," Finn said quickly. "It's my stuff."

"*Yours.*" Mustard still looked skeptical. His arms were now crossed over his chest. Man, those biceps were big.

"Yes. My computer, my equipment, my work. I've brought it down here to keep it safe."

"Underground. In a flood." This was going from bad to worse.

"Right," said Finn. "That probably wasn't the wisest choice I could have made. But I was mostly worried about other people seeing it." He held his hands out sheepishly toward Mustard. "I was sharing my room with a stranger."

"I *literally* gave you the shirt off my back yesterday."

Finn forced a laugh. "I never said I was so generous."

"You're a total sleazeball, is what you are." Mustard gestured toward the table. "So what is your all-important work?"

Finn swallowed.

"Come on, out with it. I think we've established you aren't moving until you've come clean."

"It's an invention. You wouldn't understand."

Mustard's eyes narrowed. "We won't know until you try. Just last night, Headmaster Boddy was telling me I should learn more about how this school works from star students like you. You remember the headmaster, right? Nice guy, blood's all over the floor upstairs?"

"Okay! Okay!" Finn sighed. "It's a dye."

"A dye?"

"A black dye."

"Like for clothes?"

Finn rolled his eyes. "Sure. Yes. For everything. Scientific uses. Industrial. It's black like you've never seen before. It's black like you can barely see it at all. It eats light. It eats heat. You could use it for camera backing, for telescopes—"

"For camouflage," Mustard finished, starting to nod. "To paint drones so they'd be undetectable." His eyes grew wide.

"Yes!" Finn couldn't help it. *Finally*, someone who understood what he had on his hands. Finn had kept it all so secret, for so long. Hadn't dared tell anyone, in fear that they might steal his idea or leak his secrets.

Now, he supposed, it didn't matter.

Mustard looked at the files on the table. "And you invented this dye?"

"Well, I've almost invented it." He was so close. It had

taken ages for him to devise a formula, and nearly as long for him to squirrel away enough hours in the chem lab to test it out without the Blackbrook teachers catching on to his extracurricular activities.

And, in the end, they *had* caught on. His knees starting feeling weak again, like they had that day in the headmaster's office, when all his plans had started to go fuzzy around the edges, and so had his vision.

"So why are you hiding it?" Mustard asked. "Don't you want to sell your invention to the military or some big chemical company or something? Like that Richard Fain kid did with his glue? You'd be the next Blackbrook superstar."

Finn's mouth compressed into a line. "That's just the problem—I don't want to be a *Blackbrook* superstar. I don't want to share this with the school, just because I happened to be here when I created it. Look—can I sit down?" Not waiting for an answer, he sat down on the stone floor, resting his elbows on his knees, and took several deep, cleansing breaths.

From the corner of his eye, he saw Mustard sit down across from him. When he ventured to look up, the other boy was examining him, like one might a particularly thorny math formula.

"It's in the student handbook," Finn said. "Didn't Scarlett go over that part with you during the whole new-student orientation thing?"

"You mean the honor code?"

"Yeah, the honor code, and the other stuff, too. As students of Blackbrook, our work created here is joint property with the school. It was a rule they put in place after the lawsuit with Richard Fain."

"The lawsuit?"

"He invented the glue, right? Made a mint, gave tons of it to the school—but when he died without an heir, the trustees at Blackbrook had to sue for their rights to the patent. Everything Blackbrook has is because they were successfully able to argue he'd invented the glue at Blackbrook, so that meant the state was obligated to assign the patent to them. Now we all sign explicit agreements for patent assignments at the same time as we sign the honor code. It's in your enrollment documents."

"Huh." Mustard considered this. "So, is this just for patents, or for anything? Like if that Vaughn kid writes a hit song—"

"I don't know," Finn snapped. "And it's really not relevant to me, anyway. What is relevant is, I've got a few more months I need to keep this thing under wraps and then I'm in the clear."

"Except you're not in the clear," said Mustard. "Not really. You *did* invent this dye here. According to the honor code, you have an obligation to share the patent with them."

"But that's a stupid rule!"

Mustard shrugged. "It's one you agreed to, though."

"Two minutes ago, you didn't even know the school had this rule."

"Did *you* not know it?" Mustard asked. His tone was no more than blandly curious.

Finn just scowled and looked away. He hadn't told anyone—not even Scarlett, for just this reason. Not that he worried Scarlett would appeal to his ethical obligations.

He'd always simply figured she'd want a piece of the action.

"I suppose you plan to snitch on me?"

Mustard chuckled, as if it were the stupidest idea in the world.

But how was Finn supposed to know what Captain America here thought about stuff like that? "It doesn't matter, anyway. Headmaster Boddy already got wind of it. He called me into his office last week to address a rumor that I'd been doing secret work in the lab."

"Ah, yes," Mustard said. "I heard about all the meetings in Boddy's office last week. What did he say?"

"He said I had until the end of this week to come clean. I was hoping maybe this storm might have destroyed any evidence they had against me. Then the worst they could hit me with would be an honor code violation."

"You'd get kicked out of school."

"Not the end of the world."

Mustard made a whistling sound through his teeth and stretched his legs out in front of him, which was when Finn remembered that the story around campus was that Mustard had been kicked out of *his* last school.

"Well," he mumbled. "At least I'd have the dye." If his dye worked, he'd be set for life anyway.

"So it's done?"

"No . . ."

"Then you might *not* have the dye. Or a Blackbrook diploma."

"I don't know if any of us are going to have a Blackbrook diploma after this," Finn said scornfully. "Headmaster found dead in a dorm? Flood ruins half the buildings on campus? This place might never open again."

Mustard was silent for a long moment. "Then you'd really be off the hook, wouldn't you?"

Finn wasn't sure what he ought to say to that.

Mustard leaned forward. "I gotta ask. You didn't kill Headmaster Boddy, did you? Because he found your secret?"

"No!" Finn cried.

"Yeah," said Mustard ruefully. "You seem like more of a white-collar criminal. You wouldn't kill anyone."

"Um, thanks?"

But Mustard wasn't finished. "You'd hire out."

Ouch. Finn didn't want to reflect on how accurately Mustard had pegged him. "All right. Now I get to ask you a question."

"I didn't kill him, either."

"I didn't ask that," said Finn. No, he wanted to know why the kid chose to call himself after a hot dog condiment.

"Why, because you think *I* look more like a white-collar criminal?"

"You don't look like a criminal at all. You look like a cop."

Mustard thought about this for a moment. "Fair enough. But I'm afraid in this case I'm no closer to figuring out who is responsible for this murder. It's not you, and it's not me. So who does that leave?"

"Maybe it's Rusty, and he ran as soon as he got a chance," Finn suggested.

"Possibly. Couple of the girls upstairs think it might be Peacock."

Finn said nothing.

"You witnessed her fighting with the headmaster before the storm, didn't you?"

"It wasn't Beth." Finn studied the floor as if it would have answers.

"You told Scarlett you saw her throw a candlestick at Headmaster Boddy."

"It wasn't Beth, okay?" Finn pushed himself to his feet and started packing up his things. Mustard's point about the flood was starting to make him nervous. Besides, now that Mustard knew what he was up to, there was really no point in all this secrecy.

"How do you know?" Mustard, too, stood up, dusting off his hands.

"We used to be really close, freshman year."

"But you aren't anymore."

Finn shook his head. "But I still know. She's a nice girl." As per usual, he'd been the one to screw everything up.

"You weren't the only one who saw them fighting," said Mustard.

Orchid. Of course. Well, he could just go ahead and interview everyone, then. Finn started shoving his things into his bag, but he was clumsy and hurried, and the edges of his laptop got caught. Wordlessly, Mustard held the flaps of the bag open for him.

"I never should have spread that rumor when I saw her in the office," Finn admitted. "I don't know what happened with the candlestick, to be honest. And, I mean, I probably yelled at the headmaster, too." He hadn't, but that was beside the point.

"The headmaster threatened to expel you, Poindexter," Mustard said. "When I asked Beth what Boddy wanted her for, she said it was an argument over attending a tennis match. As a spectator."

"See?" Finn exclaimed. "That's not remotely a motive for murder."

"Right," Mustard agreed. "But it was also a pretty transparent lie. I can't imagine candlesticks getting involved in that disagreement."

Finn snorted and pulled the strap of his messenger bag crossways over his head. "You don't know how much Beth likes tennis." He turned to head up the stairs in the back of the chamber. "Hey, how'd you get in here, anyway?"

Mustard looked confused. "What do you mean? How did *you* get in?"

"Through the trapdoor in the conservatory." Finn pointed at the opening a few feet away.

Mustard looked behind him, and then up at the door

before them. "I came in from the secret door behind the fireplace in the lounge."

"There's a door down there? It looked all bricked up to me." Then a horrible thought occurred to him. The passage went from the lounge, where Boddy had been sleeping, to the conservatory, where his corpse had been found the next day.

Strange.

But he shook off the chill and began climbing through the trapdoor's entrance. He'd leave the detective work to Mustard. He had plenty of things to worry about.

Mustard followed Finn out the door. "Clever," he said as he watched Finn depress the switch hidden in the brick wall that closed it off from sight once more. "If a bit less decorative than the one in the fireplace."

"Whatever, dude." Finn had no idea what Mustard was talking about, and he didn't want to spend a second more in this room than he needed to. He wondered how long it took for corpses to begin to smell. Shouldering his bag once more, he headed out.

Mustard followed him into the hall. "I think we need to get to the bottom of what Peacock and Boddy were really fighting about."

"Who's *we* in this scenario?"

"You and me."

Finn stopped short and spun around. "You're joking, right?"

Mustard stuck his hands in his pockets, looking smug.

Smug and huge. "Not really. So far, you have the most likely motive for killing the headmaster that I've managed to uncover. He'd threatened to expel you. You told me yourself."

"Yeah, well, I also told you I didn't do it."

"I wonder which one of us the cops will find more convincing."

Finn clenched his jaw. "So you *are* a snitch."

Mustard looked offended. "Or," he proposed, "you could help me."

"And a blackmailer."

"Come on. You said you and Peacock were close."

Finn let out a burst of laughter. They reached the door to the billiards room. "Yeah, but I'm the last person Beth will talk to." Maybe Mustard should try Scarlett. She and Beth seemed to be getting along great.

He'd expected Mustard to follow him inside. After all, it was their room. But instead the other boy lingered on the threshold, running his fingers over the glossy wood of the doorframe. "It's so funny. You're the only one who calls her Beth."

"I'm not into dumb nicknames," Finn shot back. "*Mustard.*"

He'd expected a defense of some sort. An argument for the validity of that preposterous name, or an emotional explanation of why he insisted on using it. But Mustard didn't react in any way, and as the silence stretched on, Finn began to feel more vulnerable than ever. He'd told Mustard all kinds of things in the last half hour, and Mustard had told him . . .

Well, practically nothing. It was possible Finn hadn't played it as smoothly as he'd thought.

"Okay," Finn said at last. "I'll help you figure out the Beth thing. But then I want to know your secrets."

"What makes you think I have any?"

Finn chuckled. "Buddy, you're a Blackbrook kid now. It's our stock-in-trade."

19

Orchid

Orchid sat on the window seat in the study as the light of the day drained away and looked out over the frozen, muddy ground stretching as far as she could see. The beautiful Blackbrook campus, which had only a few short weeks earlier been a riot of fiery colors, now looked like the set of a postapocalyptic movie. Gray, ashen, dead.

For years, it had been her sanctuary, and, to judge from the photo album Mrs. White had showed her, she now knew she was not alone in thinking of it that way. It was funny—she'd always known that Mrs. White had been a student here, back in the olden days, but she'd never really considered what that meant. The students all joked about juvenile delinquents and reform school girls, but she'd never given much thought to what might have gotten a girl sent to reform school in the last century. Hadn't reflected on how little the mansion looked like a place a girl would go to atone for her sins.

Tudor House hadn't been a punishment. Its stately carvings and marble floors might have seemed more like a palace to scared girls arriving from who knows where, with who knows what kind of trauma in their pasts. They'd found this place, and they'd found one another.

No wonder she'd always felt at home here. Well, it would have been nice if she'd found trusted friends like Mrs. White had.

Orchid looked up to see Scarlett entering.

"There you are."

Or, you know, people who weren't complete monsters.

Then again, it wasn't entirely the fault of kids like Scarlett that Orchid had never made close friends. It was kind of hard to get close to someone if you couldn't share with them any facet of who you were. When all the other freshmen had been bonding over their lives in their old schools or their hometowns, Orchid had been busy concocting her very personality. Who was Orchid McKee? What did she like? What did she want out of Blackbrook? What did she want, period?

It had been easy to figure it out in her classes. The school's rigorous academic standards slotted Orchid into a pattern of quiet studiousness. She never made waves like Finn or Scarlett, but she held her own and liked it. But the same could not be said of the social spheres in the school. She had no athletic skills to speak of, and drama club or music was right out—she could not risk revealing her background. So while the other Blackbrook kids made friends in their activities, or bonded over shared pasts, Orchid had kind of missed the boat. Even living here, in the intimate surroundings of Tudor House, she'd never gotten close to the other girls. Nisha and Atherton had been best friends from childhood, Faith and Cadence were on the swim team together, and Scarlett . . .

Scarlett had just always rubbed Orchid precisely the wrong way. Always needing to be the center of attention, always ready to step on your neck if it meant getting another foot up the ladder.

She reminded Orchid of everyone and everything she'd hated in Hollywood.

Now Scarlett came and joined her on the window seat. Orchid pulled her knees up farther toward her chest. "I checked for you in your room."

That was new. "I don't really want to be upstairs alone." At least here, she could hear the voices of Karlee and Kayla floating down the hall, and even the dim echoes of pots and pans in the kitchen as Mrs. White worked on dinner. Vaughn, she knew, was napping in the library, and Beth was doing another round of stair reps. Finn and Mustard she hadn't seen for a bit, but maybe they were still playing detective.

"Me neither," said Scarlett in a voice low enough to be a confession. She looked out the window. "Do you think Rusty will be back with the cops soon?"

"No."

Scarlett's gaze shot in her direction. "No?"

Orchid shrugged. "This isn't Manhattan. There's one deputy in the village, probably five or six more in the first town on the mainland, and they've all been flooded, too. They're probably busy rescuing people out of attics. Or they are stuck in an attic somewhere themselves."

"But . . . a homicide!"

Orchid fixed Scarlett with a look. "When Rusty left, you were pretty firmly in the suicide camp."

Scarlett ignored her. "And they must know this place will be a target for looters . . ."

Did Scarlett realize how many straws she was grasping at? "That won't magically change the number of police boats they have."

Scarlett's expression was growing frantic. "What if the looter comes back? Or what if Vaughn was right, and it was someone here?"

Orchid rolled her eyes. "Like who, Scarlett? You want to come in here and bring up Peacock and her meeting with the headmaster again? Believe me, I've already gone over it, with the new kid Mustard, and with Peacock. She's well aware we all think she killed someone."

"Well, I don't think that," said Scarlett, folding her arms.

Now Orchid was surprised. "What?"

"I spent the last half hour talking to Peacock. You're right. She *is* well aware that we've all been talking about her." Scarlett stopped. "What?"

For Orchid was staring at her, flabbergasted. "Sorry, did you just say I was *right* about something?" Man, take away the girl's phone for a day and all kinds of crazy things might happen.

"Shut up." Scarlett continued, though not cruelly. "She wants to hike out of here. Says she won't spend another night in a house where everyone thinks she's a murderer."

"She can't do that!"

"Don't worry, I talked her down," said Scarlett. "I explained that leaving now would only make people more suspicious."

"No," Orchid replied, frustrated. "I mean, it's dangerous. Look at what happened to Vaughn and Rusty."

"Oh." Scarlett considered this, looking out over the mottled, debris-strewn yard of Tudor House. "That, too, I guess."

She *guessed?* Orchid raised her eyebrows in disbelief.

"Well, I want us all to be safe!" Scarlett exclaimed. "Trust me, I've been spending all day wondering how soon my parents might be able to get a helicopter up here and get us all out. I'm sure they are thinking about it, in New York. The news must be awful. I can't imagine. I've gotten nothing at all since my backup batteries went dead. They're probably freaking out. I know you're above such things, but I've got friends and family who occasionally like to hear from me."

Trust me, thought Orchid. *Sometimes you're better off if no one cares.* Every time Scarlett brought up the media, she started feeling twitchy. And it would only get worse, once the truth of the headmaster's death became known. If a suicide was newsworthy, a murder would be a real scandal. Orchid hugged her knees and gently rocked back and forth.

Could she handle news? *Real* news? There hadn't been any news of her for years. But she could picture the clickbait headlines. They would start innocently enough.

Hotel Heiress Details Agonizing 48 Hours in the Blackbrook Murder House

Here Are the Kids Who Survived the Blackbrook Murder House (#6 Will Surprise You!)

This Blackbrook Murder House Witness Looks Exactly Like Missing Child Star Emily Pryce and Twitter Is SHOOK!

And then her sanctuary would be gone. Forever.

"You know," said Scarlett, "you should wear contacts. You look really nice without your glasses."

"I didn't ask for your input."

"Touchy much?"

Orchid groaned. "Why is it touchy if a woman doesn't appreciate unsolicited takes on her appearance? I didn't want Karlee and Kayla's makeover last night, and I don't want your opinion on my glasses today."

Scarlett pursed her lips and sat back. "Yeah, that's a good point."

You're right and *good point*, all in one conversation? Wow, this was progress, indeed.

"I guess it's hard to imagine that someone doesn't want my opinion on a subject," Scarlett said. "My opinions are so *good.*"

Orchid burst out laughing. "Maybe you should be satisfied with eighty percent of the school as your minions and stop trying to recruit the rest of us."

"Is it only eighty?" Scarlett replied. "Crap, I thought I was doing better."

Orchid laughed again, though she was also only eighty percent sure that Scarlett was joking.

"Okay," the other girl conceded. "You look like that on purpose. This no-glasses moment is an aberration. Soon you'll have them fixed and your bangs will be back in your face and we can all go back to ignoring your killer cheekbones and movie star eyes."

Orchid tensed. "My what?"

Scarlett waved her hand at Orchid. "You know, like Elizabeth Taylor or something. It's indecent." She cocked her head. "Actually, you know who you look like?"

"No." *Yes.* The blood rushed in her ears.

"Oh, what was her name? The girl from those movies, where she was an heiress. Remember?"

"No." *Absolutely* yes. One didn't forget making five horrible films in as many equally horrible months.

"I watched those all the time as a kid. My mom thought they were so gauche."

So had Orchid. Cecily had decorated their first house in a ham-handed replica of the mansion set, though. The gossip rags had a field day with that one.

"If your hair was red, you'd look just like her."

The red was a dye, too. Her hair had never been red.

The dye had irritated her scalp every week when they touched up her roots. "I thought we were done suggesting changes to my appearance."

Scarlett held up her hands. "Okay. Okay. But you *do* look like her. Ugh, what was her name?"

Maybe it was the storm, or the fact that she'd tripped over a dead body that morning. Or maybe she was just tired of lying. "Emily Pryce."

Thunderbolts didn't fall from the sky. The earth didn't crack open and swallow her whole.

"Yes! Emily Pryce!" Scarlett looked at her. "I take it you've heard that before."

"Yes."

"Must be nice. I always get one of, like, three desi actresses. And I don't look anything like at least two of them."

Had Scarlett always been this funny? It was tough to notice, in between all the scheming and gossip and shirking of the Tudor House chore chart. "I guess that just proves we need more Indian American celebrities."

"Now *there's* a thought."

There was something in the way she said it that made Orchid wonder if Scarlett already had plans drawn up to create a Bollywood West. She wouldn't put it past her, honestly. Scarlett had the soul of a producer, and Orchid didn't mean that as a compliment.

"But first we need to survive the weekend," said Scarlett. "If the murderer isn't Blackbrook's favorite tennis star, and it's not you or me—"

"Just to be clear," said Orchid, "it's *not* you?"

Scarlett ignored the dig. "Then who does that leave? It's not the wonder twins. It's not the new kid."

"Maybe it's your boyfriend."

"Finn's not my boyfriend," said Scarlett. "Right now, I'm not even sure he's my friend, either."

That did surprise Orchid, though she had always figured the alliance would crumble eventually. It was hard to trust that your friend would have your back when all you'd ever seen them do was stab other people in theirs.

Except maybe now was not the time to think about stabbings. "So you're saying he could be a killer."

Scarlett gave her a deadpan look. "No, of course not."

"Then, who?"

"The townie."

Vaughn. Orchid hugged her knees more tightly. Of all the people in the house, Vaughn was the one she couldn't wrap her head around. Was he the know-it-all jerk from history class, or the charming folk singer who had flirted with her as the fire burned down to embers?

That moment, alone in the lounge after she'd lost her glasses, she thought maybe she'd never known the real Vaughn any better than he'd known her. And when she'd stumbled over the headmaster's corpse this morning, it had been Vaughn who had kept her from having a complete panic attack.

But this afternoon, during their search of the house, he'd reverted to form. All those creepy accusations at lunch, and then stomping around the attic, kicking boxes and scoffing at the idea that anyone—murderer, looter, or entity other than a bat or a mouse—was hiding among old dress forms and spare bed frames. What was it he'd said? Something about not being able to imagine anyone wanting to hang around Blackbrook kids longer than absolutely necessary. Orchid couldn't wait to finish looking around the attic and get out of his presence.

She hadn't been thrilled when he'd showed up at the study door looking for Mrs. White, either, but he'd turned on the charm again, and not just when Mrs. White was watching. Orchid didn't get it. She thought maybe it was him showing off—the local kid trying to prove his mettle in class or with his music or offering to row to Rocky Point with Rusty. Perhaps that was why he'd been in such a bad mood when he'd come back without reaching Rocky Point. He'd failed in his quest.

Vaughn was a mystery, for sure, but Orchid wasn't ready to give Scarlett any ammunition against him. Instead, she asked, "What possible reason would Vaughn have to kill Headmaster Boddy?"

"What possible reason would any of us have?" Scarlett replied.

"Vaughn was the one who brought up the idea that it was one of us!"

"Bragging about his crime," mused Scarlett. "What a sociopath."

Orchid shook her head in disgust. "Next you'll tell me it was Mrs. White. Or Rusty." She affected a theatrical voice. *"The janitor did it!"*

"Maybe he did," said Scarlett. "Maybe they all got together. Rocky Point's revenge on the school that ruined their town."

Orchid stopped. She didn't want to admit how plausible that sounded. It would make a good headline, too. "Except Blackbrook didn't ruin the town," she pointed out. "If anything, it saved it, after the mill shut down. All that glue money allowing them to buy the land and keep all these historical buildings in such good shape. You should listen to Mrs. White—this place is her life."

"Then Vaughn did it on his own."

Oh, Orchid, when I really want to show off, you'll know it.

Which Vaughn was the real one? He could go from sweet and flirtatious to sullen and macabre and then back again, all in the course of a day. But that didn't make him a killer.

Then, she realized. "You have it in for him."

"Do not." Scarlett hesitated for a moment. "Okay, yes, he's not my favorite person in the whole world."

"Why? Are his humanities grades too good?"

Bingo. Scarlett may think the other students didn't have her number, but she was wrong. Orchid had never been the subject of one of Scarlett's sabotage campaigns, but she'd seen the girl in action before. It wasn't pretty.

"That's not it," Scarlett said peevishly, in a tone that

meant it was *exactly* it. "Do you remember the Campus Beautification Committee I helmed sophomore year?"

Orchid honestly had no idea that such a thing had ever existed.

"Remember? I wanted to tear down the old boat shed?"

Vague memories returned to Orchid of announcements and email chains. "The one by the bridge into campus?"

"Yes! It's the first thing people see when they come to Blackbrook, and it's a total eyesore. I basically had the senior class committee on board to making their graduation gift a new school sign."

As much as Orchid loved Blackbrook, she couldn't imagine getting involved in something like that. The very idea of fighting with her classmates over what color to paint the trash bins made her tired. It appeared to energize Scarlett, though, as getting her own way on matters always did.

"But then," Scarlett went on, and her tone turned ominous, "the Rocky Point Historical Society stopped us."

"The Rocky Point Historical Society?" She wondered if they were like the consultants you hired when you were on location to make sure nothing you razed or painted or hung lights from would result in a lawsuit against the studio. "*Vaughn* is in the Rocky Point Historical Society? How does he have time with all this work-study?"

"I don't know how that guy has time for any of his activities or classes," Scarlett admitted. "Time machine, maybe? But he was definitely the one who tipped them off. Apparently it's some kind of *historically significant* shack. So we couldn't tear it down."

"Pity." But it didn't make him a murderer. "Cheer up, Scarlett. Maybe the flood will wash it away for you. Act of God."

Scarlett sniffed. "You don't care about any of this."

"No," Orchid agreed. "It's not what I came here for."

"Then what did you come here for?"

"Uh, school?"

Scarlett was nonplussed. "You didn't need to come all the way from California for school, and you know it."

Orchid turned her face to the window, to the bleak, gray disaster beyond the glass. "When it started, I guess I just wanted to get away. A different life. It doesn't get much different from Los Angeles than rural Maine." A boarding school in rural Maine, where the popular kids were the ones who knew the most mathematical proofs. The whole idea had been stranger than fiction.

But what she'd really cherished—as weeks turned into months, and then years; as she watched the seasons change and her mind expand, even in her new, contracted identity—was how safe she felt. No more feeling like the walls were collapsing on her as she slept, or like eyes were staring at her every time she turned around.

No one knew her at Blackbrook. Orchid McKee was the role of a lifetime, and she loved it, mostly because not a single soul was watching.

At least, not until a few days ago. Not until the letter she'd gotten, right before the storm hit.

She thought she'd been safe when she'd heard that the bridge was closed, that the town was being evacuated. Her fortress remained, even abandoned.

But what if the person who was coming for her had already arrived? He'd said he'd see her soon. As the storm had gotten worse, and everyone around her despaired, Orchid had only breathed a sigh of relief. That was, until she'd found the headmaster stabbed to death, and everyone else in the house had spent hours arguing over whether it was a looter or, inexplicably, one of their own.

Every time Orchid contemplated the likelihood that it was neither, the sensation came back. The topsy-turvy one she thought had vanished along with her previous life. And beside it, all the enmity she'd felt for the girl across the window seat seemed petty and small. Scarlett, who she knew quite well could spot an enemy at fifty paces. Scarlett, who held a grudge like a battle-ax. Scarlett, who Orchid had thought she had pegged—but maybe she didn't know her housemate any better than she knew Vaughn, or herself.

If anyone in the house was determined and ambitious enough to out-stalk a stalker, it was Scarlett. And all Orchid would have to do was tell the biggest gossip at Blackbrook her deepest, darkest secret.

"Here's my fear," Orchid said softly. "What if it was an

intruder, but not a looter? What if they were here looking to do harm to Headmaster Boddy . . . or someone else?"

"Like who?"

Orchid took a deep breath. Her mouth fought opening, but she forced the matter. It was time.

"Like me."

20

Scarlett

Scarlett was still speechless when Mrs. White came to call them for dinner.

Scarlett Mistry was *never* speechless. She was quick on her feet, with a sharp brain and a sharper tongue. She sent lesser mean girls packing, made queen bees shake in their hives, and ensured that not a single thing ever happened on this campus without her knowing about it.

At least, that's what she'd always thought.

Today had been *very* confusing.

First there was Finn—her sweet, sneaky, spirited scientist—who, it turned out, had even been sneaking around on her. She'd never have expected it. Possibly she had trained him too well.

But she didn't have time to think about that now. For no sooner had she been rocked by the realization that her best friend was lying to her, that she discovered that there were even deeper deceptions occurring right under her nose.

Like how her housemate was secretly a missing Hollywood movie star.

Honestly, was she losing her touch?

Scarlett had grilled Orchid—Emily?—*Orchily?*—for details about her life before she'd decided to change her name and move to Maine, but the girl was as frustratingly tight-lipped about that as she'd been about . . . well, anything. Ever. It wasn't like they'd been close before the storm had stranded them all in Tudor House with no power and no distractions. And Scarlett had the distinct impression that Orchid was only coming to her now out of sheer desperation.

Honestly, her story was no wilder than the idea that one of their classmates had murdered the headmaster. Scarlett's mousy, unassuming neighbor was really a movie star, and she had a stalker who had been writing her menacing letters, and now there was a dead body in the conservatory. Scarlett didn't even need a calculator to do that math.

"Coming?" Orchid asked as she stood to leave the study.

"Yeah," Scarlett said, still distracted by the notion that anyone would willingly relinquish their hard-earned fame. Well, stalker aside. Like, hire some bodyguards, you know? Why give up being a celebrity?

"Scarlett, you know you can't tell anyone. It'll only cause more problems."

"Right. Right."

"I'm serious. No one."

Scarlett fixed her with a look. "Orchid McKee, I am known throughout Blackbrook for my exquisite sense of discretion."

But she was clearly not as good an actress as the girl across from her. "If you mean that you always know what items of gossip to keep until they are the most personally profitable, then yes, you are."

Scarlett considered this. "That's actually the perfect way to put it, thank you."

"You're only welcome if you agree with me that this is not fodder for your whisper campaigns."

Oh, no. Definitely not. She was going to allow Orchid to pay her back in a way that was far more personally profitable than that.

She just had to find some other way to convince everyone else in the house that the "looter" theory was still a go. That there was some intruder, either in the house or stuck with them on campus, who might cause them harm if they didn't stick together.

Of course, if this stalker of Orchid's was willing to stab Headmaster Boddy to get to his target, why didn't he just finish the job last night, when Orchid was alone in her room? Scarlett would have to figure that out, too, but meanwhile, she was going to stay as close as possible to her new bestie.

Darling, lost, *desperate* Orchily McPryce.

How delicious.

"I swear to you," Scarlett said in the most earnest tone she could muster, "I will never reveal your true identity to anyone without your permission."

Orchid looked taken aback. "You know, I almost believe you."

Scarlett smiled. "High praise indeed."

On the way into the dining room, they saw Finn and Mustard crossing the hall from the billiards room, and Scarlett did her best to ignore them.

"Scarlett," said Finn. "Can I talk to you for a minute?"

"Go ahead," said Orchid. "I'm going to see if Vaughn wants dinner." She lifted her lantern and headed toward the library.

"I'll save you a seat!" Scarlett called to Orchid's back. She even *walked* like a movie star. How had Scarlett never noticed it before? She might be *seriously* losing her touch.

Or maybe it was just being so disconnected from everything these past two days. No phone, no internet, no video game consoles or texts or checking the latest stats. It was beyond boring, but perhaps also it had recalibrated her observational skills. No, most human beings did not walk like that. At least not ones who weren't gunning to make top social media influencer status.

"Scarlett," Finn said again.

"I heard you," she replied with a scowl. Mustard, already halfway to the dining room, paused and turned back, a curious expression on his face. Finn waved him on. "I'm not in the mood to talk to you right now."

"What did you get out of Beth?"

"What did I *get*?" Scarlett asked, affronted. "You tell me, Finn. You seem to know a lot more about what's going on here than I do." Or, rather, than he used to. Now she had the scoop of the school.

"Don't be like that," he coaxed. He batted his eyelashes.

"I already told you that I'm sorry. And I'll tell you anything you want to know."

Too little too late. "How could I possibly trust you right now?"

"I've been working on Mustard."

Scarlett frowned. Well, that was just unfair to tease her. But no, she wouldn't be swayed by his obvious temptations. He'd lied to her. And he still hadn't come clean. She crossed her arms and lifted her chin.

"You can start by telling me everything, including everything you found out about the new kid. Then I'll see whether I'm ready to forgive you or not."

"That's hardly fair."

"*Who* is hardly fair?"

"What if I tell you everything and you decide to take it and run? I know you, Scarlett. I know what you're like."

"Huh," she said flatly. "At least that makes one of us who knows the other." And then she turned, marched into the candlelit dining room, and took a seat next to Peacock. That would show him.

"I'm starving," said Peacock. "I really hope there's real food tonight."

Finn trailed in. Peacock bared her teeth and he found a chair in the farthest corner. Karlee and Kayla were seated on either side of Mustard already. Orchid came in alongside Vaughn, chatting softly.

"Orchid!" Scarlett called, waving. She motioned to the empty seat next to her.

Orchid cast a quick—possibly regretful—glance at Vaughn and sat down beside her. She'd been defending him earlier, too. Scarlett would have to keep an eye on that. Vaughn took the final seat, beside Finn. Good riddance to both of them.

Mrs. White entered with dinner, which was ham, baked beans, and the last of the vegetable soup. "Don't worry, Scarlett," she said as she passed the crock over. "The beans, potatoes, and salad are vegetarian."

"Thank you, Mrs. White," Scarlett replied sweetly. She helped herself to beans. Mrs. White had been very accommodating of her diet since she'd moved into Tudor House and had related that several of her own friends had been vegan back in the seventies, so she was more than happy to cook with that in mind.

There was a murmur of thank-yous around the table.

"I know this has not been an easy day for you kids," Mrs. White said. "And I can't imagine it'll be an easy night, either. I want to thank you for keeping calm in the face of these overwhelming odds. With any luck, by tomorrow morning the authorities will be here and this whole nightmare will be over."

"Or someone else will be murdered," grumbled Karlee.

"No." Mrs. White's tone was firm. "It was a horrific, singular event. It was a looter, seeking to take advantage of what he saw as a fancy, abandoned house. He's long gone. He won't be back."

"You can't guarantee that, Mrs. White," Karlee said,

her voice louder this time. She turned to Mustard, who was digging in the bread basket. "I can't stay here. What if there's another attack?"

"We could all sleep in the ballroom," he suggested. "There's safety in numbers, and there aren't any windows or anything in there that might serve as an entry point."

"But that's right next to the conservatory!" Kayla squeaked. "That's where the dead body is!"

"I don't think he poses a danger at present," said Mrs. White.

Beth, at Scarlett's side, was loading up her plate. Orchid, at her other side, was still talking animatedly to Vaughn on the other side of the table. Her smile was blinding. She looked exactly like Emily Pryce.

How had Scarlett never noticed it before? Well, this would never do. She could not allow her new best friend to be so careless with her secret identity. The glasses would have to make a comeback, at the very least. And the mousy, straggly bangs, back in the face. And the anti-contouring makeup, definitely.

Strange, she'd always been so dismissive of superheroes before, but now she supposed the whole disguise thing worked better than she'd thought.

That was, of course, if Orchid planned to *keep* her secret identity, a strategy Scarlett would encourage Orchid to reconsider. Geez—*Orchid*. Scarlett should have tagged that as a fake name from the start. It was almost as bad as Mustard.

Vaughn and Peacock seemed to be in a race to see who could go for seconds more quickly.

"I think all of us being in the same room is a good idea," Scarlett said.

"You don't worry this cold-blooded murderer you imagine will take advantage of it and kill everyone?" Peacock asked, slicing her ham up with unnecessary vigor.

Karlee and Kayla looked appalled. Peacock forked a piece of ham and brought it to her mouth with relish. Then she sneered in Finn's direction. Finn pretended to be fascinated by the beans on his plate.

"We did well this afternoon with splitting into groups to search the house," Scarlett went on. "Maybe we can do three groups tonight, too, with watches, so no one is ever alone."

"Or with only one other person," said Peacock dryly. "You know, because *one of us is supposedly a murderer.*" She stabbed another piece of ham with her fork. "Question—if you all are going to be sleeping on the floor together in order to avoid being alone with me, can everyone's favorite suspect claim one of your beds? The floor actually *is* murder—on my back."

"You know," Finn said, still studying his plate, "logically, if you're *not* a murderer, you should be the one *most* worried about being left alone in the house."

"*Logically,*" Peacock shot back, "a murderer is probably someone who is already well-known for stabbing other people in the back. Right, *Phineas?*"

All other conversations ceased. Everyone looked at Finn.

Scarlett couldn't help but smile. This was going to be good.

Finn threw down his spoon. "Okay," he said. "Okay. How about you go ahead and tell everyone here why you think I'm so evil, and then I'll tell my story, and then we'll let the others decide which of us is more likely to have killed the headmaster last night."

Peacock's eyes narrowed, but she said nothing.

"Yeah," sniffed Finn. "Thought not."

"Enough!" shouted Mrs. White. "I don't want to hear any more discussions about there being a killer in this house."

"Why?" asked Karlee. "You'd prefer we just sit here, getting picked off one by one?"

Mustard cleared his throat. "I think we could bring this whole thing to a close right now if Beth decides to share with us why she and the headmaster got into an altercation last week."

"I told you already!" cried Peacock. "I asked for time off school to attend an event, and he wouldn't let me go."

No one said anything in response to that. Several people frowned. Karlee made a skeptical sort of hum in the back of her throat.

Scarlett sighed and ate another forkful of beans. If only the poor girl had come to her for advice. This was not a good way to handle the types of problems Peacock was facing. If she did end up a famous tennis star, she was going to need a good PR team.

Peacock threw her napkin down on the table, then seemed to think better of it, and used it to wrap up the rest of her roll and her ham. "That's it," she said. "I'm not staying another minute in a house where everyone thinks I'm a killer. I don't care if I do freeze, or drown, or whatever. I'm out of here." She stood up so fast she knocked her chair backward. Kayla flinched. Peacock saw it, groaned, and stormed off with the remains of her dinner.

For a second, everyone just sat in stunned silence.

"Stop her," said Mrs. White. "We have to stop her. It's too dangerous for her to go out in these conditions."

"Isn't it too dangerous for her to stay here?" Karlee asked.

Finn leaped to his feet and headed toward the door. "Beth!"

After several shocked moments, everyone followed.

By the time Scarlett and the others reached the stair landing in the hall, Peacock had her coat and boots on and was pounding down the stairs, Finn hot on her heels.

"Leave me alone!" she growled at him. "None of this would be happening if you hadn't started it."

"Is she saying Finn's involved, too?" Kayla asked.

"Miss Picach," ordered Mrs. White. "You must stop at once. I cannot allow any students to leave Tudor House during this storm."

"Go ahead and stop me then!" cried Peacock. "I'm not

just going to stand here and take these baseless accusations against me. It's—it's—" She raked her hand through her hair, and the static made all the blue ends stand out around her head like real peacock feathers. "It's crazy!"

"Peacock," said Mustard, and he stepped between her and the door. He was the only one in the house taller than she was. "Just take a minute. Think this over. Don't put yourself at risk. More than that, don't add to the suspicion that you have something to hide by running out of here. It's not a good look, any way you cut it."

And then, Elizabeth Picach, the Peacock of Blackbrook, the terror of the tennis court, pulled back her well-muscled serving arm and landed a haymaker right on Mustard's square-cut jaw.

He dropped like a rock and his head hit the parquet floor with a sickening thud.

And Peacock, possibly two times a killer, disappeared into the night.

21

Peacock

— EP WORKOUT LOG —

DATE: *December 6*

AFTERNOON SNACK: *Lemon-custard-flavored nutrition bars (210 calories, 6g protein)*

DINNER: *Ham, 10 ounces (500 calories, 30g protein), roll (80 calories)*

AFTERNOON WORKOUT: *150 stair reps, arm weight with bar, 50 crunches*

EVENING WORKOUT: *Ran across the trash heap ninja obstacle course that used to be the Blackbrook campus.*

NOTES: *YOU KNOW WHAT, I DON'T EVEN CARE WHAT THEY THINK. NONE OF THOSE JERKS MATTER TO ME ANYWAY. THIS WOULDN'T EVEN HAVE HAPPENED IF STUPID FINN HADN'T TOLD STUPID EVERYONE IN SCHOOL ABOUT THAT STUPID DAY IN THE STUPID OFFICE.*

THE SCUMBAG. HOW COME NO ONE SUSPECTS HIM????? HE'S THE ONE EVERYONE KNOWS WILL STAB YOU IN THE BACK.

MAYBE HE JUST STABBED BODDY IN THE FRONT THIS TIME.

I feel hot all over. It's freezing in here and it's like there are flames licking the side of my face. Flames of rage!

It's creepy, being all alone. And cold. If I do die, do NOT let Phineas Plum anywhere near my funeral.

22

Mustard

Mustard didn't know if it was the punch or the way his head hit the floor that had him seeing stars, but for a long moment, nothing in the hall made sense. Everyone was yelling and rushing, and somehow, in all the hubbub, someone helped him up off the floor and someone else was pressing a cold cloth to his nose and a third person was waving fingers in his face and asking him the date and his favorite color and who the president was, all quickly and without even waiting for his answers.

This person turned out to be Kayla, and his headache got a whole lot worse very quickly, until Mrs. White waved her away.

"Are you all right, Mr. Maestor?" she asked before turning to Scarlett and barking, "Get a mop for this blood on the floor!"

This was going to be the third mopping the hall floor had had in twenty-four hours.

Wait . . . Blood?

"I'm all right," Mustard said, holding a hand to his

pounding head. "Just a little dizzy for a second." He pulled his hand away. More blood. How did it get from his nose to the back of his head?

"Gross!" Kayla exclaimed. "Look! It's running all down his sweater."

"He's really bleeding," Karlee observed. "What if he needs stitches?"

"Head wounds bleed a lot," said Mrs. White. "Let me get my first-aid kit from the study." She vanished.

Mustard knew that was true about head wounds, but when it was your own blood coating your hand and making your hair and neck all sticky, it wasn't much of a comfort.

Mrs. White reappeared and pressed a rag to his scalp. "Just sit still for a minute and keep pressure on this, and we'll get this bleeding to stop." She put his hand over the rag, then handed him some pills and a cup of water. "Take these for the pain."

Mustard gave in to all of it. He sat still, and applied pressure, and swallowed the pills. He was on the bottom step of the stair landing, kind of sprawled out, while the girls bustled around him. He'd never been surrounded by so many girls in his life.

Presently, he saw another boy: Vaughn. Vaughn was standing by the big front door to Tudor House, looking out, his face like a soldier's in the midst of a battle.

Orchid stood at the door, too. They were talking. Mustard listened harder, to hear them over the girls babbling near his ear.

"—can't leave her out there."

"I know." Vaughn shrugged. "But what are we supposed to do?"

Orchid looked surprised. "You're the one who has been out there already. I kind of thought you'd want to go out again."

Vaughn snorted. "Did you see what Peacock did to Mustard? I appreciate the flattery, but trust me, she can take me. I already suffered one bloody nose today."

"So then . . . what?" asked Orchid. "We just leave her to die? You and Rusty nearly drowned, and that was during the day."

"The storm was a lot worse during the day," Vaughn said quietly. "And the storm surge. Most of the floodwaters have receded by now, and the wind's gone down. It's barely even sleeting anymore."

"It's also pitch-black out there," Orchid said. "Does Peacock even have a flashlight?"

"I understand what you're saying," said Vaughn. "But I'm worried chasing after her might only escalate the situation. Maybe she'll get cold, realize her mistake, and then either come back or seek shelter in one of the other campus buildings. Chasing her is only going to make her more upset than she already is, not to mention put whoever goes looking for her in danger. There's been enough violence."

Orchid fell silent as she considered what Vaughn had said. Mustard thought it all sounded very reasonable, though he hated that it had come to this. He shouldn't have tried to stop her.

Nearby, Scarlett was proving she'd never used a mop before in her life as she shoved dirty water around the floor in a haphazard manner that seemed pitched only to undo Mustard's own mopping job from that morning.

Above their heads, the wind batted at the tarp covering the broken stained glass, and a burst of cold wet air blew in around the edges.

If Peacock stayed out there, she might die. But so might anyone who was stupid enough to go after her.

"How did his blood get all the way over here?" Scarlett asked, dragging the mop in untidy circles over the hardwood floor outside the door to the library.

"How can you even see it in the dark?" Karlee asked.

"I eat a lot of carrots," Scarlett replied dryly.

Carrot consumption actually had no bearing on a person's ability to see in the dark. That was a myth made up by the British military during World War II to hide the fact that pilots were using radar, not gorging themselves on root vegetables. But somehow, it felt like way too much effort to say any of that out loud.

Mustard wanted to lie down, and he also had a strange inkling that it might be an incredibly bad idea to do so.

"Enough with the mopping, Scarlett," Mrs. White called. "If you want to mop, go clean up the blood in the conservatory."

"She can't do that," said Karlee. "What if it's destroying evidence?"

"What evidence?" asked Scarlett. "We've been running in and out of there all day."

Mrs. White pulled back on the cloth. "It's stopped bleeding. Doesn't look too deep. I think a bandage will suffice. You had a lucky break, kid."

"Yeah," he said blankly.

"But doesn't it just prove how violent that girl is?" Karlee asked. "What if she comes back and tries to finish us all off for guessing that it was her?"

"We don't know that!" Orchid said.

"She's certainly not acting like an innocent person," Karlee said.

"And what does an innocent person act like?" Orchid replied. "Especially when she's being accused of murder."

Mrs. White opened up the first-aid kit and pulled out some bandages and cleaning supplies.

Orchid looked at Scarlett, a pleading expression on her face. Even through the haze, Mustard noticed it.

"I don't think we can worry too much about Peacock right now," said Scarlett. "She made her choice. The real issue, as I see it, is making sure everyone in this house is safe."

"Agreed," said Vaughn. He still hadn't left his post by the door, as if, with Mustard injured, he'd taken on the part of watchman.

Mrs. White put something stinging on the back of his scalp and he hissed through his teeth.

"I still think the idea of all of us sticking together in the ballroom tonight is a good one," said Scarlett. "There's no windows, one door—we'll be secure in there."

"As long as there aren't any secret passages to the ballroom," Mustard drawled.

"There *are* no secret passages," said Scarlett.

He turned his head, and the hall swam around him for a moment. "No, there are. I found one this afternoon."

Several heads turned in his direction, all of them wearing faces that were completely dumbfounded.

"What?" asked Scarlett.

"What?" asked Orchid.

Did he not share that information with anyone? Oops. "Yeah. This afternoon. Finn and I were down in one. Finn, back me up."

Finn did not reply.

"Oh God," said Scarlett, all of a sudden. "Where is Finn?"

"He must have gone after Peacock!" cried Vaughn. "I didn't notice because we were all trying to help Mustard."

"Did he even have a coat?" Orchid asked.

"Wait a second," Mustard said, and tried to stand. "Just everyone hold on one—"

That was the last thing he remembered.

23

Plum

Finn's teeth had started chattering even before he'd stepped into the waist-deep puddle of icy water. The puddle in which he'd also lost his glasses. Which didn't matter so very much, as he couldn't see anything in the dark, anyway.

Like puddles. Or Beth.

Funny. He hadn't stopped to grab his coat or hat because he'd been so worried he'd lose sight of her in the dark.

But he had completely lost sight of her anyway. And with the power outage and the utter lack of illumination from either streetlights or windows, he had no idea where he was on campus. All the usual landmarks seemed strange and unfamiliar in the total darkness. Was it really this far between Tudor House and the science building? Or had he somehow gotten turned around in the night and was about to drop into the ravine?

He wrapped his arms around himself tighter, tucked his head down into the upturned collar of his sweater, and looked for something—anything that would give him a hint of where he stood.

There might have been a moon, somewhere behind the clouds. There must be some source of light, coming from somewhere, because Finn could just make out his hand in front of his face, and he was pretty sure the power wasn't on anywhere for miles around.

Up ahead he caught a flash of light. He picked up his pace, then stopped again as he smacked into the wet branches of a tree. Twigs and bark scratched his face.

He cursed, rearing back, slipped on a patch of ice, and went down hard onto the ground.

But it wasn't frozen earth under his numb fingertips. It was stone. One of the stone walks outside the administration building!

Finn looked up. Okay, so he was off course, but not that far off. He could just turn right from here and hopefully follow the path down the hill toward Dockery, where Beth lived.

The light flashed again, this time from far above him. He looked up and even in the darkness could make out the ornate gables and bay windows of the administration building. And the light . . . coming from a window on the third floor.

It was probably Beth. Right?

The wind buffeted him back and forth, howling like the wolves everyone said didn't live in Maine anymore. He'd stopped shivering by now, and tried to remember from his one stab at camping if that meant he was about to die from hypothermia.

It could also be the murderer. The one who had already stolen Boddy's computer and petty cash. The one he worried might have found him in the secret passageway earlier this afternoon. The one who was almost certainly still lurking somewhere on campus. Which was why he couldn't leave Beth out here alone.

Though of course she could take care of herself. Look at the way she'd laid out Mustard for daring to try to keep her from walking out a door. No one ever kept Beth Picach from getting what she wanted.

He'd liked that about her. He thought she'd liked that about him.

It's like he could never get a single person on his team. Not really. Even Scarlett had abandoned him in the end.

If he went into the building and it was the murderer, lying in wait, would anyone be sorry when he, too, got murdered? Would anyone even care? Or would Sherlock Maestor back there decide to take the information Finn had revealed to him in the secret passageway and turn it over to the school? He probably would, and they'd probably name the dye something stupid and obvious like "Brookblack" and have all the fame and money and Finn would be forgotten completely in the annals of science for all time.

The wind continued to howl.

But at this point, Finn didn't even know if he'd survive

long enough to make it back to Tudor. At least inside this building, he'd have some protection from the wind. And it was probably Beth in there, anyway.

Probably.

Steeling his nerves, he stepped out into the wind again and hurried to where he knew the doors to the admin building were. He yanked them open.

It was even darker inside.

His first step onto the carpet in the entrance hall came with a sickening squish and the crunch of ice. So the flood had reached here. Or maybe a pipe had burst, too. He wished he'd thought to bring a flashlight.

Or a hat.

It was warmer in here, but not by much. He made his way down the hall mostly by memory, and up the wide, disused marble staircase at the back. The steps were worn in the middle from generations of Blackbrook students pounding up and down them, and the first few on the lower level had frozen puddles in the indentations where other kids' feet had climbed. He skirted around them and started up. The flood didn't seem to have risen past a foot or two.

He spilled out into the third-floor hallway, which was dark and silent and looked untouched, as if the entire administrative staff had just gone home for the night. There were trophies and awards and photos of glories from Blackbrook's past in glass cases lining the halls. Nothing was broken, the way one might expect if the place were really being looted.

Every part of Finn's body hurt, and he was ready to pull down one of the big banners hanging on the wall to wear like a blanket. He was beyond cold. His toes kept catching on the carpet, as if his feet weren't lifting high enough to clear each step.

Stumbling. It was called stumbling. Why couldn't he think straight?

A few doors down was the headmaster's office. Where this had all begun. And then he saw it, another flash of light from within. Silently, he passed the threshold and crossed into the antechamber, with its hard wooden chairs, its secretary's desk, its massive wooden plaque with the Blackbrook crest.

There was a light coming from the headmaster's private chambers.

Finn had never thought about anything less in his life. Maybe his brain was frozen, too. He used to yell at characters in movies who did dumb things like this. But he was already walking in.

The room was dim, save for a single candle burning in a tall brass candlestick set on the floor next to the fireplace. It was also empty.

Finn was confused.

And then a great black shape rose up from behind the desk. Finn cried out.

Okay, he screamed.

She screamed, too, and then the air was filled with loud clunks and crashes and it took Finn a few seconds to realize her arms had been filled with firewood and she'd just dropped it all over the floor.

"What the hell, Finn!" Beth shouted at him.

"I—"

"It's not too late for me to *become* a murderer, you know."

He knew. Believe him. He knew.

"Get out of here," she went on.

"Please, Beth—"

"I said, *get out of here!*"

"I'm freezing," he said. "I mean it. Like, can't think straight, possibly losing brain cells to hypothermia, *dying* freezing. Please. I came after you without a coat, and I fell in the water and lost my glasses, and it's dark out there, and if you send me outside again, I just might die."

She glared at him, then swiped up a log or two, and crossed to the fireplace. She tossed them in the hearth, balled up a bit of newspaper, and shoved it in, too. Then she glared at him one more time for good measure, picked up the candlestick and thrust the flame at the newspaper.

When it caught, Finn thought he might cry. He fell to his knees in front of the little baby fire and held his aching fingers up to the heat.

"Well," said Beth as the logs began to glow, as the bark at the edges of the logs caught and curled into little black wisps, as he smelled wood smoke and warmth, and felt the prickle of sensation in his extremities. "I guess I'm not a murderer after all."

After a minute, he felt equal to answering. "I never said you were."

"You let *everyone* in Tudor House believe it."

Not true. He'd told Mustard it couldn't have been Beth, and Mustard had been the only one who meant it when he'd asked. "Beth, I—"

"I don't want to hear it." She sat down next to him and held her hands out to the fire. "I hate you, you know."

"You never miss an opportunity to make that clear."

"Well, I can't have you forget."

"Look who doesn't forget things," he snapped. "Or forgive them."

Beth gave him an incredulous look. The fire burnished her face bright orange. "What in the *world* have you done that would make me want to forgive you?"

"What was I supposed to do?" Finn asked. "You wouldn't even speak to me for months. Was I supposed to show up at your matches with a poster saying I loved you? Was I supposed to throw pebbles at your window until you gave in and opened up?"

"Were you supposed to let an entire house of people think I stabbed the head of this school?" she shot back. "No, but you did it anyway."

Well. Finn sat back on his heels. After a year or so he'd figured her feelings were set in stone.

The silence stretched on. He shot her a look out of the corner of his eye. She held her long arms out to the fire and stared into the flames, her icy eyes thawing not the slightest bit.

"Here's what you never did, Finn," she said at last. "You never apologized. Not once. You never said you'd do anything to make it right."

"Make it right?" he echoed. But it *was* right. That's what Beth didn't understand. "You said you weren't even sure you *wanted* to take honors chemistry. You said it might be too much of a workload with your practice schedule."

"Yes, I said all of that." She didn't look away from the fire.

"And it would have been!"

"Probably."

Finn threw up his hands in frustration. She was impossible. He'd been a good boyfriend freshman year. A *supportive* boyfriend. Tennis had been everything to Beth. He knew that. *Everyone* knew that.

She'd only qualified for the chemistry class in the first place because she studied so much with him. He'd been responsible for her fantastic grades in that subject, and she hadn't even been into it!

Only three sophomores a year got into junior honors chemistry, and it was just a stroke of bizarre luck that her name had been chosen in the lottery and not his. But Beth didn't want to be a scientist. *Finn* did. If she'd taken it, she might have dropped in her tennis rankings. She might even have quit. And then the world would have been deprived of her extraordinary talent.

Of *both* their talents. That was something, at least, that he and Scarlett had always agreed on. They never competed in their classes. She had humanities and he had sciences. That's how it should have been with him and Beth.

Beth had been dragging her feet about making a decision that spring, too. Sophomore year class schedules were due. Was he supposed to just turn in his schedule and give up the spot on the honors chemistry waiting list, on the off chance that Beth bafflingly picked science over tennis? The delay might make him miss out on other classes he wanted!

Turning in Beth's schedule for her was the easiest answer—for both of them.

"I don't get it," he said.

"Nope," Beth replied, her tone clipped. "You don't."

The warmth had started to seep into Finn's body again, but slowly. He'd heard hypothermia victims were supposed to take off all their clothes and get in a sleeping bag with another person. Somehow, he knew not to suggest that to Beth.

"So what are we supposed to do now?"

"I don't care what you do," said Beth.

"I meant about you." Finn turned, partly to look at her, partly to rotate in front of the fire. "That move with Mustard isn't going to make the people at Tudor any less suspicious of you."

"I don't care." Beth said, but he could tell by the way she was holding her mouth that it was a lie. "As long as I don't have to sit there and listen to their accusations, they can say whatever they want. It's warm up here, and there's a couch in the corner, and I have the rest of my protein bars in my bag, so we can all just wait for the cops to get here and sort it all out."

"Aren't you afraid they'll suspect you, too?"

Beth was silent for a moment. "But . . . *I didn't do it.* Yeah, I yelled at him last week, but I didn't do it. That's all you've got."

"That's all anyone's got." He looked around. "And of all the rooms on campus you could have chosen, you picked his office?"

"It's close, and I knew there was a fireplace in here."

"Beth . . ."

She stared into the flames for a long moment, then sighed. "It wasn't about the Grand Slam."

"What?"

"Why he called the meeting. It wasn't about the Grand Slam. He got a complaint in from my last tournament that I was hooking."

Finn's jaw dropped. "You were *what*?"

She rolled her eyes. "*Cheating*, Finn. That I was cheating. Get your mind out of the gutter." She shrugged and turned back to the fire. "The rules of junior tennis say that players have an obligation to accept their opponents' call, no matter how unreasonable. If a ball is in or out, that kind of thing. There aren't always refs."

"Wow, really?" Finn whistled. "How does that not get abused?"

"It *is* abused," said Beth. "All the time. And everyone just kind of looks the other way."

"But they caught you?"

Beth groaned. "How come everyone always thinks the worst of me? Okay, maybe I got aggressive in my calls in a few close games. But I'm *not* a cheater. Only, apparently, twelve opponents from 'a variety of teams at area schools'"—she made quote marks in the air with her hands—"got together and wrote Headmaster Boddy a letter claiming that this is a long-term pattern of behavior they've noticed."

Sabotage. They had banded together to eliminate a common threat. That was a tactic Finn understood intimately. "Oh no, Beth. I'm so sorry. What does that mean?"

"Well, it meant that Boddy was going to open an investigation and see if there was any truth to the claim." Her eyes welled up with tears. "Because if there was, it would be an honor code violation. I'd get suspended from the team next spring."

Right during the peak of college recruitment. She'd be ruined.

"I told Headmaster Boddy it was a smear job!" she cried. "But he said he was under an ethical obligation to investigate. But it's such crap. What does that even mean? He's going to ask the people who wrote that letter if they thought I cheated? Of course they're going to say they think it! Why else would they write the letter? They're not going to back down if they think it's about to work."

Finn shook his head. Yeah, he wouldn't back down, either. Nor Scarlett. "I'm so sorry."

"And he wouldn't show me the letter. He wouldn't even tell me who was accusing me. *That's* why I yelled at him. And, um, you know, knocked over that candlestick." She pointed at the object sitting innocently on the floor. "And that's why I came up here. I thought *maybe*, if I could see who was accusing me, if I could get my hands on the letter . . ."

"Bull," said Finn. Never try to scam a scammer. "You thought *maybe*, with the headmaster dead, if you could get rid of the letter before anyone else saw it, the whole issue might die."

Beth looked at him, lips pursed.

"I thought the same thing," Finn confessed. "Boddy caught me with some work I've been doing on the sly. He wanted a full report. That's why I was in here last week."

"Oh," said Beth.

"And when the storm started I thought if I could hide every record, every bit of data I had, I'd be in the clear. They wouldn't be able to pin anything on me. Not with everything they'd have to deal with after the storm. That's what I was doing in the lab when you saw me yesterday on the way to Tudor."

The fire crackled and popped, and all of a sudden Finn felt a whole lot less like he was about to die.

"Well." Beth seemed at a loss for words.

Funny. He might not be able to save himself, but he could still save her.

"Well." Finn pushed himself to his feet and held out his hand. "Let's go find that letter, shall we?"

Beth blinked up at him. "Really? You want to help me now?"

He sighed. "All I've ever wanted to do is help you."

She considered this. "Play tennis, you mean. Help me play tennis."

"Sure, Beth." Whatever worked.

Together they went over to the headmaster's desk. He kept it relatively neat, with only a few file folders in his inbox and—

That was weird. "It's a laptop," said Finn.

"So?"

"Well, I thought he had his laptop with him when he evacuated."

Beth frowned. "How do you know what he had with him?"

"Remember? Mrs. White told us the looter had stolen his laptop and the lockbox with the petty cash."

"Oh." Beth frowned, too. "Well, maybe that was his personal laptop and this is his work computer."

"Could be." Finn opened the case and pressed the power button. "Might be some juice left, if he hasn't been here since the power went out." As the machine booted up, a thought occurred to him. "Hey, how did you get in here, anyway? I can't imagine they left the office unlocked."

Beth bit her lip. "Um, I picked the lock. I figured, in an emergency, if I was trying to get warm, you know . . .

firewood. That I wouldn't get in any real trouble. I wasn't going to break anything or steal anything . . . valuable."

"You *picked the lock?*" Finn stared at her in wonder.

"It's an old lock," she said defensively. "I do have a couple of secret skills, Finn."

Apparently. Finn could hardly imagine what Scarlett would do with information like that. She'd recruit Beth in a hot minute. He turned back to the computer. Still had some battery life left. A password-protected screen popped up. Finn checked inside the drawers and under the leather blotter. Aha. A note card.

Old people were so reliable. He typed in the first password and was taken into the system.

"We'll search his email cache for your name," he said to Beth. "First we'll find out if the letter was emailed, or if he told anyone else about it. If we can find the digital record, we can delete it. If we don't find anything, we might have to resort to the filing cabinets."

"You just break into other people's computers all the time?" she asked.

"I also have a couple of secret skills," he replied, and opened up the email, ready to type *Picach* into the search box.

But the subject heading of the first email caught his eye.

Demolition Schedule.

24

Green

"Out of our way, or we'll punch you, just like Peacock!" Kayla yelled at him.

Vaughn didn't believe that for a second. He knew what people looked like before they threw punches. But he also knew what it felt like to be locked in. "I'm not trying to block you. I'm trying to convince you what a bad idea this is."

"We're not staying another night in the murder house." Karlee crossed her arms over her backpack straps. They were both wearing their backpacks over their puffy winter coats. Their boots were laced up tight. Their hats had sparkly pom-poms on top.

None of that would help them survive the ravine. Or whatever else waited for them out there. Vaughn couldn't get the image of the houses at the bottom of the ravine out of his head. The whole campus had been flooded. There might be structural damage to the buildings, sheets of black ice covering the pathways . . .

Murderers lurking in the shadows. No matter what, they were safer sticking together.

"If the person you're worried about is Peacock, why do you imagine you'd be safer out there, alone, in the dark, rather than in here with the rest of us?"

"Are you kidding?" asked Karlee. "Look what Peacock did to Mustard, and he was huge."

"Yeah," said Kayla. "If you're the only protection we've got left, I'll take my chances on the ravine."

"Excuse me?" Vaughn frowned.

"Yeah," said Scarlett behind them. "Excuse us? Vaughn isn't the only protection we've got, just because he's a dude. That's super sexist."

Maybe he shouldn't wade into this. "Okay, Scarlett, I see your point, but . . . just to be clear, do I have some kind of reputation as a wimp? I promise you, I can hold my own."

Scarlett raised her hand. "Calm down, John Mayer, I'm sure you're splendid."

"John Mayer?" Vaughn made a face. "Really? I'd prefer John Legend."

Scarlett rolled her eyes. "So would we *all.*" She turned to the girls. "Look—there's safety in numbers. And, you know, in having a roof over your head."

"It wasn't safe for Boddy," Karlee pointed out.

Kayla nodded her head in vigorous agreement. "We just want to get to the village. The police can help us."

"We're sitting ducks in here."

Orchid also joined them in the hall. She'd been helping Mrs. White get Mustard settled on the sofa in the study. They'd given him some painkillers, but he was still groggy.

Vaughn supposed painkillers wouldn't really help with blood loss. "What's all this?" she asked.

"We're leaving!" Karlee insisted. "Or at least we're trying to, but Vaughn is blocking us."

"Again," he clarified, "not *blocking*..."

"And we're going to punch him!" Kayla added.

Orchid broke in. "Hasn't there been enough violence in this house today?"

Exactly Vaughn's point. "I was also trying to point out that maybe they'd be safer inside than wandering out there. We still don't know who was responsible for killing Headmaster Boddy."

"Yeah," said Karlee, "but we know *where* he was killed—the conservatory—and excuse me if I don't want to stick around for that."

"Besides," said Kayla. "We're bringing protection!"

Both girls brandished their makeshift weapons. Karlee had a large wrench, and Kayla, a length of pipe.

Vaughn sighed. "Okay, fine. Suit yourselves. But keep clear of slick ice. And try to find a classroom or something to bunk down in. Don't attempt to cross the ravine. You *will* die. The currents are strong, and it's dark, and it's cold."

Scarlett rushed forward. "Are you kidding? You can't let them go!"

"I'm not actually their keeper," said Vaughn. "I'm in no position of authority over anyone in this house. If they want to go out wandering the campus in the dark like two idiots in a horror movie, what right do I have to stop them?" He shrugged. "People can have death wishes if they want to."

"But we have weapons!" Kayla insisted, waving the pipe.

"How are your grades in advanced hand-to-hand combat?" Orchid asked, crossing her arms. "Think you can take on some killer who knows enough about the topic to be carrying around some vintage fighting knife?"

"A what?" Vaughn asked.

"Didn't you hear what Mustard said this afternoon?" she asked. "Before we all started searching the house? The murder weapon used to kill Headmaster Boddy wasn't just some kitchen carving knife. It's a special military dagger."

"No," said Vaughn flatly. "I didn't." He felt very dizzy.

The statement also seemed to have a chilling effect on the two girls trying to leave. The hands holding their wrench and their pipe drifted toward the floor.

"I never thought of that," said Kayla.

"You know," said Karlee, "now that you mention it, I can't imagine why Peacock would have an antique military dagger."

"Precisely," said Scarlett. "Because it probably wasn't her. Now, why don't you go help move bedrolls into the ballroom, or clean up after dinner, or something useful?" She shooed them off.

Vaughn watched them go, unable to say anything. Unable to offer to help with the ballroom setup, or dishwashing. He was not useful here. He'd never been useful here.

He needed to go into the conservatory and take a look at that knife.

"Hey." Scarlett's hand was on his arm. "I'm glad that's defused. We can't have them wandering around campus all night."

"Yeah."

"But I am going to need *you* to go and find Finn and Peacock."

"What?" He stared at her in disbelief.

Scarlett looked back at Orchid, as if asking for backup.

Orchid seemed torn, which Vaughn supposed he should be somewhat grateful for. "We don't know who else is out there, just like you said. That—that looter, who killed Headmaster Boddy. He's probably still wandering around the campus."

Not if he knew what was good for him.

"You said it yourself!" Scarlett exclaimed. "It's dangerous out there! And Finn went out without a coat. He could die of exposure!"

"We don't even know where Finn went," Vaughn argued.

"Of course we do! He went after Peacock!"

But Vaughn simply sidestepped her, heading for the back of the house. There were bigger issues to deal with than whether or not Scarlett's boyfriend was going to freeze based on his own rotten decisions. The girls trailed behind him until he stopped and faced them. "How is this my problem? I promise you, Scarlett, when his body is found, me and the rest of the janitorial staff will get right to work cleaning it up."

She let out a sob, then quickly clapped her hand over her mouth.

Vaughn instantly regretted his words. "I didn't mean it like that. Look, Finn's smart enough to know when to find shelter."

Scarlett spent a second getting control of her emotions, then glared at him furiously, her eyes basically sparking fire. "Are you kidding? That kid is a complete moron about anything that doesn't come in a test tube. Believe me, I know him way better than you do."

"Then why don't you go find him yourself?" he shouted at her. "Why do I have to be the expendable one around here? Because I work for the school? Because I don't have money like the rest of you?"

Scarlett's mouth snapped shut.

"Don't forget, I *already* almost died once today trying to save all your butts. And we haven't talked about it that much, but I'd like to point out that there's a non-zero chance that Rusty didn't make it to the village alive."

"Wait, what?" cried Orchid. "You said you saw him on the other side! Wasn't he okay?"

"Oh, he was okay," said Vaughn. "But he was soaking wet, just like me, and he had a farther hike back into the village. Don't forget, I already made that hike once, yesterday, and it was a disaster then. Whole houses knocked down into the ravine. And a fall into freezing water like that can put a major strain on your cardiovascular system. Rusty's not a young guy. Do you know he takes medication for his heart?"

"You mean," Scarlett said, "that he might have had a heart attack on his way into the village?"

Orchid looked stricken. "I never thought of that. Oh no!"

"I don't know, okay?" Vaughn cried. He didn't like playing devil's advocate. He usually left that to Oliver. "He might be fine. He might have managed to find some police with some free boats and they might even now be on their way to save us."

"Or his body might be lying in the woods," Scarlett finished.

"I'm just trying to impress upon you how *actually* dangerous it is out there."

"But that's exactly it!" Scarlett said. "Finn is *actually* out there."

That couldn't be Vaughn's problem right now.

"With a murderer," she added.

"With any luck, the cold will get him before the looter can."

"But what if it's not a looter?" Orchid said. Her hands were clasped in front of her, as if she were pleading, but not to him. "What if it was never a looter at all?"

Yeah. That's what he was afraid of. He turned, grabbed the battery-powered lantern lighting the hall from a nearby end table, and headed toward the conservatory.

Through the tall, curving glass panels, Vaughn could just make out the ghostly outlines of trees outside. Snow and ice covered the panes in patches, and the few plants in the room sat hunched in corners, like grouchy sentinels. A line of spindly orchids graced the far table.

The body lay in the middle of the floor, still covered with a tarp.

Vaughn couldn't believe he was about to do this. He knelt as near as he could bear to get, but still beyond the edge of the dark, sticky circle where the headmaster's blood had stopped flowing, and set the lantern at his side. The light cast a broad, angled beam along the floor.

"Vaughn, no." He looked up to see Orchid standing in the doorway, holding her own lantern.

But he had no choice. He reached gingerly for the man's shoulder and tugged on it, trying to get a better view of the knife.

"It's evidence!" She came closer.

It sure was. But evidence of what? Vaughn gritted his teeth and looked. Boddy's dead face would haunt his dreams forever. He angled his gaze downward, toward the chest, and the hands—oh God, those gray, swollen hands!—and the brass hilt of the dagger sticking out of his flesh.

Abruptly, he dropped the body and reeled back as bile rose in his throat, and he coughed to keep from retching.

Orchid knelt at his side. "Are you okay? Vaughn, what is it? Are you okay?"

He knew that knife. He knew that knife. He knew that knife.

"Vaughn!" Her hands were on his shoulders. And then her eyes, boring into his. Those stunning, deep blue, long-lashed eyes.

"Breathe," she told him, like he had once told her. This morning. A lifetime ago.

Vaughn breathed, a pathetic, stuttering, broken sort of breath. "I— My grandmother had a knife like that."

Her beautiful eyes narrowed. "Your grandmother?"

"Yes," he forced out. He might still vomit. Oh no, he might still vomit all over Orchid.

"Okay," said Orchid. "It's not like they're rare or anything. Mustard said they were given to combat soldiers in wars all through the last century. Was it her husband's?"

"She didn't have a husband," Vaughn managed. Yeah, he was definitely going to throw up. He pushed her away, turned, and ralphed up all that lovely ham onto the tile floor.

He wished someone would come by and kill *him.*

After a moment, he spit into the mess, then turned to Orchid. "Sorry about that."

She was biting her lip, and then she turned and grabbed a box of tissues off a shelf and held it out to him. "Feel any better?"

No. "Yes." He took the tissues and wiped his mouth.

"Don't worry about it. Dead bodies—they're always so much worse than you expect."

"I've seen a dead body before." He covered the mess he'd made with a few more tissues and wiped it away. He tossed everything in the trash, then plopped back down on the floor near the lantern. "I found my grandmother in her house."

"The same one who owns"—she gestured vaguely to the corpse—"the knife like that?"

"Yes." The knife *just* like that. But it couldn't be, could it? Every time Vaughn got close to considering it, he felt like throwing up again. Maybe Orchid was right, and every soldier in the last century had a knife just like that one.

"I'm sorry," Orchid said. "That must have been so hard."

It had been nearly impossible. Vaughn still didn't know how he'd survived it. Those months had been such a blur. Gemma dead, and then the whirlwind that followed, and the next thing he knew, he was a freshman at Blackbrook, with hardly any memory of how they'd managed to arrange it while the world was falling apart.

And then, miraculously, Orchid sat down beside him, as if it didn't matter a bit to her that he'd just puked on the floor. "I've seen a dead body, too," she admitted. "My . . . uncle. He was hit by a car right in front of me. It was speeding toward me, and he pushed me out of the way."

"I'm so sorry," Vaughn said.

"It's okay. It was a long time ago. Nearly five years. And not only did I throw up, I fainted. And then I had what my mother insisted on calling a nervous breakdown . . ." She laughed mirthlessly.

"Your mother said that to you?" Orchid must have been little more than a child! "It was probably the stress.

People say crazy things in grief, and if her brother had just been killed—"

"Oh, it wasn't her brother," Orchid said quickly. "It was . . . complicated. My mother isn't the nicest person in the world. Families are . . . complicated."

"Yeah, I get that," said Vaughn. He cast another glance at the corpse.

Orchid was quiet for a moment. "I changed everything about my life after that. I was so scared of putting anyone I cared about in danger ever again. But sometimes it feels like danger is following you."

Yeah, well, there was nothing he could do about that. Never had been. "I should wash the floor."

"That mop's never seen so much use!" Orchid said, cracking a smile. "Especially in here. I love Mrs. White, but she has this whole theory that a garden's not a garden without a little dirt. Too much of a hippie, I guess." She lifted a hand to show a smear of dust on the heel of her palm. "Look at all this. I don't think she's mopped in here for ages."

Vaughn lifted his own hands. Spotless. He looked at the floor where he sat, glowing under the arching beam of the lantern. The floor looked freshly scrubbed all around him, and the lantern illuminated a clean swath of tiles all the way from the door to—he turned—the corpse.

What a small puddle of blood it was, underneath Headmaster Boddy. What an insignificant amount, for a man to have died here, on the spot. It had been a while since Vaughn studied biology, but he seemed to remember that the human body held more than a gallon of blood.

This didn't look like a gallon.

He thought back to this morning, when the tarp covering the window had blown down and the whole hall had been flooded with water.

He thought of Scarlett, cleaning the floor after Mustard's minor injury and claiming she'd found his blood halfway down the hall, by the library.

"Vaughn?" Orchid asked. She waved her hand in front of his face.

What possible reason would the killer have to make it seem like the headmaster had been killed in the conservatory instead of—

"The hall," he blurted.

"What?"

He shook his head. "Headmaster Boddy was stabbed in the hall. He bled all over the floor. He bled down the hall and into the conservatory."

"What?"

He swallowed thickly, hoping not to vomit again. "And someone cleaned it all up."

Orchid considered this. "That doesn't sound like a looter."

"No," said Vaughn softly. It sounded like someone who was trying to hide the fact that anyone had been stabbed at all. No one was going to go hanging out in the cold conservatory in this storm. They might not have found the body for hours yet. Maybe even days.

Maybe even at all.

The murderer would have had ample time to return to the scene of the crime and hide his evidence. Maybe he'd already tried to do that this morning, and instead found a house filled with people who already knew his secret. And if the people in the house knew, they, too, were a liability.

"Where's Scarlett?" Vaughn asked as he pushed himself to his feet.

"I don't know," said Orchid. "That's weird she didn't follow us back here . . ." She jumped up, too. "You don't think she went after Finn all on her own, do you?"

"Are you kidding?" Vaughn said darkly. "That's *exactly* what I think." Stupid geniuses like Scarlett and Finn. They always thought they knew best. He hurried from the room and down the hall toward the library, shining his lantern at the walls and floor.

How had they not seen it before, when everyone was supposed to be searching the ground floor? There was a smudge of blood on the wall by the billiards room. A smear on the floor near the baseboards. Of course, they'd been looking for an intruder, not for clues.

Headmaster Boddy had stumbled by all of them while they slept, fighting for his life.

He burst into the library and grabbed his coat.

"What are you doing?"

"Going after them, of course." He zipped himself in

and pulled his hat down over his ears. "Stay here. Find Karlee and Kayla and Mrs. White. Stay with Mrs. White!" At least that was a level of safety he could promise.

"You just said it wasn't worth the danger for you to look for him!" She grabbed his arm.

"Things have changed." If Vaughn was there, he might be able to mitigate the damage. At the very least, he would prevent too many questions.

Orchid gasped. "So you think the looter is still a danger?"

The looter! Scarlett hadn't realized how close her theory was to the truth! Sure. "Yes. I think they're in a lot of danger." He hurried to the front door. "Do you have a key to this door?"

"Of course I do." She dug in her pocket and held it up. "Here."

He grabbed it and yanked open the door. "Lock this behind me, and don't open it up for anyone who isn't Finn, Peacock, or Scarlett."

"Or you?" she added.

"You know what? Don't open it for anyone," he ordered. "Promise me."

"Why?"

"Because I think I know who the killer is," Vaughn said. "And he hates Blackbrook kids."

25

Scarlett

Okay, it was a lot darker out here than Scarlett originally thought. And maybe her eyesight wasn't as good as she expected, carrots or no. She'd bundled up as well as she could, and brought a flashlight, a backup flashlight, and a lantern, but still couldn't see much beyond the paltry circle of light they cast.

Had she ever been in darkness? *Real* darkness? It never got remotely dark in Manhattan, which was why her parents had invested in top-of-the-line blackout curtains in all their apartments. There was that time, on the transatlantic cruise, when the ship had briefly turned off all the lights so the people standing on the deck could see the Milky Way. And once, she'd gone to float in a sensory deprivation tank—for about five minutes, until she'd freaked out and pounded on the lid to be released.

Darkness, she decided, was as inconvenient as weather.

"Finn!" she screamed for the fiftieth time, but the wind caught her voice and carried it up into the sky. This wasn't getting her anywhere. She hefted Finn's winter coat under her arm and hoisted the lantern higher. "Phineas Plum!"

If she found him alive, she was going to kill him herself. How dare he scare her like this! Just because they'd had some little fight didn't mean she didn't still want to take care of him.

The cold was biting, intense, but Scarlett didn't care. She had her anger to keep her warm. But she still made sure to keep a healthy distance from any puddle, even the ones that looked shallow. The last thing she needed to do was fall into icy water.

She remembered what Vaughn had said, about freezing water putting a strain on your heart. If Rusty had had a heart attack on the other side of the ravine, what were the chances of anyone finding him before it was too late?

If Finn fell into the water here on the Blackbrook campus, what were the chances that she would be able to get to him in time?

"FIIIIIIIIIIIIIIIIIINN!"

Far above her, she saw a light. She looked up at the building across the way—the administrative building, if her internal map of the campus was still on track—and saw a figure silhouetted in one of the upstairs windows. It waved—or at least it looked like a hand passing back and forth quickly. She peered through the darkness, trying to make out the person's features, but the flickering light in the room cast too many shadows.

"Finn?" she called.

The figure waved again.

That was good enough for her. As quickly as possible, and skirting as many puddles as she could, Scarlett ran toward the administrative building. The entrance door on the ground floor was slightly ajar, and as Scarlett sprinted inside, her boots squelched against the soaked carpet in the hall. She ignored it and headed for the stairs. If she was counting correctly, the person she'd seen would be on the third floor.

Which was where Headmaster Boddy's office was.

Scarlett stopped dead on the steps. Why would Finn have gone to the headmaster's office? He'd been looking for Peacock.

Unless Peacock, too, had decided that of all locations on the campus to escape to, the place she most wanted to be was the scene of her original crime, where she'd first attacked the headmaster several days earlier.

That would *not* have been Scarlett's first choice.

There was, of course, another option. Scarlett took a tentative backward step down. Maybe the person in the window hadn't been Finn at all. Maybe it had been the looter, back to see what else he or she could steal from the headmaster's office.

Carefully, silently, she turned and started back down the stairs.

"Scarlett?"

The echoes in the stairwell did something funny to the voice. She couldn't tell if it was Finn. She held up the lantern, but it didn't make it that far. The person held up a flashlight, but shone the beam directly down toward her, forcing her to protect her eyes from the glare. "Finn?"

"Get up here."

She took a few steps toward him. "You ran out without your coat or anything. I was scared to death about you!"

"Hurry!"

"Put down that flashlight. You're blinding me."

"Oh, sorry." The light dropped. Purple circles floated in Scarlett's vision as she climbed the remaining flight. She blinked rapidly, and at last, the glow of the lantern fell on Finn's face. She breathed a sigh of relief. He was smeared with dirt, and his glasses were gone, but he was alive.

"You look a mess."

"Come on," he said, his voice so eager it was almost unrecognizable. "You won't believe what we've found."

He led her down the hall and directly into Headmaster Boddy's private office. A fire burned in the grate, and Peacock stood behind the big teak desk, her face illuminated with the comforting bluish glow of—

"A computer!" Scarlett cried. "This building has power?"

"No," said Peacock, not as regretfully as Scarlett would have. "But the computer still has some battery power left."

"Can it connect to the internet?" Maybe they could contact the authorities from here. The later it got with no word from Rusty, the more worried Scarlett became that Vaughn had been right and the old man had never made it back to the village at all.

"Wi-Fi's down, Scar." Finn pulled her around to see the screen. "But don't lose your focus. That's not the point."

Before her, she could see what looked like scans of architectural drawings and plans. These kinds of things she knew well from a lifetime of sitting at her parents' knees and watching them pore over plans for their latest hotel or chalet. "What's this?"

Finn was grinning broadly, and his eyes were wide with excitement. "It's plans for the new science department. Isn't it gorgeous? Isn't it huge?"

"New science department?" she said, confused. The plans showed soaring atriums and spacious classrooms and lecture halls. It was, she had to admit, very pretty. But how had she never heard of this? Wouldn't there have been updates in the school newsletter? Wouldn't she, the head of the Campus Beautification Committee, know all about it?

Or maybe she was as clueless regarding this as she'd been with noticing there was a movie star living down the hall. Here she'd been battling with Vaughn over the fate of an old boat shed, and Boddy had plans to raze half of the campus and put in an entirely new classroom building?

"They're supposed to build it in the spring!" Finn bounced on his heels. "State-of-the-art. Should be finished in time for classes in the fall. This is amazing, isn't it? Amazing."

"So soon." Scarlett narrowed her eyes. Headmaster Boddy had shut down a beautification project at the start of the school year, saying Scarlett should spend more time concentrating on her honors classes. But now she supposed he didn't want her wasting time refurbishing buildings slated for destruction.

Still, why all the secrecy? Unless Boddy, too, wanted to circumvent the wrath of the Rocky Point Historical Society.

"I wonder if they'll have to delay construction, thanks to all this flooding," said Beth.

"And, you know, the murder of the headmaster," Scarlett pointed out.

The historical society would only get involved, though, if Blackbrook planned to demolish any of the old buildings. She clicked through the images, showing the new construction from different angles, and an overlay to show its location on campus. She peered closer at the scale. This couldn't be right.

"Is this Tudor House?" she asked, pointing to a spot on the overlay drawing.

"I can't read that without my glasses," Finn admitted.

"Yes," Beth confirmed. "What does that mean?"

"I think it means they're building it on top of the Tudor House location," Scarlett said.

"That would make sense," said Finn. "The email we found this stuff in was called 'Demolition Schedule.'"

"What!" Scarlett cried. "They're demolishing my *house*? This spring?"

Finn made a face. "Oh yeah. That sucks."

That was putting it lightly. Scarlett had hoped to stay in Tudor for all her senior year, too—especially now that there was bound to be crowding in the other dorms, with all the storm damage. She couldn't believe that Headmaster Boddy would attempt to keep the plans a secret until it was a fait accompli. That was . . . diabolical, even to Scarlett.

More shouts came from outside, and they rushed to the window.

Scarlett could see Vaughn picking his way through the muck, just as she had, and shouting their names.

"Well, it's nice he finally listened to me and came looking," she drawled. She pounded on the window and he looked up at them, then went running toward the building.

Scarlett turned to face the others. "So, are you guys coming back to Tudor while you still can, or are you altogether too cozy up here together?"

Finn rolled his eyes. "Beth just felt like she was under attack back there."

"Yeah," said Peacock. "No thanks to Finn."

"You felt like you were under attack, so you attacked Mustard?" Scarlett said.

"I mean . . ." Beth shrugged. "I guess I punched him."

She really didn't know her own strength. "He's still passed out."

"What!" Finn shouted. He turned to Peacock. "Jeez, how hard did you punch him?"

"It wasn't the punch," Scarlett said. "He hit his head on the floor when he fell."

Peacock buried her face in her hands and groaned. "Well, now they're all sure I'm a murderer."

"It's okay!" Scarlett said quickly. "He's not bleeding or anything anymore. I think he just passed out from standing up too quickly. Or something." Although, he should have regained consciousness by now if that was the case, right? Maybe he had a concussion.

"I'm going to go to jail," Peacock grumbled. "Do you think they have tennis courts in jail?"

"Oh yeah," Finn drawled. "Just like at country clubs."

Vaughn appeared in the doorway to the office, panting hard. "Hey," he said warily. He stepped in with his arms outstretched, as if he were waiting for someone to strike.

"Hey," said Scarlett easily. "I found them."

"Everyone okay in here?" Vaughn asked. "Everyone . . . alone in here?"

"As opposed to what?" Finn asked. "You mean, are we under attack from the murderous looter?"

Vaughn's arms lowered. "Yes. The looter. You haven't seen anyone else on campus?"

"No, man," said Finn. "And, honestly, I'm starting to doubt there ever was a looter. We've got Boddy's computer right here."

"Though it may just be his work computer," Beth clarified. "Maybe what the looter got was his home computer . . ."

Vaughn's mouth had become a thin, careful line. He looked at each of them in the firelight, as if weighing his options. Scarlett felt uneasy.

"Dude, what's wrong with you?"

"Let's go back to Tudor House," he said abruptly. "I think it's better if we're all there together."

"Yeah," Scarlett agreed. She hated how much she was agreeing with Vaughn these days. "Like I said, we have to enjoy it while it lasts."

He looked at her curiously. "What does that mean?"

"Oh!" Finn perked up again. "You have to see these plans of Boddy's we found. He's going to knock down all of the outer campus, including Tudor House, to build a big new science complex."

Vaughn's lips parted in shock.

"Leave it to Boddy to only care about the sciences at Blackbrook, huh?" Scarlett said to him. "The roof leaks in the English Department building every thaw, but you don't see him throwing any money toward the humanities."

"The gym could use some work, too," said Beth.

Vaughn didn't say anything for a long moment. "They're tearing down Tudor House?"

What was he so upset about? It's not as if *Vaughn* lived there.

"Yeah," Finn went on. "I guess it's been some big secret. Not even Scarlett knew about it, and she knows about everything."

"I can't believe I'm going to have to find a new place to live." Scarlett shook her head. "Man, what a bummer. That place is a part of Blackbrook history."

"Maybe they'll have to delay," said Beth. "You know, to finish the murder investigation—which, by the way, I had absolutely no hand in."

She was making her argument to Vaughn, but he still seemed lost in his own world. Typical townie. Well, no wonder. If he'd freaked out over some stupid old shed, she imagined he'd be catatonic at the thought of losing such a gorgeous mansion.

And then the fog seemed to lift and Vaughn looked at Scarlett, an unreadable emotion in his light eyes.

"Do you think Mrs. White knows?"

26

Orchid

So weird. Orchid had thought Karlee and Kayla had gone to help Mrs. White in the kitchen. But when she walked over there to report the latest departures from the house, as well as Vaughn's bizarre declaration that he knew who did it, she'd found the kitchen empty. A storm lantern still burned on the table, but there was no sign of the proctor or the two female students. Next, she checked the ballroom, but it was also empty, and she didn't see the girls' bags in the vast and shadowy corners of the room.

She wondered if instead of helping Mrs. White the other girls decided to sneak out the kitchen door into the backyard. The kitchen door was unlocked, and Orchid debated whether she should lock it. Vaughn had seemed to indicate that they were in danger from the outside, so she went ahead and locked the door.

Only, if Karlee and Kayla had gone out, and thought better of it, how would they get back in?

She sat down at the kitchen table, playing Vaughn's words over in her mind. He'd been so intense—going after the dagger, figuring out that Boddy might not have been murdered where they'd first assumed—she'd thought they were on the verge of a major breakthrough. And then . . . he'd run out after Scarlett.

Who could Vaughn have meant when he said he knew who the killer was? Of course, Vaughn was a townie. He knew everyone for miles. It made sense, too, that a looter who came to Blackbrook was a local, someone who could even have known what kind of valuables might be found in Tudor House.

If Vaughn was right, then it wasn't Orchid's fault at all. The killer was some local hooligan with a grudge against the headmaster of the fancy private school and the rich and spoiled kids who went there.

Except . . . Orchid McKee was also a rich and spoiled private school student. Either way—stalker after Emily or killer on the rampage against Blackbrook—she was a target.

She looked out through the kitchen window into the blackest night.

Silence reigned. Well, silence and the distant howl of the wind.

Be in touch soon.

This was precisely what was not supposed to happen. Orchid alone in this house. That's why she'd confided in Scarlett this afternoon. Maybe the others were just upstairs.

She thought she heard a thump, and nearly jumped out of her skin. She sat perfectly still, not even daring to blink, and listened, hard, for ten seconds. The sound did not repeat. All she heard was the faint howl of the wind from outside.

Dread rose inside her like a living thing, twisting around her organs and clawing up toward her throat. She wanted to whimper, like a puppy left alone in the dark. But she didn't whimper. She hadn't in years.

Mustard! He would still be in the study. And he was out of it—injured and drifting in and out of consciousness—but it didn't matter, anyway. Because there was nothing, really, to be afraid of. She just didn't need to sit in this big empty house alone. She could be with him. Safety in numbers, and all that.

She fairly ran from the room, and down the empty, dim hall. Scarlett and Vaughn had taken all the lanterns, and she'd left her flashlight in the kitchen. She leaped for the door to the study and sprinted inside, heart pounding as if she were really being chased.

Mustard started at the sound. "Hello?" His own lantern glowed dimly on an end table. Orchid leaned over and turned it up, making him squint.

"It's Orchid," she said. "How are you?"

"Groggy." He blinked. "Where is everyone?"

Exactly what Orchid wanted to know. "Well, Peacock took off."

"Yeah." Mustard lifted a hand to his head, touching it tenderly. "That part I remember."

"And then Finn took off after *her*. And then Scarlett went after *him*. And then Vaughn—"

"Okay, I get it. Who does that leave?" He started to sit up, then put out his hand as if to steady himself on the arm of the couch. Mrs. White had wrapped a big bandage around his head. "Whoa. How much blood did I lose, exactly?"

"It didn't look like that much," Orchid said. "But who knows? Didn't Mrs. White give you some painkillers, too? Maybe that's what's making you feel so out of it."

"I don't think ibuprofen has that effect."

"Are you sure that's what she gave you?"

"No." He blinked rapidly, like he was fighting to keep his eyes open. "I feel sick to my stomach, too."

"That might be the blood loss," said Orchid. Unlike Mustard, however, she was already feeling better, shut inside this little, cozy room. The fire in the hearth had burned down to glowing red coals, and the big shades were drawn. It was safe here. Quiet, except when a gust of wind blew down the flue, with its muted shrieks and squeals. "Anyway, I just went looking for Karlee and Kayla, who I'd thought were in the kitchen helping Mrs. White clean up, but they seem to be gone, too, which I suppose shouldn't surprise me, given they'd packed up their stuff and insisted on going until Vaughn talked them out of it."

"Wait, so everyone is gone? Except us?"

"And Mrs. White. Now you see why I got freaked out." Another distant murmur from the wind. "Not to mention what might happen to them out there. It's still pretty bad."

"Hopefully this will be the last night," Mustard said. "Rusty should have alerted the authorities by now."

That reminded her of what Vaughn had said. "If he made it. Who knows how bad it might be in the village. Vaughn seemed worried that the dip in the freezing water might have done a number on Rusty's heart."

This seemed to worry Mustard momentarily, but he shook it off. "I'm sure it's fine. I bet he's just letting us sweat it out. I heard him talking to the headmaster last night when we were all sitting in the lounge. He thinks this whole house is filled with spoiled brats."

Rusty and half the population of Rocky Point.

"Remember, when he left, Scarlett was still arguing that the headmaster committed suicide. I'm sure he got to the village and found people who needed a lot more dire help than we do."

"Yeah," she conceded.

"Or, he just left us to our own devices," Mustard joked. "Maybe he secretly hates Blackbrook and Blackbrook kids and this was his way of getting revenge."

Orchid's eyes widened. "Murdering Headmaster Boddy?"

Mustard frowned. "No . . . leaving us here with a dead body."

She sat back against her seat. "Oh. Right." Then she recalled what Vaughn had said.

I think I know who the killer is. And he hates Blackbrook kids.

She swallowed. "You don't think—"

"That Rusty killed the headmaster and skipped town?" Mustard shook his head, then stopped, obviously regretting the motion. "No."

"But doesn't it make sense?" she asked. "I mean, more sense than—" More sense than that she had a stalker who had tracked her down out here in the wilderness, broke into the house, stabbed her head of school, and then mopped up all the blood and shut the door on the corpse . . . only to leave before seeing the object of his obsession at all?

Oh, crap. She'd told Scarlett her secret for nothing, hadn't she?

Orchid felt like a moron.

"More sense than what?" Mustard asked. "Than that the school's star tennis player stabbed Boddy over not letting her skip school to watch a tournament? Yeah, sure. I guess. But in the end, I think it's like Mrs. White said—someone came in here thinking they could case the joint, ran into Mr. Boddy, and stabbed him. Just a simple home invasion gone wrong. I bet if we go into the conservatory, we can find whatever window he forced entry through." Mustard thought for a second. "You know, it is a little weird that Boddy heard him all the way across the house, but maybe the headmaster was up making sure everyone was in the bed they were supposed to be in when he caught him."

Orchid pounced on that. "That's just it, though! Vaughn and I discovered that Boddy hadn't been stabbed in the conservatory. There are splatters of blood all down the hall and even into the conservatory. We think he might have been stabbed in the hall, and then either stumbled into the conservatory or was dragged there. And then the killer tried to mop up the blood so no one would see."

Mustard listened, horror blooming on his face. "Is that why the tarp was pulled down this morning? To flood the hall and help wash away the blood?" He tried to sit up more, then winced. "I mopped today too! I helped destroy evidence!"

"So have I," argued Orchid. "And doesn't it seem like if someone tried to clean up the mess, it's much less likely it was a looter who found himself in the wrong place at the wrong time, and much more likely that it was someone in this house . . . trying to hide what they did. Someone who really knows how to clean up after themselves."

Mustard was breathing hard. "And you think Rusty Nayler stabbed the headmaster in the middle of the night? Why?"

"I don't know." She shrugged. "Maybe they got in a fight."

"I can't imagine what about," Mustard said. "I spent a good hour hanging out with them last night while you were getting your hair braided. They were just talking about the damage and the cleanup."

"Maybe Headmaster Boddy was pushing too hard for quick repairs," said Orchid.

"Not at all. If anything, he seemed really chill. Rusty

was talking about starting as soon as the tide went down on the science lab, but Boddy told him not to rush and to focus on the student dorms. Which I guess makes sense, as we're going to need housing for the kids, but most science classes can meet in other rooms, at least to start."

The wind howled again. Screamed, really. A very human scream.

Mustard and Orchid stopped talking and looked at each other.

"That sounds like it's coming from outside," she said.

"No," said Mustard. "Closer." He looked at the mantel. "Do *you* know about the secret passage?"

"No. I mean—rumors. But, wait—you said you'd found one, right?"

"Yeah. Me and Finn."

"Where?" she asked.

"In the conservatory. And the lounge." Mustard waved his hand in that general direction. "Sort of . . . connecting them."

The wind screamed again. It sounded like a woman.

It also sounded really close. Far too close to be coming from the conservatory, the lounge, or points in between.

"We can't just sit here," said Orchid. Or maybe Mustard couldn't do anything but sit there. Maybe he was still too dizzy to move. "We have to find the source of that sound. What if it's Mrs. White and she's hurt?" What if someone was *hurting* her?

"Maybe there's another secret passage," he said.

"Sure," said Orchid. "Because if you're going to put one secret passage in a house, why not put one in every room?" The more secret passages you have, the more women you can torture, right?

"The entrance to the last one was in the fireplace," said Mustard. "Are there any—carvings—on the mantel anywhere?"

"What kind of carvings?"

Mustard grimaced. "Um . . . naked men? Naked men wearing maple leaves?"

Orchid gave him a skeptical look. "Are you talking about the naked man on the mantle in the lounge? He's tiny. How is that an entrance to anything?"

"It wasn't. It was the, um, way to open it." He gestured vaguely at his lap.

Orchid blinked at him. "Okay, then." She stood and crossed to the mantel, but it was just smooth, curved wood. "Well, this mantel's pretty plain. There's no anatomy carved in it at all." Tall bookshelves graced either side of the fireplace along the wall, lined with knickknacks and mementos from Tudor House's past. No naked men there, either.

"Okay." Mustard seemed to be thinking. "Look for something that doesn't belong—loose paneling, a seam where there shouldn't be one, a hinge . . ."

He still hadn't gotten off the sofa. Orchid's breath was coming in fast pants as her fingers tripped across each object and book on the shelf, jiggling them in turn to see if they were the magical switch that would open the secret door. Even if she found this passage, was she supposed to go down there alone to where a killer might be torturing Mrs. White? Ten minutes earlier, she hadn't even wanted to sit in the kitchen alone.

Her fingers snagged on something and she looked. A book, stuck, perhaps, to the varnish from years of disuse. She tugged again, but it didn't move. She looked closer. The cover was leather, with a gold embossed maple leaf on the spine, but no title or author. She put her hand along the top edge and felt not the edges of bound pages but smooth wood, and a small indentation, inside of which lay . . .

A switch. She pulled it, and a section of the bookcase shifted ever so slightly, like a door swinging on its hinges. Swallowing, she pushed the door open. Beyond lay a sweep of stone wall and a curving set of stairs heading down into blackness.

Orchid's breath caught in her throat. "A secret passage . . ." She whirled to look at Mustard, who was struggling to stand.

"I'm coming. Just give me a minute."

She gasped. "No way. You can barely walk."

"You want to go down there alone?"

"No," she admitted, "but let's be honest, what choice do I have?" Mustard would only be a liability down there. If he fainted, there was no way she'd be able to carry him. She looked around and grabbed a poker from the fireplace set. "At least I have a weapon."

"Get me the tongs or the shovel or something," Mustard said. "In case someone else comes."

That seemed fair. She fetched him his own iron, delivering it to him on the sofa, and Mustard tossed her his headlamp.

"Don't forget a light."

Right. She put the headlamp on and, shouldering the fireplace poker, returned to the entrance to the secret passage.

Okay. She could do this. She was Orchid McKee, and she was strong, and she was smart, and she was about to walk into a pitch-black passageway in search of a screaming woman.

This was nuts.

"Go!" Mustard hissed at her back. "Before it's too late."

She went.

Within three steps, the curvature of the stair caused the firelight from the room above to fade almost to nothingness. Her headlamp illuminated nothing but an empty passageway for several feet. It was cold down here, and damp, and the plain stone walls were close and rough. After walking for a few more yards downhill, the passage veered up again, and turned to the left.

Here, Orchid stopped and forced herself to take several deep calming breaths. She couldn't hear anything over the roar of blood in her ears. She wasn't sure if she should call out to the screaming woman.

She especially wasn't sure what it meant that whoever it was seemed to have stopped screaming.

She checked behind her, but there was nothing back there but darkness. She couldn't even see where she'd entered from.

Why couldn't this be like the passages in some adventure movie, lined with quaint oil lamps? She'd even take a couple of tiki torches. But now, this was a horror film, and she was the character who stupidly went into the basement alone.

What was that? There were sounds. Just around the corner—thumps and squeals and sobs.

Oh no. Mrs. White! She was coming.

She turned the corner and stopped dead.

Before her was a tiny, stone-walled chamber. In a few places along the wall, her headlamp caught the glint of metal pipes and shelving.

And on the floor, squinting up at her and writhing, bound hand and foot, with a rag covering her mouth so all Orchid could hear of her shouts was high-pitched mumbling, lay Kayla. Beside her, unconscious, but otherwise in the same condition, lay Karlee.

She dropped the poker and rushed over, pulling the gag off Kayla first.

"Who did this to you?"

"I don't know!"

Of course not. Thanks, Kayla.

She yanked on the ties binding the girl's wrists, but they didn't come undone. "What do you mean you don't know?"

"I mean it! Karlee and I were ready to leave, remember?

And then Vaughn stopped us. And then—" Her voice caught on a sob. "Then I was in the dark, and all tied up. I thought I'd been kidnapped. Then I thought maybe I'd been killed. I'd been killed and death was just blackness and not being able to move. Forever . . ." She started sobbing, hard.

Orchid wrestled with the impossible knots for another minute, then gave up. She swung her head around the room, looking for something she might cut the rope with.

This place definitely looked like the lair of a killer. The shelves were lined with cans bearing no labels, canvas bags filled with mystery items, and boxes marked AMMO. From hooks on the wall glinted the metal butt of a hunting rifle and a small silver revolver in a case.

No scissors. Maybe she could loosen the knot with the edge of the fireplace poker. She retrieved it from the ground and turned back to Karlee. "Okay—"

But there was another light in the room now. At the top of a previously unseen set of stairs stood Mrs. White, holding a lantern and looking more disappointed than appalled.

Orchid dropped the poker. "Mrs. White!" At least she was okay.

Mrs. White clucked her tongue at Orchid. "Oh, dear. What happened here?" Then she came farther down the steps and set the lantern on the table. In the brighter light, Orchid could see that Karlee's scalp was wet with blood. She also saw the wrench and pipe the girls had been wielding, abandoned in a corner alongside their backpacks.

Mrs. White knelt down to touch Kayla's bonds. "Are you all right?" she asked in a tone that made Orchid want to weep with relief. Finally, there was a grown-up here who could handle matters.

But when the girl nodded, Mrs. White merely patted her on the head, then reached down, grabbed the gag, and shoved it back into Kayla's mouth.

Kayla let out a muffled scream.

"Mrs. White!" Orchid shouted.

"You're right. It's not really keeping her quiet, is it?" The woman turned and she had, in her hand, a combat knife, just like the one that had killed Headmaster Boddy.

Oh.

The realization hit Orchid with the force of a winter storm.

Mrs. White killed Headmaster Boddy.

She tried to sprint toward the passageway, but Mrs. White cut her off, backing Orchid toward the corner of the room farthest from the exits. On the ground, Kayla whimpered. Beside her, Karlee began to stir.

"Please, Orchid," Mrs. White said, her eyes wide, her voice desperate. "Don't make this difficult. I've already had a terrible day."

"Mrs. White," she cried. "What's going on?"

"I don't know," she replied. "Nothing makes any sense. All I ever wanted was just to stay here, and to keep my secrets secret. Surely you know what that's like."

Orchid's breath caught in her throat. She wanted to make a run for it, but what about the other two girls?

"It's getting out of hand," Mrs. White said. "I didn't plan any of this."

"Okay," said Orchid inanely. "Then just let us go?"

The look on the older woman's face was enough to break Orchid's heart. "I'm afraid it's too late for that, though. If only you hadn't gone into the conservatory this morning. All I needed was a few more hours to hide the body down here . . ."

"Mrs. White—" Orchid gasped.

And then, out of the darkness came a lumbering form. Mustard crashed into Mrs. White from behind, knocking her to the ground. The knife went clattering out of her hand and skidded across the floor.

"Quick!" Mustard called. "Help me!"

From underneath him came a muffled squeak. "I think you've got it handled. Get off of me, you giant oaf."

Kayla squealed a muffled protest.

Orchid grabbed the knife in one hand and the poker in the other. "Okay, let her up."

Mustard rolled off Mrs. White, but she didn't spring up and attack. No, she scuttled against the wall and laid there, panting deep shuddering breaths that soon turned into racking sobs.

Mustard pushed himself to his feet. Orchid, unsure of what to do, handed him the knife.

"I'm glad you came, after all," she said.

"Yeah, well, we'll see how long I can stay upright. I feel like I'm going to pass out any second."

"That would be the sleeping pills," said Mrs. White from the floor.

"What?" Mustard snapped.

"I gave you sleeping pills instead of painkillers. You were noticing a bit too much." She looked at the floor, dejected. "I should have drugged all your dinners."

Kayla spit out her gag and started squealing again. "Oh my God. We're going to sue this school for everything it's got! Oh my God, you have no idea."

Mrs. White glanced over at Kayla. "I think I had the right idea with the gag."

Orchid shook her head in disbelief. "You killed Headmaster Boddy."

Mrs. White squeezed her eyes shut and drew her knees up to her chest. "I guess I did."

"Why?"

The woman's narrow shoulders raised. "I don't know. Even now, I don't know. It doesn't seem real, does it? We were fighting—we were fighting about that stupid window. He said it didn't matter if we fixed it or not. In four months, this house would be gone."

"Gone?" Orchid's eyes narrowed.

"Some new development." Mrs. White curled even farther into herself. "He didn't care that I'd lived here my whole life. He didn't care that this *was* my whole life. Blackbrook boys are the worst."

Beside her, Mustard was undoing the bonds on Karlee. "Her head is still bleeding," he said. "We need some first aid."

"I'm so sorry about that," said Mrs. White. "I wasn't thinking. I saw them in my secret space and I just flipped. Like I said, things have really been spinning out of my control this evening."

"You could have killed us!" Kayla cried.

"You *did* kill Boddy," Orchid said. She hadn't lowered her poker.

"I know." There were oceans of regret in Mrs. White's cracking voice. "I wasn't thinking when I stabbed Brian, either. I just— I couldn't bear to lose it."

There was a pounding overhead.

"Let us in!" Scarlett's voice. "It's locked!"

Orchid heard the kitchen door opening.

Mrs. White didn't so much as look up from the ground. "You know, we still had the occasional drill in these shelters when I was a student here. In case the world ended. In case of attack."

"Look!" Finn's voice. "Another secret passage!"

"We were supposed to be safe down here," she said.

Feet echoed on the stairs and Finn appeared at the entryway, with Scarlett and Beth right on his heels. Their eyes went wide as they witnessed the scene before them.

Scarlett gasped. "Is everyone okay? What happened?"

Tears flowed down Mrs. White's face as Vaughn, too, appeared at the door to the secret passage. In his hand, he held Orchid's keys, but he didn't look at anyone but Mrs. White.

"Vaughn," she sobbed. "I'm so sorry. Please tell her I'm so sorry."

And then she put her head down on her knees, and wept.

27

Mustard

Mustard had never been much of a fan of coffee, but as it was the only thing keeping him awake, he was more than happy to down pot after pot as the night went on. He wasn't willing to take his eyes off Mrs. White.

They'd put her in an armchair in the study, and on Mustard's insistence, they'd tied her feet to the rungs of the chair.

"Is this absolutely necessary?" Vaughn had asked.

"She drugged me," said Mustard. "She knocked Karlee unconscious. And, in case you're forgetting, she killed a man last night."

"I'm not forgetting," said Vaughn. "I just don't think she's a flight risk."

"No," agreed Mrs. White. "I'm not a flight risk."

Mustard sat across from her, in the hardest, most uncomfortable chair he could find, hoping it would also help keep him awake. The others wandered in and out with reports on how Karlee was recovering, or with fresh infusions of caffeine, but he wasn't going to take his eyes off the killer until she was in police custody.

His father might even be proud of him again.

At one point, Scarlett came in with Plum to confirm Mrs. White's story about the imminent demolition of Tudor House.

"We saw it all right there on Boddy's computer in his office," Finn said. "They want to knock it down in the spring to make way for a new science building."

"His computer was in his office?" Mustard asked. So it had never been stolen at all.

Wait, of course not. Mrs. White was the person who'd said they'd been robbed. She was the origin of the whole looter theory. Mustard looked at the little old woman, sitting primly in the chair, her hands folded over the folds of her broomstick skirt.

They'd better double-check those knots.

"What were you doing on Boddy's computer, anyway?" Scarlett asked. "I never got a chance to ask before."

Plum averted his eyes. "We were trying to connect to the internet."

But Scarlett could pinpoint her friend's evasions as well as Mustard now could. "Yeah, right."

Plum groaned. "I'll tell you later, okay?"

"You'd better."

Those two seemed to have buried the hatchet, though Mustard wasn't entirely sure that was a good thing, for the school or the world.

"Peacock wants to talk to you," Scarlett said to Mustard. "I think she's waiting to apologize."

"Let her wait," Mustard replied coldly. He'd let Plum convince him that Peacock wasn't violent. Maybe she hadn't murdered Boddy, but she'd almost killed Mustard. He'd clearly underestimated the women at Blackbrook, to his detriment. They weren't gentle or helpless, or even very cunning.

But they did pack one hell of a punch. Whatever he'd been taught at Farthing, it was all wrong.

Scarlett turned to their prisoner. "Mrs. White, I'm sorry. I'm sorry about your house. I love it here, too, and I think what the administration is trying to do sucks."

"Thank you, dear. It hardly matters now." Mrs. White's clasped hands got even tighter.

"Well, it's not gone yet. I don't know how Boddy thought he was just going to do this without an outcry from the student body . . ."

"That's probably why he kept the plans a secret," Plum broke in.

Scarlett clucked her tongue. "I wish you'd told me, Mrs. White, rather than resort to such drastic measures. I do know a little about this field. I could have helped."

"I wish that, too," said Mrs. White. "And I should probably stop talking now, for . . . evidence reasons."

"I'm not a cop," said Mustard.

"No," Scarlett pointed out. "You're a witness."

Mustard didn't deign to respond to that. Scarlett could

comfort the killer as much as she wanted. Didn't make Mrs. White any less of a murderer.

Mrs. White was more talkative when Vaughn came in the room half an hour later with a shawl he'd rescued from Mrs. White's bedroom and a bag of chocolate-covered espresso beans from Orchid, for Mustard.

"In case you were getting sick of coffee," he said, handing Mustard the bag. "I'm happy to take over for an hour or two. If you want to sleep."

"That's all right," said Mustard. It would not be his first all-night watch duty. Though it might be the first he'd attempted under the effects of sleeping drugs and a head injury. "Although, if you could watch her for a minute while I go to the bathroom?"

"Careful, Mr. Maestor," Mrs. White drawled. "I bet you aren't aware I've known Vaughn since he was born. I was his mother's godmother. He might assist me in becoming a fugitive from justice."

Mustard looked at Vaughn.

Vaughn rolled his eyes. "I'm not the criminal in the family. Trust me."

Mustard didn't entirely, but he also thought it would be a risky move for the other kid to take, since, if Vaughn did let Mrs. White go, everyone would know who was to blame. He limped down the hall to the toilet, and when he got back, it was to find Vaughn situating some more cushions around their prisoner's thin frame and wrapping her shawl around her shoulders.

"I don't understand," he was saying softly. Neither of them noticed Mustard standing at the door. He leaned against the jamb and listened.

"Neither do I, Vaughny," she replied. "It all happened so fast. I don't think—I don't think I meant to hurt anyone, really. I had the knife—just in case. And then when Brian told me about the house . . . " she trailed off. "I just panicked. Everything today was me panicking. Olivia would be so disappointed in me."

Vaughn looked down at her and sighed. "Gemma wouldn't judge you."

"She would so! My temper, getting me into trouble again. Getting me into the worst trouble of all. She never lost her temper like that. Always said revenge was a dish best served cold."

"Yeah," Vaughn scoffed. "Cold as ice. She never did get around to that revenge of hers."

"That's okay," said Mrs. White. She patted Vaughn's hand. "Someone else will. And they'll do it right. Not like me."

Vaughn suddenly noticed Mustard's presence and stiffened. "The offer still stands, you know," Vaughn told him, as Mustard entered the room. "You look like you're about to pass out. We can take shifts."

"I don't think so," replied Mustard. Not after that little exchange. Bad enough the two were old friends from Rocky Point.

"Suit yourself." Vaughn leaned over and kissed Mrs.

White on the cheek. "I'll find a way to help you with your defense, Linda. I promise."

"Don't you dare," Mrs. White responded. "You graduate Blackbrook and you get out of this town, Vaughn Green. Get out before it swallows you whole."

Vaughn didn't respond.

When they were alone again, Mustard couldn't help but bring it up. "So you killed him in the heat of the moment?"

Mrs. White lifted her chin. "You're neither a cop nor my lawyer, young man. And I'd be interested to know if this trick you've pulled with the rope might count as kidnapping."

"Well, you'd know best about kidnapping," he replied.

Silence reigned in the study for several minutes.

Finally, Mrs. White spoke again. "I suppose the others won't be by to see me."

"What others?" Mustard responded. "The ones you tied up and hit over the head or the one you pulled a knife on?"

"Orchid and I got on famously," Mrs. White said. "Just this afternoon we were going through my photo albums and talking about the good old days at Tudor House."

And then the old woman had pulled a knife on her and confessed to a murder. Tended to put a damper on even the most promising of relationships.

"I thought she might understand how important this place has been to me. It's been my refuge."

"Where did you get the knives from?" Mustard asked.

She shrugged. "I've had them forever. My friend and I found them down here when we were young. I had one on me last night for protection. I was worried about looters, you see." Her eyes filled with tears that glistened in the dying light of the fire. "I was only trying to protect my charges."

And then she bowed her head and wept. Mustard, too, felt an oddly powerful desire to comfort her, but what kind of comfort could he offer? She was a murderer, a criminal, and she knew what was coming for her.

In a similar way, Mustard knew what it was like to spend the night alone, waiting for the authorities to come and decide your fate. Not even kind words from a stranger made a difference in those moments. Tears were a sort of release.

So he sat in silence and let her cry. It went on and on as the fire burned down to embers, and not even Orchid's chocolate-covered espresso beans could make a difference.

When next he jerked awake, the grate was cold, Mrs. White was asleep, her head nodded forward in her chair, and there was the gray, dead light of dawn pushing through the corners of the drapes.

More than that, he heard the sound of voices coming from outside.

He leaped from the chair, ignoring the pounding in his head, and ran for the front door. He undid the lock and opened it wide.

Two police officers stood on the front porch in foul-weather gear and waders. They introduced themselves, and then the female one said, "We got a report from a Blackbrook staff member that there's been a death in this house. Are there any adults in the house we can speak to?"

Mustard heard the others coming up behind him. "There's one adult in the house, Officer, but I feel I should warn you, she's confessed to the murder."

"Murder!" exclaimed the officer. She looked disbelievingly at her partner.

Mustard cast a quick glance behind him. Plum stood there, and Scarlett and Orchid and Peacock and Vaughn Green. Karlee and Kayla must still be asleep.

But it was over.

"Yes," said Mustard. "Headmaster Boddy was murdered by Mrs. White. In the hall, with a knife."

28

Peacock

— EP WORKOUT LOG —

DATE: *December 8*

TIME WOKE: *6:00 a.m.*

MORNING WEIGH-IN: *144 lbs*

BREAKFAST: *Oatmeal with strawberries, bananas, almond butter (450 calories, 10g protein), matcha green tea*

LUNCH: *Grilled chicken salad with 1 cup brown rice with hemp and chia seeds (700 calories, 35g protein), lemon water*

AFTERNOON SNACK: *Apple (100 calories), 4 dried figs (84 calories), 1 serving salted almonds (160 calories, 6g protein)*

DINNER: *Zucchini noodle lasagna with ground turkey and a fresh salad (750 calories, 40g protein), small dish of lemon sorbet (60 calories)*

MORNING WORKOUT: *Cardio (Zumba), and 2 miles on treadmill*

AFTERNOON WORKOUT: *2 hours court time*

EVENING WORKOUT: *½ hr Pilates and ½ hr strength training*

NOTES: *It's so nice to be back to a normal schedule. Mom and Dad made sure we didn't have to stay in that crummy police station any longer than absolutely necessary. And Finn made sure I have nothing else to worry about, either.*

I guess I can forgive him.

My backhand has suffered, probably due to muscle mass lost during the storm. I need to up my court time over break.

29

Green

Vaughn wasn't sure why they couldn't just stay in Tudor House. Sure, it was a crime scene, and the power was still out across the entire penninsula of Rocky Point, but the crowded, cold police station back on the mainland was no nicer. Especially after the ride across the frozen, choppy bay in the police boats, which was the equivalent of getting slapped in the face with icicles for half an hour.

The police were rather stunned by the story the students had to tell about the previous day, but as Mrs. White readily confessed to the entire thing, the cops quickly gathered that it was best to shunt the children out of the way before the minor scandal turned into something major.

Karlee, Kayla, and Mustard were briefly taken to the hospital to get treated for their injuries, and then they came back to the police station as the cops questioned all of them about the events in the house. Pretty cursory questioning, too, in Vaughn's opinion, but he supposed they had a willing confessor and not much reason for serious digging.

Thank goodness for small favors. He shuddered to think what would happen if they started comparing notes about his behavior over the weekend.

After that, before Vaughn even realized what was happening, everyone's parents showed up to whisk their kids away in town cars and—in Scarlett and Finn's case—a Mistry Hotels helicopter. Local law enforcement didn't seem particularly interested in making them stick around, especially given the weather disaster they were also dealing with, as well as the prestigious positions held by most of the students' parents.

Blackbrook kids could bend even murder to fit into their schedules.

The last to go was Orchid, who was the only one, out of all the kids—besides himself, of course—who didn't have either a parent or a lawyer—or both—to meet her at the police station.

"Where are your folks?" he asked her.

"On safari in Africa," she replied smoothly, then stopped, biting her lip. She took off her crooked glasses and folded the lenses, giving them a rueful look. "Actually, I don't know who my father is, and I don't really speak to my mom about anything other than money. So . . ." She lifted her shoulders. "They might actually be in Africa. Or maybe on a trip to the moon. Who knows?"

"I'm sorry," he said. "Families are complicated, right?"

"Yeah," she replied. "And I've been lying about mine for so long it's second nature."

Vaughn caught his breath. His heart pounded in rhythm: *Me too. Me too.*

She hesitated for a moment, then looked up at him, her bright blue eyes shining fiercely. "The truth is, I've been emancipated since I was twelve. I've got no one looking out for me."

Vaughn was struck with two equally powerful sensations: sympathy and envy. "I—I don't know what to say."

She laughed mirthlessly. "Neither do I, Vaughn. Sometimes I think all I ever do is lie about who I am, and where I'm from. But I'm beginning to think that's no way to become the person I really want to be. I think I need to start telling the truth."

Vaughn could definitely see the benefits of that. Only, he had no idea where to start.

He walked her out to her waiting town car. "I guess I won't be seeing you next semester, huh?"

"Why?"

"You're joking. You're not coming back to Blackbrook!" He was astonished. "After all that's happened? The murder and everything?"

"Blackbrook is my school!" she protested. "'To make men of knowledge and integrity,' remember?!"

Yeah, but Orchid could transfer to anywhere. Vaughn had no other option. "I just figured . . ."

"You figured wrong. As bad as everything was, I was actually kind of relieved at how it turned out."

Vaughn didn't follow. "You mean how you have been

living with a"—he stumbled over the word—"murderer all year?" He still had a hard time imagining that Linda White could kill anyone.

Even though you were all too quick to believe it of Oliver.

But Oliver had been threatening revenge on Blackbrook since the beginning. There'd been a corpse. There'd been that knife.

He's still your brother.

The thought did not do anything to put him at ease. Not after learning what Linda White was apparently capable of. Vaughn hadn't slept at all last night. Wasn't sure he ever could again.

"Yes," she admitted. "Because at least this death didn't have anything to do with me."

He remembered the story she'd told him about her uncle, who had died protecting her from a speeding car. *How lucky she was, to be able to think there was nothing you could have done to prevent this tragedy.* Vaughn wasn't quite there yet.

She went on. "I just have to get a few things sorted in my life and then I'll be back. You can count on it."

Her words hit him hard, and when he looked up at her face it was to see the hint of a smile. Vaughn had spent his life not counting on anything. At least, not on anything good.

"Besides," she added, "I can't run away every time something horrible happens. How many do-overs can a girl get?"

"I don't know," he said. "How many have you had already?"

Orchid just smiled, leaned in, and gave him a peck on the cheek. "Stay cool, Vaughn."

No one had ever called him *cool* in his life.

"I'll see you in history class."

All the warmth fled, but he waited until the door shut behind her to mumble, "No, you won't."

History wasn't Vaughn's subject. It was Oliver's.

After Orchid was gone, Vaughn sat around the police station on the mainland for hours, until someone realized he was there and arranged to have him sent back to Rocky Point on a patrol boat. More icicles stinging his face. He hadn't changed his clothes since yesterday. He didn't want to think too hard about what he must have smelled like when Orchid kissed his cheek.

Which was too bad, because that's basically the only thing he was capable of thinking about the whole ride back.

Things at home were about as awful as he'd expected. No power, no heat, and no water. His neighbors were all begging one another for spare firewood and canned food. He emptied out the pantry for them and then wondered where Oliver was hiding out.

He had a pretty good guess.

The bridge to the Blackbrook campus was still out, but Vaughn knew he could still get across the ravine at his secret place. He'd managed it yesterday. After crossing, he followed the edge of the ravine back to the road until he found what he was looking for.

The boat shed still clung to the side of the cliff, right by the entrance to campus. It must have flooded in the storm surge, but now it just stood there, as dingy and dilapidated as ever.

Scarlett had been right. It was an eyesore.

But Oliver would have killed before he let anyone tear it down.

Vaughn peeked through a crack. The inside was lined with spoils—from ages ago, and some new acquisitions his brother must have claimed after the storm. Oliver was in there smiling smugly and calculating the worth of his hoard, looking for all the world like a particularly sociopathic dragon.

Vaughn didn't bother knocking on the ragged scrap of tin that served for a door.

"Ah," he said, entering. "So there *was* a looter, after all."

His brother looked up, and grunted. "Yeah. Too bad there wasn't really a lockbox with thousands of dollars in it." He tapped the corner of his bad eye in recognition of Vaughn's handiwork.

The black eye hadn't been Vaughn's finest moment, but he was just a tiny bit pleased to see how swollen it had gotten since the previous day. Peacock wasn't the only one who could throw a punch.

Plus, Oliver had hit him first. But Vaughn escaped with nothing more than a bloody nose, a small price to pay to ensure that Oliver wouldn't be able to take his place in the house again.

"Look at all the trouble you caused," Vaughn said.

Oliver looked affronted. "*Me?* You're joking. *I* didn't kill anyone."

"You know very well what you did." They'd almost torn each other apart, thanks to Oliver's manipulations.

His brother only straightened, and that cruel, clever light came into his eyes. "Yes, well, *they* never will, will they?" Vaughn scowled in contempt and turned to leave the shed, but Oliver caught him by the arm. "Will they, brother?"

Vaughn shook him off. "Of course not. What good would it do? What difference would it make?" Mrs. White had panicked and assaulted the girls and drugged Mustard all by herself. She might not have done it if Oliver hadn't convinced everyone in the house to suspect one another, but it was of her own volition. A few more charges cops could pile on top of the *homicide*.

"I imagine it would make quite a difference to *you*."

Oliver was right. He was always right about things, always one step ahead of Vaughn. It was stunning *he* wasn't the one who had gotten into Blackbrook. He certainly had the mind for it, as he'd proved time and time again.

"So what are we supposed to do now?" Vaughn asked.

Oliver sat back down. He picked up some piece of science equipment he'd likely stolen from the Blackbrook labs and polished a lens. "I can't imagine why anything would need to change. The plan is the same. Everything is the same."

Vaughn thought of Orchid and her easy laugh, and her promise to return to Blackbrook after the break.

Sometimes I think all I ever do is lie about who I am, and where I'm from. But I'm beginning to think that's no way to become the person I really want to be. I think I need to start telling the truth.

What he wouldn't give to tell Orchid everything.

To act like a normal high school student for once in his life. To actually *be* one. Vaughn Green, the kid with the guitar. Not Vaughn Green, who couldn't remember the names of the kids in half his classes, because he wasn't the one *at* half his classes, and Oliver had never been much for making friends.

To actually take history with Orchid next semester.

"I don't think I want to do this anymore," Vaughn blurted.

Oliver fixed him with a look. "That's not really an option."

"What if it is?" Vaughn tried to keep the pleading tone from his voice. He knew how much his brother craved it. "I could just finish school. Like I'm supposed to. And you can do . . . whatever you want. Look at all this stuff you have. It's worth a fortune."

"No!" Oliver slammed his hand down on the table. "We're not changing course. I don't care what happened in that house. It's not over."

"Things at Blackbrook are going to be different now," Vaughn said quietly. "The storm, the scandal . . . It's not like before. The school is going to be under fire."

Oliver held up the lens, so all Vaughn could see was a big amber-brown eye, identical to Vaughn's own. "Good," he said. "Perfect time to strike."

Acknowledgments

Thank you to everyone at Hasbro and Abrams who have made this madcap project possible. Thank you to Kara Sargeant for being a sounding board and to Russ Busse for seeing me through the storm. Kate Testerman: You couldn't have found me a more perfect match! Also thank you to Kyla Linde, Leah Cypess, Sarah Brand, and Jennifer Lynn Barnes for brainstorming help; Michael McCartney and Dan Peterson for Mainer tutelage; Mari Mancusi and Jacob Beach for *Clue* cheerleading and tech support; and of course my darling family for their patience, love, and eternal eagerness to play board games and mess around with mansion maps. Finally, my eternal devotion to anyone even marginally involved with the beloved 1985 classic movie, as well as my parents, who thought nothing of letting us bring along our battered VHS tape of *Clue* on every road trip growing up. I could know a foreign language; instead I know that movie's script by heart.

DIANA PETERFREUND is the author of thirteen books for adults, teens, and children, including the Secret Society Girl series, the Killer Unicorn series, *For Darkness Shows the Stars*, and *Omega City*. She has received starred reviews from *Booklist*, *School Library Journal*, and *VOYA*, and her books have been named in Amazon's Best Books of the Year. She lives outside of Washington, DC, with her family.

A killer is behind bars, but another semester brings new dangers and long-time enemies to the halls of Blackbrook. Turn the page for a sneak peek at the next installment of the spine-tingling trilogy!

PROLOGUE

Rusty

There weren't a lot of jobs in Rocky Point, Maine, especially after the lumber mill shut down. And custodial services didn't exactly pay a mint, even at a fancy school like Blackbrook Academy. But Rusty Nayler knew the secret of success:

Rich folk played by a different set of rules.

In that way, Rusty could still be a part of the game. He held the keys to every lock in the school. With Rusty on their side, a desperate student could find their way into the labs after hours. They might even get late-night access to the contents of their teacher's desk drawers.

For a price.

And then there were the . . . extracurriculars. Blackbrook had a curfew, and strict policies about drinking and private shenanigans in the dorms. As a member of the staff, Rusty was tasked with upholding those policies.

But he could also be convinced to look the other way, or even help hide the evidence. It was extraordinary, the things that money could buy.

Over the years, Rusty had amassed quite a tidy sum from Blackbrook students with too much money and not enough sense. It was a nice gig. Certainly, the perks made it easier to ignore the jeers of students when he was mopping up their messes or emptying their trash cans. He never responded, but he did keep it in mind when he set his fees.

That was part of the game. He never could understand the locals who wouldn't play along. Those like Linda White, who knew the rules as well as he did but rejected every chance to take advantage of them. Those like young Vaughn Green, who refused to even believe the game existed and that he was part of it . . . whether he liked it or not.

Or so Rusty had always thought. He'd given Green a job when the boy first came to Blackbrook, scholarship in hand, eyes shining with delusions Rusty didn't have the heart to dispel. Green might be a Blackbrook student, but he wasn't really one of them. For two years, he'd watched the poor kid working himself to death, trying to play the game against those who'd already bought themselves a winning hand.

But then, the storm had come. Green had shown a different side of himself that day.

It took a murder for him to get a clue.

And in the weeks that followed, Rusty saw how Green was sneaking around and taking advantage of the chaos that had followed the storm. Little wonder. Ever since the headmaster's murder, Blackbrook was in free fall. Parents had yanked their precious youngsters' enrollment. The administration was forced to cut back on staff hours and even terminate a few jobs. Everyone had to look out for themselves.

That's what Rusty was doing out here, at midnight, forcing a stubborn old lock buried in a tangle of knotty vines. He should have charged more for this task. But some deserved favors. Those who had weathered the storm by Rusty's side definitely counted.

The student had remained silent the whole time Rusty struggled with the lock. Usually, they never stopped talking, always ready to explain in great detail how they weren't really a cheater or a degenerate or a thief but that *this* was a special circumstance.

Not this time. Maybe his companion knew there was no point in lying.

Rusty hacked away at the vines until the creaky door budged. No one had used this tunnel since Prohibition. Lord only knew what might be hidden away down there.

He cast a careful glance at the kid. "Okay. We're in."

His companion nodded once and climbed past him into the hole in the vines. Rusty eased in, too, casting the weak yellow beam from his flashlight around the dirty stone walls riddled with invading roots, mold, and creepy-crawlies.

"What are you looking for again?" he asked skeptically.

"I didn't tell you the first time."

Fair enough. But Rusty was sticking around, anyway. There'd be hell to pay if something happened in this death trap and got traced back to him. Blackbrook was under enough scrutiny, and the interim headmaster wasn't about to let things slide.

But it was all Rusty could do to keep up. The kid wasn't even using a flashlight. He turned a corner, then another, and all of a sudden, Rusty knew exactly where they were headed.

"Wait a minute—"

But Rusty was the only one who stopped. He shone the beam up over the familiar walls.

"You never said this was where we were going."

Rusty turned, but the kid had vanished.

"Hey!" he hissed, suddenly *very* conscious of who else might be listening. "Where'd you go?"

His flashlight beam flickered as he cast it about the dank space, illuminating mossy walls and detritus washed up in the flood. Generations' worth of odds and ends.

"Get back here!" Rusty whispered into the shadows. But the kid was gone.

His light faltered again. Rusty tapped at the base of the flashlight. He should have put in new batteries before this little outing. In the darkness he thought he heard some shuffling, and when the light came up again, it shone on more junk. Decades old, by the look of it. Rusty had no idea how the papers and pictures and boxes and blankets had survived the flood. He peered closer. A hobo's hideout? But then he saw the school crest, and the name on the papers.

Oh. *Him.*

Just another enterprising young Blackbrook cheat. Fifty-odd years of thieves and degenerates. Rich folk with their own sets of rules.

He heard footsteps at his back. At last, they could get out of there.

His flashlight flickered again, but not before he saw the face of the person approaching.

"It's you," blurted Rusty Nayler.

They were the last words he would ever speak.

The mystery continues in:

IN THE STUDY WITH THE WRENCH

A **CLUE** Mystery BY

DIANA PETERFREUND